H

FOR PETE'S SAKE

This Large Print Book carries the
Seal of Approval of N.A.V.H.

FOR PETE'S SAKE

Geri Buckley

Thorndike Press • Waterville, Maine

Published in 2005 by arrangement with The Berkley Publishing Group, a division of Penguin Group (USA) Inc.

Thorndike Press® Large Print Americana.

The tree indicium is a trademark of Thorndike Press.

The text of this Large Print edition is unabridged.
Other aspects of the book may vary from the original edition.

Set in 16 pt. Plantin by Minnie B. Raven.

Printed in the United States on permanent paper.

Library of Congress Cataloging-in-Publication Data

Buckley, Geri.
    For pete's sake / by Geri Buckley.
        p. cm. — (Thorndike Press large print Americana)
    ISBN 0-7862-7822-6 (lg. print : hc : alk. paper)
    1. Large type books.   I. Title.   II. Thorndike Press
large print Americana series.
PS3602.U2647F67 2005
  813'.6—dc22   2005010541

To Geno,
all the way to the moon and back . . .

As the Founder/CEO of NAVH, the only national health agency solely devoted to those who, although not totally blind, have an eye disease which could lead to serious visual impairment, I am pleased to recognize Thorndike Press* as one of the leading publishers in the large print field.

Founded in 1954 in San Francisco to prepare large print textbooks for partially seeing children, NAVH became the pioneer and standard setting agency in the preparation of large type.

Today, those publishers who meet our standards carry the prestigious "Seal of Approval" indicating high quality large print. We are delighted that Thorndike Press is one of the publishers whose titles meet these standards. We are also pleased to recognize the significant contribution Thorndike Press is making in this important and growing field.

Lorraine H. Marchi, L.H.D.
Founder/CEO
NAVH

* Thorndike Press encompasses the following imprints: Thorndike, Wheeler, Walker and Large Print Press.

Prologue

A sultry July in the Florida Panhandle

Old Mrs. Lang died at that time of the month — when the sheriff hauled the drunks in for cooking more moonshine than pancakes at the Vet's pancake breakfast. Danny Benedict found out about her passing when he went to Langstown's only hospital to visit her. Hers was a private room, naturally, because her endowment had built the hospital.

The woman of his acquaintance was ninety years young and had lived a long and very peculiar life. But she wasn't what held Danny's attention.

Her granddaughter Pete was.

Pete had a lovely tush, round as an apple, and legs just the way Danny liked them — one on each side and all the way up. She wore a short jean skirt and a tank top, and the view as she leaned over her grandmother's deathbed . . .

Yes, it was an insensitive observation. Irreverent. But Danny couldn't help himself. Guys simply didn't come with the ability to multitask when scoping out a delectable woman.

Just because Mrs. Lang was on her way home to glory didn't mean Danny couldn't admire the scenery. At least he had the presence of mind not to voice his racy thoughts.

Instead, he introduced himself and said, "I didn't mean to intrude on your grief."

"We were expecting you," Pete said. "Grandmother told me you were driving down from Atlanta to strategize about Jackson's divorce case. I didn't know you two were acquainted until my brother asked her to recommend a lawyer and she suggested you."

"Your grandmother and I met many years ago, and I'm flattered that she remembered me."

They had met a decade or so ago to be exact. Mrs. Lang had been among Danny's first clients when she finally tired of her husband making mattress moves on everything in a skirt. What she'd lacked in material wealth growing up, she'd made up for in ambition and an overactive imagination. The old dear had wanted attention, and Danny had obliged.

But he felt no need to share any of that with her granddaughter. As it turned out, nothing ever came of the divorce. The case died as quietly as Mr. Lang did when he had a massive heart attack before Danny could file proceedings.

"Since Jackson's a public figure," Danny added, "my official story is that I'm here on a fishing trip. I want us all to be reading from the same page in case it comes up."

"Of course, sure. You have a place to stay?"

"I've rented the cottage next to your grandmother's house for a few days."

"They say you're a good divorce lawyer. I read somewhere that if you'd handled Lilith's case, she would've gotten the Garden of Eden *and* the mineral rights. Is that true, or just luck and a lot of hype?"

"I'm not quite that mercenary," he said. "The people who walk through my office door want one thing, and I make it a point to deliver. My job isn't to right wrongs. It isn't to fix what's broken. It's to get my client the spoils of war, and that's what I do. And I'm good at it."

He noted her gaze and lifted the lattice pot of hellish red begonias he held. "Since I was here, I was going to leave these, then clean up before I paid my respects. I'm sorry for your loss."

Pete accepted the flowers and offered a

stiff but sympathetic smile.

"Thank you," she said. "That's very kind of you. I thought I'd stay with her until the funeral home came."

Danny nodded and turned to leave her with her grief, then thought better of it and paused just before he reached the hallway. She lingered at the foot of the hospital bed, gazing toward the nurses' station as if steeling herself for the next grim surprise.

"Would you like some company?" he said.

"Oh, you don't have to —"

"But I'd like to, if you don't mind. Unless you want to be alone . . . ?"

She considered a moment.

"No," she said, her smile warming up. "That would be nice of you."

When she turned to set the flowers on a nearby end table, Danny had the ridiculous feeling of having passed some sort of test. His line of work had sharpened his ability to read people.

"You two were close?" he said.

Pete nodded.

"Grandmother was the last of her contemporaries, and she was ready to go. I think we both were ready for this. It was time."

Being the matriarch of a small town's

founding family had given Mrs. Lang a powerful hold that she wielded unsparingly. Was Pete anything like her grandmother?

Danny hoped not, for her grandmother didn't have secrets . . . her secrets had her.

Chapter 1

Revenge is a dish best served cold.
— Pierre Choderlos de Laclos (1782),
Les Liaisons Dangereuses
(*Dangerous Liaisons*)

When Pietra Lang's granddaddy had an affair, it was infidelity. But when her grandmother found out, it became murder . . .

Or so Eugenié's chicken bones said.

Pietra, better known as Pete to her friends, might have grown up accepting the Cajun housekeeper's mysticism, but a message about an old murder was a doozie to pull out from the great beyond, even for Eugenié Thibodeaux. Pete squinted at the mangled chicken carcass scattered on the kitchen's wooden cutting board, trying to divine more than good soup stock. She failed.

"Bones don't lie," Eugenié said.

Maybe they do.

The uncertainty niggled at Pete.

Eugenié's foresight was usually half a bubble out of plumb but seldom entirely off beam, like the summer the bones told her Pete would meet up with tall, dark, and good-looking. She did. He turned out to be a horse.

At any other time, Pete would've jogged upstairs and pried the straight scoop from her grandmother. That wasn't possible now though, since the old gal had died yesterday. She had been a woman steeped in potent Southern roots, emotional, unpredictable, touched with charisma, and given to histrionic flourishes. Not much about her antics could surprise Pete anymore.

Still . . .

"And this murder'll be revealed when?" Pete asked the housekeeper.

Eugenié shrugged and scraped the chicken pieces into a steaming pot, the multicolored glass bracelets on her wrists tinkling an exotic rhythm. Her funeral white turban and caftan made her dark eyes intense and fathomless within her smooth brown face.

She might have been fifty or eighty; Pete couldn't say. She'd worked for the family for thirty years and never seemed to age.

"Bones don't tell when, missy, just what."

That could mean five minutes or fifteen years from now, so Pete quashed her curiosity and planted her feet squarely on the temporal plane.

"My schedule's packed," she said around a mouthful of warm buttermilk biscuit. "What with the family coming in, the Fourth of July committee giving me fits, and burying Grandmother, no way I can squeeze in a scandal or anything else right now. No time."

"Everything has a time," Eugenié said, nodding. "You'll see." Then she made a shooing motion with her hand. "Now, scat! I got me plenty of hungry people to feed . . . and haul them catfish outta my kitchen."

Pete shoved away from the granite countertop, telling herself not to be ridiculous. She neither put stock in the housekeeper's predictions nor ignored them.

But murder?

Then again, given all the wrinkles in the Lang family, she had good reason to feel a nagging sense of unease.

Homicide in a prominent Southern family was definitely juicy news, the stuff of prime-time sudsers. And watershed scandals were nothing new to the Langs.

They had made their money the old-fashioned way — they inherited it — and that was a strike against them in the media, for no matter how justified an act might be, wealth equaled power and, to some people, guilt.

Temperatures neared ninety-five degrees and climbing in Langstown, a small town nestled in the Panhandle. Live oaks. Southern Baptists. Quiet money.

Outside, the air was thick and stifling. Barely any breeze moved through the red, white, and blue bunting that festooned the upper balcony railings of Grandmother's home in celebration of the upcoming holiday.

The one-hundred-twenty-year-old antebellum house was Pete's pride, her first project in Langstown to be restored to the grandeur and romance of the Old South. At that moment, seventy-five of the town's most influential were enjoying her handiwork as they milled about deep in the shade of the wide verandahs or beat the summer heat in the air-conditioning that billowed starched organdy curtains through the opened French doors.

They had dropped in to pay their respects as much as to rhapsodize over Eugenié's homemade beignets served with café au lait. Later, there would be barbecue ribs, ham, Cajun slaw, macaroni salad, and enough cakes, cookies, and pies to induce insulin shock served on banquet tables spread with red-checkered tablecloths under the shade of towering live oaks. So it was a sure bet no one was leaving short of an earthquake.

Pete had slipped into an unadorned black cotton sheath dress to play hostess, a role she'd relinquish to her mother, Racine, once her private plane landed from Los Angeles. A devotee of Our Lady of Accessories, Racine lived to hobnob.

She also believed in marrying well and often, a philosophy subscribed to by her older daughter Phoebe but one not shared by her younger daughter. Her greatest regret was that Pete had yet to land herself a captain of industry.

The year Pete turned thirty, Racine finally accepted that her younger daughter loved working in historical restoration and would likely never leave the sleepy rural community. That same year Racine revised her matrimonial hopes for Pete down to simply a man with a pulse.

Once Pete had greeted the mourning visitors, she roped her long-time friend Albert into helping her lug the cooler full of heavily iced catfish filets down to the old boathouse where Grandmother's fish freezer sat. The July 4th committee, which Pete chaired, planned a catfish fry as part of the town's annual Independence Day activities, but Eugenié needed the fridge space in the house for the extra guests.

Albert was both a curiosity and a fixture in Langstown. He lived in Tallahassee but often made the ninety-minute drive to play escort whenever Pete represented the family at a county fund-raiser or a historical society function.

The two of them got along so well because they were kindred spirits. Through the years, they'd both subjected themselves to blind dates, even when they knew the inevitable outcome would still be two people looking for something other than what they'd found.

Today, he wore his usual Hawaiian print shirt and Sperry top-siders with no socks but had opted for dark cargo shorts and a black armband as concessions to her grandmother's recent passing. They crossed the manicured carpet grass and down the winding crushed oyster-shell pathway, Albert struggling with his end of the heavy cooler, thanks to a two-pack-a-day habit, while Pete led the way.

Three of her grandmother's dogs tagged alongside, on the lookout in case one of the pond mallards decided to launch a frontal attack. Grandmother had named the mutts after her favorite all-female group, the Andrews Sisters.

A Walker/Yellow Lab mix was the alpha, while the ancestry of the other two was in doubt beyond a bit of Terrier, a lot of dark fur, and a shared fondness for shredding lacy underwear. Pete had learned to like Jockey thigh-highs in self-defense.

Behind them, the whir of car tires crunching over the gravel driveway mixed in with muffled voices, the metallic slam of car doors, and the constant whine of crickets. A pair of squawking mockingbirds strafed a blackbird that was too close to their nest, and a hound dog bayed somewhere off in the woods, probably scenting a deer. The mouth-watering aroma of smoked ribs saturated the air.

"Good God," Albert wheezed, sweating freely. "Whose idea was this? I'm in no shape for manual labor."

"C'mon, couch potato, just a little farther."

"I prefer divan diva, if you don't mind." And on that note, Albert stubbed his toe on a protruding shell but quickly recovered. "Geez, I think I dropped my 'nads back there."

"Don't worry about it," Pete said, trudging on through a swarm of no-see-ums. "You don't use them anyway."

"Like you can talk. I know nuns who see more action."

"Don't go there. You sound like my mother."

"At least I'm looking. You? You're doing nothing but biding time with that bean-pole mortician."

The sun beat on Pete's face and melted her makeup. She could feel it sliding down her cheeks. Gauging by the sticky feeling under her arms, her deodorant wasn't putting up much of a fight, either.

"Vonnie Miller's a nice man," she said. "Safe."

"Safe is the last thing a man wants to be called, unless it's being said at his parole hearing. Trust me, toots. Keep looking. You can do better. The right man is out there just waiting for you to find him."

How often had Pete heard that? Too many to count. Racine quoted the trite saying like scripture, especially around the holidays.

"So how come I have to do all the looking?" Pete said. "Why can't he look for me for a change?"

"Fat chance of him finding you here in the boondocks."

About then, the plastic handle slipped out of Albert's sweaty grasp. He swore and jumped to save his toes as his end of the cooler slapped the ground with a grating screech, forcing Pete to either drag the cooler or stop. She stopped.

One of the blue-haired guests you-hooed to Pete from the upper verandah and waved. She shaded her eyes, recognized Mrs. Conroy, one of her grandmother's friends from the Eastern Star, and returned the wave.

"What's the old bag barking about?" Albert asked.

"I have no idea," Pete said, nodding and smiling toward the verandah as if she understood the woman's every word. "Probably another pitch for her grandson, the air-traffic controller from Memphis."

"Good-looking guy?"

"A salad bar of neuroses."

"Never mind then," Albert said. "But while we're on my favorite topic . . . spill your guts about Danny Benedict. Have you seen him yet? Is he as gorgeous as his pictures? I want all the details."

"Yes, yes, and he's not your type."

Albert deflated.

While he consoled himself with a smoke, Pete slid the black scrunchie off her wrist and bunched her brown hair at the back of her head to lift it off her damp neck. The humidity had turned her new 'do into a mass of frizz.

She debated how much to share with Albert.

He knew Benedict was a high-powered divorce lawyer. They'd seen pictures of him in *People* magazine, usually with some celeb's ex-wife stuck to his side like a hair on a biscuit. But Albert didn't know Benedict came to meet with Pete's older brother Jackson.

Jackson intended to ditch his wife of ten years so he could marry his podiatrist. Because he was up for reelection to the state legislature in November, he understandably decided it was more politic to keep this business low profile.

The problem was that Albert and Jackson disliked each other, had done so from day one. Whenever they were in the same room, it was like watching two dogs square off in the middle of a junkyard. So as much as Pete adored Albert, low profile meant not sharing that tidbit with him.

Thinking back on meeting Benedict at the hospital, she recalled casually elegant clothes, an expensive shirt and creased slacks, smoky brown eyes, and a sensuous mouth. He was the kind of man her grandmother would say could walk into a room and tame women like snakes.

"Benedict's okay," Pete said, "if you like the tall, blond, and devastating sort."

Albert snorted. "It would be tough, but I could force myself to get used to it."

"I'm sure his dog loves him, too."

Another puff and Albert flipped his cigarette into the boxwood bushes, so Pete hefted her cooler handle and continued toward the boathouse.

"The man didn't have to come to the hospital," she added more to herself than to Albert, "but he did. He's okay."

Out of her league was more like it. She was a plain, ordinary woman with plain, ordinary tastes. From what Pete had read about Benedict in the gossip sheets, she was no match for a man who kept a string of glamorous women and waltzed through them faster than kudzu through the backyard.

Up ahead of her, the boathouse overlooked a spring-fed lake that had been stocked years ago with large-mouthed bass, bream, shellcracker, and bluegill. Pete never cared for fishing, but as a kid, she used to come down to the lake to watch the wood ducks fly in at dusk to nest in the reedy wetlands on the far edge.

Now as she approached, a hungry bass

exploded on an unsuspecting frog that snoozed close to the seawall. The surface of the murky water churned foamy white for a second then quieted into gentle ripples.

The building itself was a rustic, gloomy catchall outbuilding, seldom used since Granddaddy Lang had passed away the decade before except by mud daubers and doves that homesteaded the opened rafters. In his day, it was rumored, the boathouse was often the scene of stolen kisses and illicit rendezvous with women of abandoned character who seemed intent on picking the gold out of his teeth.

The design was utilitarian — Pete's favorite euphemism for functional and buttugly. Apparently, Grandmother had liked it that way, because she had refused to include the outbuilding during the restoration of the big house.

Pete never understood why. Too many memories, perhaps. Now that the old gal was beyond fussing, Pete made a mental note to spruce up the facade to give it more character and more integrity with its surroundings.

She unlocked the metal door and stepped gingerly past spiders and grinch-green tree frogs waging a turf war over the clutter of sprinkler parts and rusty fishing lures that littered the warped wooden shelves. The place smelled old and musty, like the inside of an unwashed running shoe.

"Ye gods and little fishes," she said, "when do you suppose was the last time this place was cleaned out?"

"We'll herd the livestock later," Albert wheezed with an impatient hand wave. "Open the freezer, toots. Chop, chop. I'm dying here."

"You sound like an old fud."

"Knowing you has made me an old fud."

"Yeah, yeah, the wailing wall is around back."

Then Pete turned, yanked open the ancient upright freezer, and stopped short.

"Oh, my aching . . ."

Her mouth worked, but no more words came out.

She slammed the door shut as quickly as she'd opened it, then swallowed hard.

"What now?" Albert griped.

"Did you have a good breakfast?" Pete said after a moment.

"Grits and eggs, my usual. Why?"

"You may be seeing it again."

Then, afraid to look, afraid to confirm what she'd seen, Pete inched the door open until it swung wide on its hinges.

And there it sat, her worst nightmare and Eugenié's damned chicken bones in the flesh.

Of everything that could be left over in her grandmother's freezer, the last thing Pete expected to see was the barefoot bleached blonde who was defrosting inside.

Chapter 2

On the far side of the lake from the imposing Lang mansion, Danny Benedict was crouched in prickly thigh-high swamp reeds, fighting a water-soaked pine log for possession of his favorite fishing lure. The log was winning.

And it was all Pete Lang's fault.

A man knows the instant he looks at a woman and says to himself *this one* that someday she'll break his heart. But he looks anyway. He can't stop himself.

So it was last night at the hospital, and so it was a minute ago. Danny's gaze had been glued to Pete's trek down the pathway until she disappeared into the boathouse, instead of on where he was casting.

Who was the guy with her? Boyfriend? Lover? Danny preferred to think none of the above.

But that was exactly the kind of thinking that could lead to trouble.

When a man made himself a public entity, he became a target for gossip, innuendo, envy, and lies. So no matter how people perceived Danny based on his public persona, he followed one cardinal rule in his private life: never mix business with pleasure.

He never — ever — got involved with a client. Same for a client's ex or sister. They could turn just as messy and interfere with Danny's working relationships.

No, definitely hands off Pete Lang.

His career came first.

He wondered how she would taste.

As he tried to free his lure from the snag, he silently debated which was more irritating: women, dealing with every miserable aspect of partners who wanted out of relationships that had gone sour, or fishing. Right then, it was a toss-up.

"Ain't no use tugging, mister."

Danny swatted at the gnats flitting around his baking nose and squinted up toward the voice. Sweat trickled into his eyes.

A grimy-faced boy with no discernible teeth scrambled down the grassy dam, a cane pole slung over one skinny shoulder. A bobber, a split-shot, and a wiggler flopped from his line.

"I take it you have a better idea?" Danny said, rising and swiping the sleeve of his worn-in T-shirt across his forehead.

"Sure do."

Before Danny could ask what, the kid sidled up beside him and whipped out a scaling knife half his size and sliced through the murky water near Danny's feet. Danny's fishing pole popped free just as Danny hopped to avoid the sharp-looking blade.

He lost his balance and splashed backward, landing hard on the seat of his tan Columbia shorts, dredging up silt, and scattering minnows in all directions.

"Weren't no call to flinch, mister. Shoot, I ain't even come close to chopping y' toes off."

Danny's knowledge of kids was spotty at best, but as cold water and gritty sand filled his shorts to his waist, he figured this one for eight going on thirty-five.

Unrepentant, the kid pocketed the knife and then reached down toward the log, coming back up with a split-tail mirror lure dangling from a snarled mass of fishing line.

"Reckon this sorry thing is yours?"

"Hey, I paid six bucks for that," Danny said.

The boy looked to the lure held high in his dripping fist then back to Danny and pronounced with worldly wisdom, "You was robbed."

About then the unmistakable click of a camera shutter claimed Danny's attention. He glanced over his shoulder to the knee-high Bahia grass on his left just as a man lowered an expensive Nikon from his face and flashed a grin.

Danny swallowed a groan.

No introductions were needed. Danny recognized Niles Pollard; it was hard not to. The man had a face for radio.

Pollard was a bear of a man with a splotchy complexion that matched his deep-auburn hair. A well-known freelancer in peepshow publishing, he had a checkered personal history.

He was one of those photo journalists who pumped up his bank account by selling exaggerated stories along with the most unflattering photos money could buy. He'd built a career pursuing the beautiful and celebrated like they were moving targets.

"There are more than a few people who'd pay plenty to see you flat on your ass, Benedict," Pollard said.

Contrary to his words, he edged into the yellow flowering weeds and red clay mire at the shoreline and extended his hand.

"Thought you were still taking dirty pictures somewhere in California," Danny said, clasping the proffered hand with his muddy one and gaining his feet.

Pollard wasn't exactly a friend, but fortunes changed too quickly for Danny to overtly antagonize any member of the tabloid press. He never knew when one might come in handy.

Danny bent down and rinsed the mud off his hands. In this heat, the rest of him would air-dry in no time.

"Naw," Pollard said. "No money in it, not when you can turn the channel to an award show nowadays and catch an eyeful for free. Who's the kid?"

"He's not a kid. He's a kamikaze."

"M'name's Jimmy Boswell," the boy said and had the nerve to smile. "And fishin's m'game."

He scrubbed his wet palm down his faded cut-offs and extended his hand. Danny shook it automatically.

"For five bucks, mister, I can teach you to fish. Gimme ten and I'll catch 'em for you."

"Enterprising little snot," Pollard said. "Isn't he?"

"Put a sock in it," Danny said and then turned his attention back to the kid.

Pollard took no offense. He just chuckled and started snapping pictures of the white cowbirds that watched them from their front row seat along the bank.

"What makes you think you know so much, Mister Boswell?" Danny said.

"I know fish. And I know there ain't none in them thunder reeds yonder. This time of day, the big boys keep to the bottom where it's cool."

"Miss Lang lets you fish here a lot?"

Concern flashed in the kid's eyes.

"I ain't trespassing, mister. Y'can ask Miz Pete."

The kid gestured toward the mansion for emphasis, and Danny's gaze followed. He hadn't seen Pete come out of the boat-house.

What was she doing in there? Better yet, what was she doing in there with that other guy? Danny's curiosity wanted to know.

"I tell you what," he said, reaching in his pocket. He pulled out a few soggy bills and counted them. "I sure would like to take some fish to Miss Lang. Catch me a couple of your big boys in the next few minutes, and this eight dollars is yours."

The kid's expression lit up.

"Hold out for ten, son," Pollard said, fiddling with his camera lens. "He's a lawyer. He can afford it."

Danny shot the photographer a glare and peeled off two more bills.

"Ten dollars it is," he said.

The boy stuck his hand out, palm up.

"Half up front."

"Don't you trust me? You can see I'm good for it."

"You a lawyer, ain'tcha, mister?"

Pollard clapped Danny on the shoulder.

"Kid learns quick," he said.

"You've been watching too much television," Danny grumped as he handed over five bills.

Satisfied, the boy nodded and sauntered off around the bank, scattering cowbirds and looking every inch the serious fisherman.

Once he was out of earshot, Pollard said, "So what's a divorce shark like you doing in Podunk?"

His demeanor was a little too casual to suit Danny.

"Getting older," Danny said, bending to rescue his sinking rod and reel. "And a funeral."

He strolled over to where his tackle box sat and flipped open the lid. Pollard replaced his lens cap and let the camera dangle from the strap around his neck. His light blue shirt was blotched with dark sweat stains, and his face was turning medium rare.

"Yeah, I heard about old lady Lang kicking the bucket," he said, shading his eyes with a meaty hand. "You a friend of hers?"

"She and my aunt were good friends," Danny fibbed, digging out a filet knife. He leaned his rod against the top of the box. "I thought the least I could do was pay my respects."

"Never took you for the sentimental type."

"Even a lawyer has a heart."

Pollard snorted.

"So what are you doing?" Danny said, cutting the tangled line from his lure. "I can't imagine there are any sleazy back-alley stories around here."

"Jackson Lang's campaign manager hired me to photograph him on the stump."

Danny grabbed his chest in mock horror.

"Be still my heart . . . a legitimate job?"

Pollard shrugged.

"Everyone needs a hobby. Don't think I could trust a politician who didn't try to hijack the press to further his political goals."

Once Danny rethreaded the line through the eyes of his fishing pole, he checked the barbs on his lure to see if they were still sharp after being hung up on the stump.

"And naturally," he said, "you hope to mine the gold out of the political dirt."

"Of course. Who knows, if I don't die of boredom first, I may luck out and snap Lang boffing the nanny."

His eyes held smug knowledge. Satisfied the barbs didn't need filing, Danny retied his lure and checked his drag.

"Now who's fishing?" he said.

Pollard gave a careless shrug.

"It was worth a try."

About then, a large bass struck the baitfish not far off shore. Dragonflies skittered over the water's surface.

Danny flicked his wrist and cast his lure dead center in the ripples the strike left behind. With ten-pound test line, he could bring in a twelve- to fifteen-pound bass if he played him right.

"You're wasting your time," he said. "The hot news right now is that some farmer's chocolate Lab had a litter of eighteen. It made front-page headlines of the weekly. That's about as exciting as it gets around here . . . except for fishing. Want to try your hand?"

Pollard shook his head and turned to go back up the dam the way he'd come.

"No thanks," he said. "I can't stand fishing. I prefer catching."

And that's what worried Danny.

Both Pete and Albert stood dumbstruck in front of the opened freezer, staring at the contents. Albert regained his voice first.

"Ain't this different," he said.

"Putting your nuts in a vise is different," Pete snapped. "*This* is a disaster."

And she pointed an accusing finger at the blonde in the freezer.

"Get up out of there," she said. "Whoever you are, the joke's not funny."

Tattooed. Waxy complexion. Dark roots. Squeezed like a block of government cheese into a yellow Chanel suit for which she appeared twenty-five pounds too heavy and five hundred dollars too poor to own, the woman didn't move.

"That outfit is so Jackie O," Albert said, wrinkling his nose in distaste, "minus the class and pillbox hat."

Pete swallowed hard. Jackie had been Grandmother's fashion icon. On closer scrutiny, damn if the button-down jacket and matching pencil skirt didn't look exactly like the suit Grandmother had worn to Pete's college graduation.

Albert edged Pete aside for a better view.

"I ain't so sure it's a joke, toots."

Following up on that thought, he leaned forward and nudged the woman's bent knee.

Nothing.

No twitch, no smile, no kiss my ass.

"She's dead?" Pete whispered over his shoulder.

Albert straightened and said, "If she ain't, she sure missed a damned good opportunity."

Very dead. Oh, yes, this was different all right, and it had Grandmother written all over it.

Pete slammed the freezer door shut again.

"Keep calm," she said, sucking in air so fast she was on the verge of hyperventilating.

"Calm is good," Albert echoed.

"No reason to panic."

"None at all."

"There's a simple answer for this, and a logical solution."

"Of course, there is." Albert mopped his sweaty forehead on his sleeve. "And we can talk all about it when I come see you on visiting day at the state bed and breakfast."

Prison?

"Let me think, will you?" she said.

While Pete plopped down on top of the cooler to rest her suddenly weak knees, Albert reopened the freezer door and fluffed his shirtfront, trying to redirect any coolness.

"At least her tattoos are spelled right," he muttered, his breath barely frosting. "Wonder who Fritz is?"

Pete jerked her chin up, her eyes wide, her morning biscuit churning in the pit of her stomach.

"No," she said. "You're kidding, right?"

"Check for yourself." Albert shot her a questioning glance. "You know him?"

Pete edged her face around the door and squinted at what little could be seen of the woman's tattooed arm. The rest of the design was hidden by the jacket's three-quarter-length sleeve. Then she groaned with rising anger.

"Fritz was Grandmother's . . ." How to put this politely? "It was her pet name for Granddaddy."

"Ouch." Albert grimaced. "No wonder the old gal saw red. He would've been wiser not to share their little intimacies with his —"

"Floozy?"

"I was gonna say mistress."

"Same thing." In full rant, Pete jumped to her feet. "Unfortunately, my grand-daddy wasn't the kind of man who both-ered to spend much time thinking, at least not with the head on his shoulders."

A half-second later, Albert chuckled.

"Shall we go dig him up so you can beat him senseless?"

"Very funny. But I would, if I thought it'd do any good." Pete breathed in a deep breath of stale, hot air. "Now, I'm the one who's got to fix this mess."

"I imagine your grandmother counted on it."

"Why do you say that?"

Albert shrugged.

"Houses . . . people . . . scandals," he said. "That's what you do — you fix things. You're good at it, and you're dependable."

Pete frowned.

"You've just described the Maytag man," she said.

Shrugging off that dismal assessment, Pete pushed a flyaway lock of hair behind her ear. Some people might call living in a rural town boring, but she liked the slower pace and craved the orderliness of the qui-eter life. It suited her spirit.

Besides, she had her work. No way could

it be said she was collecting dust like the rest of the country folk.

"Okay, I take it back," Albert said. "You're a wild child, and I'm clueless why your grandmother would've thought anything different."

"Will you be quiet and let me think?"

He shut up then and gave Pete a wide berth as she paced the short width of the boathouse, her sling-backed sandals click-click-clicking on the concrete skirting. The stifling humidity made her dress stick to her like a second skin. She tried fanning herself with her hand and got little relief for her effort.

In the distance, thunder rumbled like cannon echoes of a long ago war, the sound too familiar and too far away to be much more than a teasing promise of cooling rain. Not a breath of air stirred the muggy interior.

There was no denying that Pete's granddaddy had been a rascal when he was alive, one who couldn't keep his pants zipped. Grandmother, like most women of her era, had cultivated the grace and charm that allowed him to think he was king of his castle, but everyone knew she was the undisputed queen of the realm.

So it didn't take much for Pete to figure

that Miss Fritz was probably a failed palace coup.

How she got in the locked boathouse and stuffed like a Christmas turkey inside the old freezer was the mystery. But solving it would have to wait.

"We've got us another problem," said Albert.

"Just one?"

Pete whipped around and stared where he pointed to the water puddling on the concrete floor. The stain oozed from under the freezer and wormed its way along the plyboard on the outer wall.

"Ye gods and little fishes," Pete said again.

She wasn't up for more nasty surprises.

Albert squatted on his heels, checked the coils at the back of the freezer, and then shook his head.

"There's no reviving this old box. It's giving up the ghost good and proper."

The heat and humidity in July were no joke. Just what in blue blazes Pete was supposed to do with Miss Fritz now was the question, and it was a biggie.

One word and the folks in the main house would gallop down to speculate and ogle for themselves. Pete didn't relish that prospect just now.

"Is your mother heading in?" Albert said, standing and brushing clods of dust and cobwebs off his hands. "Your brother and sister?"

Pete nodded, feeling the perspiration that drenched her face trickle down her hairline.

"Don't remind me. Mother's on the way. Phoebe's driving down from Atlanta with her CEO du jour, and Jackson was coming anyway to marshal the July 4th parade. They're all due in any minute. One at a time is bad enough. All three should be a real picnic. Now this . . ."

"Then it's settled," Albert said. "Miss Fritz yonder is beyond our help and —"

"Maybe we should call the sheriff?"

"Not so fast. Look, Pete, when you're in the grave, it doesn't much matter to you how you got there. As I was saying, her troubles are over. Yours are just starting. Think about it. If word gets out, you could be facing charges as an accomplice."

"Me? What about you? You're in this, too."

"I don't think so. That whole prison thing . . . those boys traipse around in stripes. I don't do stripes. They make me look fat." Shaking his head, Albert pointed his finger. "Nope. Possession's nine-tenths

41

of the law. And she's in *your* freezer . . ."

"Hold up on the handcuffs. I know as much as you do about how this woman got here, which is *nada*."

Albert shoved his hands in his pockets and rocked back on his heels, his ruddy face the picture of consolation.

"That's the beauty of conspiracy. The right hand can get the left in a lot of trouble. Your grandmother's gone, Pete. Save what you have. Save your family."

Pete had to admit Albert had a point. If an investigation ensued, there was no telling whose pants were going to get dropped.

She and her grandmother had always stuck together. Pete was there as her grandmother grew old, fixing her makeup when her fingers turned stiff, putting in a wheelchair ramp when walking became painful, reading the rag mags when her eyesight faded. Finally, they had stuck together when Grandmother slipped into a coma after suffering a stroke.

A scandal featured on Page Six or splashed across the tabloids could ruin the family, ruin the town, and especially tarnish the memory of Pete's beloved grandmother.

As far as Pete could recall, Langstown hadn't been the scene of a murder since the 1940s, when the owner of the Five and Dime came home from the war and caught his missus playing pirate and slave girl with a Bible salesman. Theirs was a quiet community not far south of the Alabama border, where no one locked his door or feared his neighbor, where they had so many eccentrics because they had so much family, where children learned the tenets of Southern hospitality from the cradle: open your home, open your heart, and open your fridge.

A grandchild of a lost war had founded the town and fathered the Lang family fortune when he started a turpentine store in the middle of nowhere. Southerners can never resist a losing cause, and the first old man Lang was no exception. Aside from the store, the stifling humidity, and the gargantuan bugs, there was nothing for miles but trees . . . selling at twenty-five cents an acre.

Now, six generations and ten thousand acres of prime Florida timberland later, not only did the Langs hold political sway in the county and the state, but with the death yesterday of Grandmother Lang, the South lost its belle of the ball, and the town lost its favorite matriarch and main benefactor.

"You're right," Pete said.

She opened the freezer door again, hoping against ridiculous hope to find it empty.

No such luck.

Miss Fritz was definitely still there.

After a resigned sigh, Pete said, "I'm not about to sit by and watch my family go down like the *Titanic*. Grab that end."

She closed the freezer door and positioned herself at its side, her shoulder against the metal and her feet braced on the concrete floor.

"What're we doing?"

"Unplug the damned thing! You're going to help me push the freezer into the swampy part of the lake."

In mid-reach toward the electrical plug, Albert halted, shook his head, and refused to budge.

"Oh, that's subtle. Don't you think someone's bound to notice?"

In answer, a low, authoritative voice came from the doorway behind them.

"Someone already has."

Chapter 3

Danny thought Pete was adorable . . . and in very deep shit.

She and the party animal in the pineapple print shirt had been too preoccupied to notice Danny's sudden appearance, not that he'd bothered to advertise his approach in the first place. After all, it hadn't escaped his notice that the boathouse occupied a spot that was peaceful and discreet, so Danny was half expecting to stumble upon some form of nooky fest in progress.

In case he did, he'd decided to feign surprise and had a practiced apology waiting on the tip of his tongue. But he never got a chance to use it.

Instead, he was blindsided by a scene worthy of Leopold and Loeb. Too bad Danny wasn't Clarence Darrow, though. By the looks, Pete would be needing a criminal lawyer, and a damned good one at that.

What the hell was she thinking?

Danny's eyes had acclimated to the dimness inside the stale-smelling boathouse just in time for him to catch a gander at a bimbo stuffed into a fridge that looked older than gunpowder, while the woman of his fantasies directed the bimbo's disposal with the élan of a Mafia don.

Was Pete nuts?

Danny couldn't decide.

She gaped at him across the sweltering silence. He gaped at her, and the short and burly party animal's hint of a smile congealed as he turned pale enough to faint.

Danny let them both stand in front of the sweating freezer box while he remained near the doorway. In those few seconds, he couldn't help but register that Pete's skin glistened. Her kissable mouth was moist and pink, and her nipples torpedoed through the clingy top of her dress, showing the shape God gave her.

No surgically altered blowup doll here. And he should know. Too many clients strutted through his office doors sporting plastic racks that started at around ten thousand dollars and went up. Not Pete. He'd bet last year's W-2 on that. She looked to be all natural woman, hot and gorgeous.

Danny felt a little shiver below his beltline. But it wasn't the flames of desire that flushed her cheeks.

It was guilt.

She looked away first, but then her soft gaze slowly wandered back to his. Such an unexpected shy move electrified Danny's imagination and deployed every protective male nerve he owned. The cool-headed attorney in him kicked into gear without him giving it a second thought.

"I guess you know how bad this is?" she said.

"I've got an inkling," he said, then nudged his chin toward the party animal. "Who're you?"

"Albert Rhinehold," Pete cut in, gesturing between them. "Meet Dan . . . Dan Benedict."

Danny acknowledged the introduction with a curt nod and then pointed the tip of his fishing rod toward the fridge.

"And the late unlamented? She a friend of yours, too?"

Pete snorted. "Hardly."

"Well, that certainly clears everything up."

The party animal chimed in about then, spitting out words so fast he was dribbling them down his chin.

"Hey, man, this ain't our doing. You gotta believe us, Dan-Dan. Miss Fritz ain't a friend of ours, no way, shape, form. Never saw her before in my life — had nothing to do with her present circumstance — have no clue who left her here like a forgotten science project —"

"So how come you know her name?"

"We don't." Pete crossed her arms over her chest, hugging herself. "She's got more tattoos than a Navy lifer. The name was just a try for a polite level of educated insult."

"Miss Manners would be proud," Danny said.

"Look, I have an alibi," Albert continued, swiping his palm across his chin. "I was —"

"Then you know when she was put in there?"

"No, but whenever it was, I'm sure I was busy that day —"

"Okay, calm down, don't make an opera out of this." Danny propped his fishing rod against the nearby cracked shelving and dropped his tackle box and the stringer of bass to the concrete floor. "No one's accused anyone of anything."

"Yet," Albert added and mopped the rest of his ruddy face, his gaze sober. "We're in the buckle of the Bible belt, don't forget. You, straight-boy, the cops'll question. Me, they'll hang."

Danny went quiet for a second, figuring that bit of information probably left Pete Lang unattached and the door open for him to indulge his newfound fascination with her. Mister Albert Rhinehold had just become Danny's new best friend.

"Anyone else know about this?" Danny said.

"Just us three," Albert said.

"And whoever filled the freezer," Pete reminded him.

"Oh, yeah . . . right." Albert nodded and put a cigarette to his mouth that he'd pulled out of his shirt pocket. "So that's four."

Danny stepped closer, taking in the perfume of her skin as he did. She had great eyes, bedroom soft with dancing flecks of brown and gold. No color-enhancing lenses here.

"Don't even think about lighting that," he said to Albert, then glanced around, ready to get this business done with so he could move on to more pleasurable pursuits. "Got a cell phone on you? Or do we need two cans and a string to contact the sheriff?"

Her beautiful brown eyes narrowed, interrupting his incorrigible thoughts, and she shook her head.

"No way," she said. "The fewer people who know, the better."

"I wasn't planning on calling a press conference," Danny said, "but neither am I interested in getting my butt barbecued for failing to report a crime."

"And I can appreciate that."

"Can you?"

"Of course, but since it's my family that'll be hurt by this, I think we'd better keep it between us for right now."

"That's something I can't promise to do, Pete. A lawyer has a duty not only to his profession but to himself. We have to do the right thing here."

"I understand that, too."

"No, I don't think you do. What you're asking isn't a matter of what's right; it's what's expedient."

On a sigh, she said, "You and I need to talk. Albert? Why don't you take the catfish back up to the house? I'll take care of things here."

And without even a token protest, Albert jumped to the task and upended the cooler by the handle.

"You got it, toots. No problemo."

"Need help with that?" Danny asked, watching him strain.

"Let me get it, Dan-Dan." Albert shook

his sweaty head. "You may want to have children some day."

Seconds later, Albert was out the door and struggling up the oyster-shell pathway, tugging the reluctant cooler behind him. Danny heard the screech of plastic bottom scraping ground shells above Albert singing irreverently to himself: *Ding-dong the Fritz is dead . . .*

"And Albert?" Pete shouted after him. "Keep your mouth shut!"

After receiving a waved acknowledgment, she stepped back from the sun-bright doorway and turned toward Danny.

"Can you trust him?" Danny said.

"Of course. He's my friend. Don't you trust your friends?"

"I trust them all right. I trust people to do what's in their own self-interest."

"That's rather cynical, isn't it?"

"Realistic. There's a difference. We can all be counted on to look out for ourselves and nothing more."

"Spoken like a true lawyer. Unlike you, Mr. Benedict —"

"Funny, I was Dan a moment ago."

She stopped and gave him an open, honest look that said he'd surprised her. He wasn't sure why he did, and he was intrigued enough to stick around to find out.

"All right. Unlike you, Dan, I don't treat relationships that are important to me as if they're potential lawsuits."

That hurt.

Of course, she didn't. She shot from the lip, defending her friends to the death. What an innocent. Danny liked that about her. But now wasn't the time and this wasn't the place to argue it out.

"Would you say —" she started.

"No, I wouldn't," he said, "and certainly not loud enough to make the neighbors curious to come see for themselves."

She offered a self-conscious nod and lowered her voice.

"So?" she said, pointing toward the freezer. "How're we gonna keep this out of the campaign fodder?"

We?

"Are you kidding? We're not."

"Whose side are you on?"

"My client's. That's why we're not hiding a crime. Murder is bad enough, but covering it up is a PR nightmare."

"And what makes you so sure this was murder?"

He cocked an eyebrow and gave her a look that subtracted one hundred IQ points straight off the top.

"I think we can pretty much rule out suicide," he said. "There have got to be a dozen easier ways to do yourself in than by turning into a Popsicle."

Pete grimaced.

"I meant how do you know it wasn't an accident?"

"Because in my line of work, I've learned that a wife scorned is a scary prospect."

When Pete's eyes widened, Danny realized he'd come too close to breaching attorney-client privilege.

What a mess.

Lang's case was turning out to have more wrinkles than a Shar-Pei puppy.

"You think my grandmother had something to do with this then?"

"Don't you?"

Pete didn't have to say yes. Danny could read it in the tilt of her head and in the cute way the skin between her eyebrows crinkled in thought.

"The freezer doesn't prove my grandmother did it," Pete said. "The authorities would have to prove a relationship existed."

"Now where did you learn that?"

"Perry Mason, Mike Hammer, Philip Marlowe . . . TCM is my favorite television channel. Well, it's true, isn't it, about proving relationship?"

It was cruel to argue with such naïve logic, but Danny gave it a shot anyway.

"For your information, Pete, in most homicides, the victim knew the killer. That's why cops focus their attention on the victim's immediate circle. I don't think it'd be hard for them to start here and work backward and find a connection."

"Grandmother wasn't the killer type." Pete hiked her chin up a notch. "Whatever happened between them, I'm sure it wasn't planned."

"That's still at least second-degree murder. Ignoring the facts doesn't change them."

"Aren't you interested in truth?"

"Truth doesn't count in law. Only proof. And with your grandmother gone, we can't disprove diddly-squat." Then Danny did a little fishing. "If you had knowledge, you'd be culpable in the eyes of the law."

After a worrisome moment, Pete shook her head.

"I loved my grandmother. I was prepared for her passing because she'd become dissipated and frayed. She was ready. She'd lived a rich and fulfilling life, and she was ready to go. But I wasn't prepared for this. I didn't know anything until today. Please believe me. That's God's honest truth."

Danny did believe her, not only because he wanted to, but because he remembered all too well Mrs. Lang's voice on that day she'd sat in his office.

She'd had good recall for a woman of her advanced years. She'd also sprinkled it with a good ration of bullshit.

Her story had included her dirt-poor beginnings, marrying into money, and yearning to be accepted by Langstown's snobby old guard. How, initially rebuffed as an unsophisticated gold digger, she'd persisted with gusto. How her husband had kept a number on the side . . . several of them, in fact. And how she'd offed one of her husband's bimbos.

Accidentally, of course.

Speaking of believability, well, there had been none at the time. Civil lawyers rarely heard such spontaneous and ripe confessions.

Cheating?

Yes.

Stealing?

Maybe.

Murder?

No way.

That only happened on daytime television.

Back then, Danny hadn't given her

whopper a second thought. Now, he wished he had.

"It looks bad," he said, raking his fingers through his sweat-matted hair, "but it's going to look worse when the tabloids get wind of this story."

Pete gasped and sagged against the freezer door.

"We can't let that happen," she said. "We won't, right?"

Her eyes were bright, determined, and demanding, and Danny knew with absolute certainty the memory of them would nag at him late into the night.

We again?

He leaned back against the rickety shelving and folded his arms loosely across his chest.

"We might not be able to stop it," he said and then informed her of his earlier encounter with the photographer hired by her big brother's overeager campaign manager.

"Even more reason," Pete said, "why we should wait to talk to mother and Jackson first about Miss Fritz."

Before Danny could utter much beyond a groan of disgust, he heard thin music flowing from somewhere on a channel of muggy air, then a woman's voice pierced the hot curtain with a shrill, "You-hoo! Pietra? Are you still in the boathouse, dear? If there's room in the freezer, we've brought shrimp . . ."

"Oh, no, Mrs. Conroy," Pete whispered. "She sucks up gossip like a Hoover deluxe. If she goes to open the freezer —"

Pete's stricken gaze shot from the ancient fridge to the empty doorway and back again, and every muscle in her body seemed to tighten. Gauging by the rapid sound of footsteps scrunching on the pathway toward them, the woman outside intended to barge in to the boathouse rather than wait for an answer.

There was no time to head her off.

Indecision hung in the sultry air between Danny and Pete for one awkward moment, along with a palpable sense of sin. Then, as if they were of one mind, they acted.

Pete grabbed the front of Danny's T-shirt with frantic fingers and yanked him to her. A second later, Danny claimed her lips with his as he flattened her against the front of the old freezer door, molding the two of them in a frenzy of knee, thigh, pelvis, and breastbone, their bodies rubbed soft by pure heat.

Misdirection.

It was a simple trick magicians used all

the time to lure the audience into seeing only what they were supposed to see. Danny hadn't meant to get carried away with the pretense, but Pete made it so easy to lose himself in her touch.

She was stunning to his senses, and he moved in tandem with her as they explored each other's mouth, all to give Mrs. Conroy something less damning to talk about.

Danny was vaguely aware of the older woman's squeak of embarrassment and quick departure. Somewhere in the midst of creating their diversion, it registered in the back of his mind that he looked like pond scum and probably smelled like it, too.

God love Pete. What a sport she was. Apparently, she was the kind of woman who saw things in her own way and chose to blink at unpleasant facts.

Not many women would be so generous of spirit.

On the other hand, though, not many women would use Danny as bait to lure attention from the dead body that was stuffed in the box at her adorable backside. And God only knew there certainly weren't that many women Danny would even consider letting use him.

But the reason he did so now came down to one inescapable truth: when a man has a desirable woman in his arms, he does things he shouldn't do.

"Will you give me a little time?" Pete said, breaking off the kiss and pushing breathing room between them.

"Back to that, are we?" He stared at Pete's luscious mouth, took a calming breath to slow his racing heart, and let it out in a resigned sigh. "You realize I could be jeopardizing my whole career?"

"Nothing will happen, I promise. And just so you'll know everything's on the up and up, come up to the house right now if you want and we'll talk to Mother and Jackson together. They should be arriving any time."

Dissenting opinions echoed in Danny's head, but he ignored them.

"Let me get cleaned up first," he finally said, nodding, "and then I'll join you. A half hour, tops."

"A half hour," she said. "Come in the back way. It's shorter from your cottage."

Danny agreed.

Business first.

Then, whatever this thing was that was happening between Danny and Pete . . . He'd worry about it later.

Chapter 4

Danny's rental was nestled in the shade of an eighty-foot-tall magnolia. It was a small and cozy cottage reminiscent of a bygone era and was close enough in foot traffic to the Lang mansion to suggest it had once been part of the sprawling estate. Now, to the casual viewer, it sat on the fringes of the property like a cast-off lover and seemed ignored to the point of indifference.

But as Danny was fast learning about things connected to the Langs, looks were deceiving.

His client might have been footing the bill, but it was Danny's confidential assistant for the past nine years, sixty-two-year-old Flora Gorman, who had arranged for his accommodations. Her romantic sentimentality and fondness for him was reflected every time Danny stepped foot into the white cottage.

Judging by the island resort design, Danny guessed the two-room house was probably built in the 1930s as a caretaker's lodge. Or maybe it was always meant to be a private bungalow?

He was certain no low-rent Lotharios entertained here, though.

To Danny's eye, the lush setting spoke of quiet money and lots of it and was designed to keep lust on a slow burn. He should know. His mother was Henrietta Foster, one of Atlanta's much-sought-after and highly acclaimed interior designers.

As he'd learned at her knee, mood lighting and artful details could turn any space into a miniature paradise. Less was always more to drive a man stark raving mad with desire.

Here lovers could patter barefoot across authentic hardwood floors through air turned balmy and soft by lazy paddle fans suspended from the cathedral-beamed ceiling. A fluffy duvet was piled high on a gauze-draped king-size bed that sprawled in the middle of the great room.

Hugging the walls were a kitchenette, a wicker loveseat, and an intimate café table for two. A tub/shower bathroom was tucked away in a separate, smaller room. The whole place was a slow, subtle seduction in a clean, beige and white palette, right down to the monogrammed towels and pillowcases.

All the cottage lacked was a gallon of Cherry Garcia ice cream, a tub of whipped cream, a six-pack of condoms . . .

And a woman for Danny to share them with.

Fresh out of a cold shower, he stood naked in front of the French doors that opened out to a lattice-enclosed private porch and air-dried himself. The rich perfume of late-blooming magnolia blossoms kissed the air. Below the porch, a leering yard gnome waded in a pond of yellow daylilies.

Danny grabbed his cell phone off the nearby wicker nightstand, attached the portable hands-free speaker and microphone, and dialed his private office number. Flora answered on the second ring.

"Any messages that can't wait?" he asked while he toweled his hair.

"Only your mother. She's hosting a dinner next Friday and wants you to round out the table."

News of a root canal would've been more welcome.

"What she wants is grandchildren," he said, chucking the monogrammed bath sheet to the floor.

"Can't blame her for trying," Flora said. "Every mother wants to see her son settle down with a nice girl."

Danny picked up his hairbrush and turned to his reflection in the oval wall mirror.

"Then why does she always manage to sandwich me either between refugees from a rehab catch-and-release program or reincarnations of the Bitch of Buchenwald?"

"You're too particular, you know that?"

"You weren't at her last dinner. The woman on my left had a face like a walnut, and the one on my right wore makeup applied with a hand trowel. I've learned to fast on Fridays. Look, if Mother calls again, tell her I'll phone her later. And tell her to stop meddling. Speaking of which . . . I've got a bone to pick with you, young lady."

"With *moi?*"

Danny sighed and tossed the brush on the bed and then rummaged through his bag to lay out his underwear.

"Don't play innocent," he said. "Tell me, how did you hear about this place?"

"Oh, so you like?" Flora said.

She sounded entirely too cheery to suit Danny.

"It's too froufrou," he said, "and the shower's small. Now, answer my question."

"Froufrou? Daniel, what you're experiencing is artistic self-expression, a dwelling geared toward the socially enlightened —"

"Cut the crap. It's a love nest, and you know it."

Caught red-handed, Flora copped to her shenanigans without a shred of remorse.

"Representative Lang's assistant suggested it when I asked," Flora said. "The way she described it, I must say it sounded yummy."

He uncapped his deodorant.

"Please, as his lawyer, I don't even want to think about how she came by her endorsement."

"Better to have a place and not need it than to need it and not have it, *n'est pas?* You're in a small town, after all. I'm only thinking of your best interests."

And in her own way, Flora always was.

Some people drift into your life like you've known them forever. For Danny, Flora Gorman was such a person.

She was a throwback to the days of June Cleaver and other mythical moms who cheerfully put hubby through medical school and then baked cookies for the next twenty-seven years until the last of the kids pointed his late-model Beemer toward an Ivy League college. Danny had handled Flora's divorce pro bono when she'd had no money, no job, and no prospects, and was staring down the barrel at middle age, begging crumbs from a gray-headed husband who was hemorrhaging money into a forty-foot sport yacht and a trophy wife.

Flora was a survivor who'd grown as tough over the years as a bus station steak, but through the phone line, her smoky voice held a torch singer quality and made her sound younger than her salt and pepper hair attested to.

"You're too good to me," Danny said, "but do me a favor?"

"Name it. I live to serve."

"Stick to the job, and quit trying to arrange my love life."

He walked into the bathroom to fetch his cologne.

"What love life?" Flora said. "You don't have one. That the rumor mill claims you're taken by every cocaine-sniffing starlet and anorexic model that struts down the runway is the biggest hoax since Bill Gates said size doesn't matter."

It was moldy news to Danny that he was considered a prize catch. His all-too-brief but famous fling with a candy heiress had spawned his alleged philandering ways and had helped make him a tabloid favorite even before his client list swelled with the names of the wealthy and media-obsessed.

The truth was, his heiress had taken him to hell in a handcart, but what a lovely ride it had been.

According to the press, he dated a plethora of babes, so they quickly labeled him the womanizer who would forever remain a bachelor. The reputation wasn't accurate, but outside of committing matrimony, there wasn't much he could do to dispel it. Few in the paparazzi bothered to look beyond the surface and notice that he was so busy working that he wasn't seeing anyone in particular and hadn't been in a relationship for several years.

Danny wasn't a womanizer, not really, but then he'd always been a great fan of irony.

He slipped his undershirt over his head, and in an effort to nudge Flora off a topic he didn't care to keep defending, said, "Wait a minute, are you saying size does matter?"

His effort failed.

She laughed out loud and then said in a conspiratorial whisper, "Really, counselor, everyone knows it can be a long way to England when you're paddling a rowboat." Then louder, "But that's neither here nor there. How can I be guilty of trying to arrange something that doesn't exist?"

"Look, I'm happy with my life the way it is," he said, stepping into his briefs.

"No, you're not. You're getting older. You need stability, a family, someone to talk to when you come home at night."

Talking was the last thing Danny could think of to occupy his nights with a woman.

"And you need to worry about staying employed," he said. "Don't start with me, Flora."

"All right. Fine. Have it your way. You are, after all, the boss."

She conceded that point too sweetly for Danny's taste, but he said, "Thank you," and left it alone.

"You're welcome."

"I'm glad we're straight on that."

"Was there ever a doubt?"

"Can we go back to the part where you live to serve?" He retrieved the dental floss he'd left by the sink, and switched the subject to his chief investigator. "Has Mary Ruth checked in?"

"About an hour ago," Flora said.

"When she calls in again, tell her to drop everything. I need her to check into a missing person for me."

"Trouble in paradise?"

"That's what I'm trying to avoid. Are you clear to copy?"

Danny heard papers ruffling, and in his mind's eye he saw Flora flipping through her ever-present steno pad before she said, "Go ahead, shoot."

He slicked his damp hair with the brush again and then pulled into tan slacks while he rattled off a brief sketch of Miss Fritz and her circumstance for Flora to pass on to his investigator. It would suffice until Danny met with Jackson, Pete, and their mother. Once he laid out the legal ramifications, then together they could coordinate which propeller head would do spin and which press agent they'd sic on damage control.

The little bit Danny knew wasn't much to go on, but if anyone could dig up anything on the dead bimbo in old Mrs. Lang's freezer, it was petite Mary Ruth Marshall. Her passion and tenacity for her job defied the odds.

She resembled a gymnast and radiated sunny, good-natured charm, yet she never took prisoners. On a bad day, one cross word from her could drop a grown man like used dental floss.

"Watch yourself, Daniel," Flora said. "You're an officer of the court, and you're flirting with disbarment."

"Only if I abetted my client in the commission of a felony, which I haven't done, and I'm not going to do."

"Plus there's a little matter of obstruction, accessory after the fact," she added, and he could almost hear her shake her head. "Those carry jail terms. Promise me you won't get in over your head?"

"I'll be fine."

"Bet Davy Crockett said that, too, as he toddled off to the Alamo. Anything else I can help with?"

"Maybe," Danny said, pulling a navy blue polo shirt out of his garment bag. "Jackson Lang has a sister . . ."

"Phoebe? Now there's a field that's been plowed before."

"You know her?"

"Not personally, but I know people who do. She holds court with all the best Wall Street weenies. In fact, I think I heard that she used to be tight with that airline CEO who was just sentenced to five to ten in the Club Fed somewhere in that area."

"I meant the other one. They call her Pete."

"Oh. Don't know much about her at all. I can make a few calls if you want."

Danny was quietly tending his own thoughts when Flora suggested into the protracted silence, "Or you can find out for yourself. She's down there, isn't she?"

"Yes, she lives here in town."

"Have you met her yet?"

"Briefly, yes."

"And? Daniel? What am I hearing?"

"Nothing," he said, coming back to himself. "I just took a shower, and I'm getting dressed."

Then he slipped the shirt over his head and thought sure Flora would know better than to tread on his temper again.

Did he ever think wrong.

"Don't try to bamboozle me, Daniel Benedict. I've known you too long. This Pete person . . . is she nice? She better be nice . . ."

Heat rose within him along with the memory of the squishy, slurpy sound two sun-drenched bodies make when they lock in a steamy embrace.

"She's got bedroom eyes," he said before he caught himself.

A flutter of a heartbeat later, Flora said, "I love it when you distill an issue down to its essence. So when are you going to ask her out? Or have you already?"

"Don't order the wedding flowers just yet," he said, slipping his bare feet into tasseled brown loafers. "I haven't asked her out, and I'm not going to, either. You know these things can get messy, especially with a shutterbug on the loose, and messy is the last thing I need on my plate. I can't go there."

"Can't or won't?"

"Does it matter?"

"You know, Daniel, it's not totally unheard of for relationships to last. Some actually manage to do it for forty or fifty years."

"So you keep telling me."

"You're such a cynic about love."

"Not love. Marriage."

Down through the ether and into the room exploded a loud sigh of long-suffering patience.

"Really, Daniel, you're a dandy lawyer, but a bit thick in the noodle at times. As my grandma used to say . . . never up, never in."

"Your grandmother said that? She play for the Braves or who?"

"It might've been my grandfather. My point is, you can't sit around waiting for your ship to come in. Sometimes, you have to row out to it."

Danny rummaged in a zippered compartment of his bag until he found his brown alligator belt.

"I've got to run," he said, barely curbing

his impatience. "I'm due at the Lang Mansion for a meeting with the family. Don't forget Mary Ruth. I'll check in with you later."

He started to say good-bye when he heard a frantic, "Daniel? Daniel!" coming back at him.

"Yeah?" he said.

"Be a good guest and hang the towel back on the rack."

That snapped him to attention, and he gave the cottage's nooks and crannies a quick perusal.

"Have you got x-ray vision," he said, "or is this room on tape?"

"Neither — I have a father, two brothers, and almost thirty years with a husband and three football-playing sons, none of whom ever learned not to toss a wet towel on the carpet. It's a guy thing."

Grumbling about bossy females, Danny bid Flora good-bye and then dutifully swiped the towel off the floor to hang it over the shower curtain rod. The terry cloth flopped him in the face, so it was hard for him not to see, really see, the fancy script monogram. To his secret delight, instead of the JL of his libido-driven client Jackson Lang that Danny expected, he stared at a very suggestive PL.

Too bad his golden glow of anticipation wasn't destined to shine long.

His client was a politician in a reelection year. Pete Lang was his client's sister. That combination alone spelled trouble with a capital L for loser.

Add in that they were hiding a dead body in the family freezer, and the arguments in favor of Danny keeping a professional distance slapped him in the face hard enough to knock the fillings right out of his teeth.

No, a compelling reason would have to arise before Danny would break a perfectly good work rule of never mixing business with pleasure.

That silent debate settled, he gave himself one last check in the mirror and then threaded his way along the footpath leading to the rear of the Lang Mansion. As he walked, though, one nagging question remained unanswered.

How in the world was he supposed to keep his hands off Pete when he got a chubby just thinking about her?

Pete wasn't good with surprises. Never had been.

She lacked whatever chromosome all southern women seemed born with that allowed them to meet the unexpected with a plate of fried chicken and stoic acceptance. Perhaps that lack explained why dumping a dead body in the murky lake water had held a certain logic and appeal on first blush and why the taste and feel of Dan Benedict left her heart beating fast and her good sense scattered.

No other explanation fit. His kiss had lasted for little more than a blink, but in that snatch of time, she was ready to nominate it as one of her all-time favorites.

Once she caught her breath, she could hardly believe she had dared to commandeer his attention with the closest thing to a sexual panzer attack. Pete Lang didn't do those kinds of things.

It had to have been her evil twin. Whatever the man had thought of Pete before, she was certain his assessment went down a steep hill very fast after her impromptu lip-lock.

After Pete had watched Benedict disappear among ancient oaks flocked with lichen-colored wisps of Spanish moss, she'd checked that no one else was hanging around the boathouse and then she'd made sure the rusty metal door was securely locked behind her. No telling who else Grandmother had given a key to, but Pete refused to worry over the possibilities just then.

It was the people who didn't have a key that she wanted to make sure couldn't stumble upon the freezer contents before the family could decide on a plan of action.

In a jumping, yipping stampede that resembled a free-for-all scramble for cheap Mardi Gras beads, Grandmother's three mutts hotfooted it along with Pete toward the mudroom that was off the kitchen. One stern word from her at the back door quieted the two Terriers and the Yellow Lab for half a second before the three of them bolted across the yard after a suicidal squirrel.

When Pete slipped inside the back door, cool air greeted her along with the mouth-watering spicy aroma of shrimp jambalaya and a nagging sense of bad juju.

Something was up.

A hubbub of voices floated through the cavernous hallway leading from the front rooms. Half the town must have arrived in the minutes she'd been detained in the boathouse. She listened for a moment, caught snatches of conversation, and distinctly heard her name dropped once or twice.

Pete mentally winced. It didn't take a genius to peg Mrs. Conroy as the horse's mouth.

The old lady had probably torn into the house, arthritic knees flying, and promptly launched into a graphic yarn for the benefit of the other ladies in her over-seventy Sunday school class. Good grief, by tonight, what she thought she'd glimpsed in the boathouse would be blown out of proportion and spread all over the county.

No way Pete was used to being the topic of gossip. Her family, yes. Pete herself? No. She preferred to remain in the background.

This time she had no one to blame but herself, though, so other than marching into the front room and sharing a much worse scandal with all and sundry, Pete opted to let the speculators chew over her for a while.

What else could she do?

Rather than brave the herds of inquisitive mourners just yet, however, Pete hightailed it up the back stairway toward the privacy of the third floor guest bathroom to freshen up and put on her battle face first.

That she might also want to look better when Dan Benedict saw her again had less than nothing to do with it.

Over the generations, the house had undergone several face-lifts. The second and third floors had morphed into a rabbit warren of niches, alcoves, and doorways, with more than a couple of cubbies secreted behind innocent-looking decorative wall panels.

Antiques burnished by time and history cluttered each room. The playroom held some of Pete's favorites: Erector Sets, a Fort Apache play set, Tinker Toys, Lincoln Logs, and odds and ends bought off the Fuller brush man.

As a kid, Pete had delighted in touring the old house with visitors.

Now the sight of a heavyset man browsing in the hallway ahead of her caught her attention, and not in a positive way.

Sunlight danced on his reddish hair as he poked his head into doorways. He didn't appear to be doing much else, but his nosiness was enough to raise her hackles.

There was no reason for anyone outside the family to venture beyond the first floor. Pete wasn't hosting an open house, and it was bad manners of this guy to be so presumptive.

The fringed Bakshaish hallway runner muffled her steps as she came up behind him.

"May I help you, sir? This floor is usually reserved for family only."

Startled, he whipped around and pasted on a patently false smile. His hellfire-pink sunburn proclaimed him a tourist and not a local, and the camera dangling against his chest tagged him a nuisance.

"I was looking for the bathroom," he said. "I think I got lost."

His excuse sounded a little ripe to Pete's ears.

"You certainly did, mister — ?"

"Pollard." He extended his hand. "Niles Pollard, Miss Lang. I'm sorry about your grandmother."

"Thank you. Have we met?"

"I recognized you from your pictures downstairs. Your brother did mention I was coming, didn't he?"

No, but Dan Benedict had.

Pete figured it was wiser to keep that information behind her teeth. The less she said to a member of the press, the less crow she'd have to eat later.

"Of course, Mr. Pollard," she said, shaking his hand, "you're Jackson's campaign photographer. Is he here already? I

78

didn't see him come in."

"He's due any minute. I came ahead."

Now was as good a time as any to set some ground rules.

"Mister Pollard —"

"Niles, please."

She offered him a practiced smile and extracted her hand from his sweaty grip.

"Well, *Niles* . . . as you can see, Jackson doesn't campaign up here. Now, if you'll go back down these stairs, you'll find four bathrooms on the first floor. One off the foyer. One off the dining room. One off the laundry room. And one out in the pool area."

"Really? That many?" he said and mustered a chuckle. "It's a wonder I missed them."

"Yes, it is, isn't it?"

She crossed her arms over her chest and waited.

After an awkward moment, he grinned and said, "I have a confession to make —"

"Let me guess . . . you weren't actually hunting for the john."

"Not much sneaks by you, does it?"

"Sometimes I amaze even myself. What were you looking for? Anything in particular?"

"You," he said.

Her throat dried up.

For all Pete knew, she had Jimmy Hoffa in drag defrosting in the locked boathouse. What a career-maker that would be for some reporter lucky enough to stumble upon the body's hiding place. Dumber things had happened.

She could see the tabloid headlines now: *Rep's Demented Sis Refuses to Talk After Death.*

The question was, how lucky was Niles Pollard?

He canted his head to the side in much the same irritating know-it-all manner as Pete's tenth-grade English teacher when he'd handed her an F for a book report on a book she hadn't read.

With an aplomb borne of too much practice, she contrived to look calm and pointed at her chest with an index finger.

"You were looking for me?" she said, wide-eyed. "Why, I'm flattered. Whatever did you need me for?"

"To see if you wanted to confirm or deny the rumor I've heard about you and a certain well-known lawyer caught going at it like Energizer bunnies."

Pete's nerves were shot, and her brain was spinning. For a moment, she almost laughed out loud with relief.

"Really?" she managed to say. "Who's your source?"

"A little bird."

"Goodness. Which species? The bespectacled blue-haired chin-wagger by chance?"

He deflected her barb with a chuckle and said, "Well? You two an item now?"

"As if," she said on a low snort.

"Yeah, I couldn't see you as Benedict's type, either."

Her chin snapped up.

"Oh, and what type is that?"

"Young. Blonde. Big tits —"

"Thank you, I get the picture." She got it too well and didn't need a scum-sucking reporter to catalog her shortcomings for her. "For the record, we were not cavorting."

"Sure sounded like you were doing something."

"What I do is none of your business."

About then Niles snapped her picture before Pete could raise her hands to block the shot.

"Hey! Stop that," she said, seeing little white lights dance in her vision. "My brother's paying you to take pictures of him, not me. How about following your nose back down the stairs, Niles, and if I catch you butting it in again where it doesn't belong, I'll talk to Jackson about cutting it off. Fair enough?"

"Whoa, hold up a minute," he said. "Are you threatening me?"

"Why, yes," Pete said, hands planted on her hips. "Did I stutter?"

His eyes widened and then he smirked.

"Assertive women are very sexy," he said, lifting his camera again. "C'mon, smile for me, honey."

"Pollard, I'm not your *honey*. Now waltz your happy ass down those stairs, or so help me —"

"All right, all right," he said, lowering the camera back to his chest. "I'm going. No need to get your thong in a bunch. Some people are so touchy."

Pete stood there, staring at his retreating back.

"What a jerk," she muttered to the stately walls, sorry she'd lacked the nerve to toss the crude and hairy man ass over teakettle down the stairs for emphasis.

Her big sister wouldn't have hesitated. Phoebe had a knack for verbally skewering a man before he realized he'd even been pricked. She relished the role of speaking the truth as she saw it and damn the consequences. Too bad Pete wasn't more like her.

As Pete watched the camera hound disappear from sight, her stomach wrapped in tight knots. She didn't believe for one moment he would let his curiosity sit idle.

No, she'd encountered his type too many times over the years and recognized it the way she knew the music of her own name. Niles Pollard was trolling for a honking big piece of dirt to make a quick buck.

And if Pete and Benedict didn't do something in a hurry, Pollard just might find more than any of them bargained for.

Chapter 5

Minutes later, Albert met Pete at the bottom of the stairs with a frenzy of worry on his face and car keys in his hand.

"Have you any idea, toots, what the grapevine is saying about you?" He looped his arm through hers and snatched her close to his side. "I leave you alone for a few measly minutes, and you turn into Hester Prynne. I'm surprised there's not a big red A stamped on your forehead."

Pete felt a blush heating up her neck.

She wished she'd had time for a leisurely shower rather than just the quickie face wash and body spritz she'd done. At least she'd managed to drag a brush through her hair and slap on some smoothing cream to tame the frizz. She'd also ditched the schoolgirl scrunchie in favor of sweeping her long bangs behind her ears and letting the loose ends of her hair graze her shoulders.

The style was a stab at a sleek, more glamorous look, but glam wasn't in the cards for her. With her hair's fine texture and the humidity, her hairdo simply fell flat.

"Is the talk that bad?" she said.

"The natives are in a feeding frenzy out there, and you're the main course. What in the world happened after I left you two?"

"Long story," Pete said, then pointed at his key ring and turned his probing questions aside with one of her own. "Going somewhere?"

"Back to Tally," he said. "I love you more than my Fat Boy Harley, but I'm getting gone while I can. You're handling Miss Fritz, and Eugenié's already read me the riot act about the catfish —"

"What did you tell her?"

"Nothing, I swear! Just that the freezer was busted beyond repair and we'd have to put the catfish somewhere else."

"And she bought that?"

"Sure, why not? She's too busy cooking."

"Always stick close to the truth . . . that's good thinking. What did you do with the fish?"

"She told me to shove the cooler out of the way so she wouldn't fall over it, and I did. Now, before I hit the road, spew about Dan-Dan. Is he a man's man or what?"

"Or what," Pete said, heading down the hallway.

"Did I also mention he's rich, successful, and as dapper as they come?"

Pete abruptly stopped walking, pulled back, and stared at Albert, her teeth set and her face drawn into a frown.

"Aren't you forgetting something?" she said.

"What's that?"

According to the adage, wisdom came with age. What a crock. In some cases, age came alone.

Pete tapped the corner of the chair rail on a nearby wall panel to reveal a broom closet tucked away beneath the stairs, and gestured inside.

"Step into my office for a moment," she said, "won't you?"

Her tone brooked no argument so Albert ducked inside, and she followed him in, plunging them into darkness with the closing door. The old church cathedral aroma of lemon and bees wax surrounded them, conjuring images of cowl-necked monks lining a musty nave and reverently chanting *Invitatorium for the Dead*.

A string dangled overhead, attached to a naked lightbulb on the ceiling. She yanked on the string and the bulb flared to life, transforming the closet interior into an Orwellian interrogation chamber.

Glaring yellow light created skeletal shadows out of a rack of brooms, sweepers, and mops hanging on one wall and flickered in and out of several well-stocked shelves of cleansers, detergents, and polishes on the other wall.

"There's a dead body down there, you chowder head," she said in a forceful whisper. "Not only is hiding a dead body highly illegal in this state, but she's *defrosting,* and I don't think you're appreciating the fact that it's going to get ugly around here real quick if we don't find somewhere else to put her!"

Albert stared at Pete as if she had something he didn't want to catch.

"I'd love to help," he said. "Shall I waltz the problem up the mountain where the guru of hit men lives so he can perform the necessary incantations and blood rites that will keep our pert little fannies out of the poky?"

Exasperated, Pete started to spit something back at him but then thinned her lips.

"I thought you were my friend," she said.

"Oh, no you don't. I'm wise to your tactics. Dumping a guilt trip on me won't work." Albert shook his head and pointed to his chin. "Take a close look at this adorable puss. Is this the face of someone who knows about hiding dead bodies? I don't think so. Thank you."

"If you stay and help, I'll sit you next to Benedict at supper."

"On the other hand," Albert said, brightening, "bribery works very well. Okay, how's this for an idea: we call down to the Thriftway and ask to use their fridge."

"That sucks swamp water."

"Reckon it's too public?" he said, thoughtfully scratching his jaw. "The Grab 'N Go then? They have a walk-in beer cooler."

"Oh, please."

"Clancy's Restaurant, the long salad bar fixture thingy? We could straighten her legs out maybe and . . ."

Pete shook her head vigorously on that ghastly thought.

"Why not your mortician boyfriend, Miller? Having him around ought to be good for something. Let's give the old boy a ding-a-ling."

Then she listened, amazed, as Albert proceeded to trump himself.

"What's one more body?" he said. "We'll stick her in a corner . . . He won't notice."

"Are you completely nuts?"

"Hey, I'm learning from the master, Miss Pete *I-think-dumping-her-in-the-lake-*

is-a-good-idea Lang."

Pete dragged her fingers through her hair, ruining any chance she might have had for not looking a wilting mess.

"My grandmother is reposing in Vonnie Miller's funeral home. Not only do I expect half the Panhandle to come to her viewing, but I wouldn't sully her memory by putting her in the same room with that . . . that other woman."

"It ain't as if we have to bail her out of a cheap hotel, toots. At this stage in the game, I really don't think she'll mind the extra roommate."

How could Pete argue with such an iron-clad endorsement?

Easy, but she wasn't listening. Another ugly thought had occurred to her, and she gasped, almost choking on a fresh surge of humiliation.

"Vonnie!" she said, doubling over and cradling her hot face in her hands. "I'd forgotten about him. What if he hears the gossip?"

Vonnie Miller was a slim man, with a wistful face and guileless eyes, the kind of innocent countenance that beckoned a woman to put her arms around him and hug him and look after him. Grandmother had liked him, calling him a nice young man from a good family.

Pete was fond of him; protective, too. He was comfortable to be around. Safe. Vonnie never asked for more than she was willing to give.

He was single, never been married, owned a thriving business, and adored Pete. They hadn't gotten around to talking about rings or proposals or forever yet, but everyone in town assumed it was just a matter of time.

She straightened, propped her elbow against a shelf, and let loose a laugh that bordered on hysterical.

"What am I saying? There's no 'if' about it. Once he hears I was in the boathouse kissing another man — a stranger, at that — it's over. He's done with me. He probably won't speak to me again, and who would blame him?"

When Pete paused in her rambling for much needed breath, Albert jumped in with a gleeful chuckle and said, "It was time to move on, anyway."

"Easy for you to say. This is a small town. The pickings are slim."

"Will you please forget the dweeby undertaker?"

"I can't. My sister can be promiscuous, but people around here expect better from me. Vonnie expects better."

"Then he'll just have to lower his expectations. You and Dan-Dan were actually smooching?"

Forehead resting in her palm, Pete nodded.

"Oh my," Albert said, "and here I thought the old bags were just flapping their gums. I'm shocked. I'm stunned. I'm aroused. Tell me all about it, toots, and don't leave out a single juicy detail."

That did it. She latched onto the clump of hair sticking out of the neck of Albert's shirt.

"Hey!" he said, smacking at her clenched fingers. "Careful, the shirt's silk."

"Don't you understand?" she said into his face. "How we're going to get out of this mess is a tad more important right now than the fact that Dapper Dan Benedict is a good kisser. I'm suffering torment of biblical proportions here and —"

About then the door swung open and Pete and Albert squinted into Benedict's impassive face. Her stomach lurched to her toes.

How much had the man overheard? With her luck . . . everything.

Who wanted to lead a life of quiet desperation, anyway? Not Pete. She seemed fated for hers to be completely public.

She'd always prided herself on being one, if not the only, person in her family who was resolute and in control. The absolute last thing she wanted was to appear as a desperate, plain-Jane mess in front of Dan Benedict, but, oh brother, was it too late. That boat had already sailed.

Releasing the stranglehold she had on Albert's chest hair, Pete blurted the first thing that popped into her head.

"A flying tarantula," she said and then expanded on her theme. "We cornered him in here."

Benedict squeezed in to the small room and let the wall panel swing shut behind him.

"Guess it's a good thing he could fly then," he said. "The little fella would've had a hell of a hike from the Southwest to Florida. Did I hear my name mentioned?"

Caught between laughter and irritation, Pete said, "Don't you get tired of sneaking up on people?"

"Actually? No. I kind of like doing it." And then he had the nerve to smile. "Am I interrupting something?"

She squirmed under his tender regard. It didn't escape her notice that he was a man who could move from casual elegant to T-shirt and shorts and back again and wear both looks with effortless ease.

By comparison, Pete looked like beef stroganoff an hour later — gray and lumpy.

"At least you're honest," she grumped.

"You sound surprised," he said, feigning hurt. "I'm wounded."

"I am surprised. Aren't you the guy who's not interested in truth?"

"Truth and proof are two different things," he reminded.

Albert tapped Benedict on the shoulder and said, "I hate to be the rut on the road to romance, Dan-Dan, but I just want to reiterate how much I'm counting on you to parlay our tushies out of this mess."

"Speaking of which," Pete said, and Benedict swiveled his attention back to her. "How did you know where to find me?"

"The voices in the wall as I passed," he said. "I figured it had to be either a poltergeist or you, and I don't believe in poltergeists. Don't bother explaining. I take it you like being different?" Then he spotted Albert's keys and jabbed a finger in his chest. "And you . . . don't even think about going anywhere. We are all in this together."

Albert sobered.

"Gotcha," he said, shoving his car keys

into his front pocket. "What's our plan?"

Benedict cocked his head toward Pete, crossed his arms in front of himself, and said, "Ask Mustache Pete here. I'm only the hired help."

Pete huffed and regarded him dubiously. "Watch it, buster. I do not have a mustache."

"Yet," Benedict added, startling a grin out of Albert.

She thwacked her friend on the arm.

"He said it," Albert whined, "not me."

"It's gangster slang," Benedict said. "Means a crime lord of the old school." He turned the full brunt of his warm and engaging brown eyes on her. "Y'know, the big cheeses rubbed out by George Raft, John Garfield, James Cagney — that bunch. You did say you liked old movies, remember?"

No, so far her day was lasting a month of Sundays; she didn't remember mentioning old movies.

"Never mind," he said. "It's lost something in the translation."

That Benedict went to the trouble to remember what she liked gave Pete a funny feeling of uneasy pleasure.

"Well, you do have a plan," he said, prodding her back on topic, "don't you?

That is, short of raising the dead or making us accessories to murder?"

She didn't, but doggone if she'd admit that to him. Instead, she tried to ignore the intensity of his nearness and spoke to Albert, improvising as she went.

"Once everyone's here," she said, "I'm calling a family conference in the library. I need you to stick around and play host while Dan and I are with them behind closed doors."

"Closeting yourself from your guests is rude," Albert said. "What should I say y'all are doing in there, electing the pope? People are gonna ask."

"Tell them we're going over arrangements," Benedict suggested.

At the same time, Pete said, "Make something up," and gave a dismissing wave of her hand. "I don't care. Break out the bourbon —"

"This early? We'll all go to hell. It's not even noon."

"It's a risk we'll have to take," Pete said.

"Just ply the drinks," Benedict added, embracing the idea, "and maybe no one will notice anything's up. Think you can handle that?"

"It's kinda hard to do a dog and pony show without the pony." Albert beetled his brow, seemed to come to a decision, and then offered a slow, wicked grin. "But it just so happens I majored in good pours in college."

The self-assurance entering his tone forewarned Pete.

"Please tell me you're not going to un-cork some of Delford Cooper's moon-shine," she said. "The fumes alone could strip the chrome off a trailer hitch."

He gave her a gentle pat on the noggin.

"It ain't the Fourth of July until we've broken out a little libation to whet the ole whistle. Leave it to me, toots. I promise I'll do you proud."

Not totally convinced but too grateful for the help to argue further, Pete leaned over and kissed her friend's cheek.

"Your wish is my command," he said and snapped to a salute.

"In that case," Pete said, "go forth and mingle. PDQ."

"Aye-aye, captain. I'll be at the front. Holler if you need me." To Benedict, he snapped his fingers, pointed, and said, "I'll catch you later at supper."

And on that note, Albert ducked out of the closet and soldiered on toward a covey of holy rollers.

Left alone to share the intimate space

with Benedict, Pete surreptitiously inhaled his clean scent and admired the sexy way his hair fell into a boyish bed-head tousle. Random clusters of hair offered a mere suggestion of a part, while an untamable fringe slipped over his forehead.

He remained silent through her perusal, letting her drink her fill of features that she would trace in her dreams.

No one could deny he was as good-looking as they came. But he wasn't just another pretty face. His was a face with substance.

Unlike the pinstripe-clad shysters who sported manufactured tans, Benedict had the rugged bronze skin of a man at home under the sun, the sort of reflective soul who could rescue hurt animals or build a house. Sharp. Diligent. Muscled.

A delicious temptation.

Beautiful brown eyes were set against high, tight cheekbones and perfectly framed a toothpaste-ad smile that was guaranteed to rattle a female to her bones. Looks, talent, charisma, and intelligence — what more could a woman ask for?

Even his name affirmed his measure, for Dan meant judgment. Pete managed to stifle a guilty sigh.

It was too late to put the genie back in the bottle. She stood a better chance of finding the Holy Grail among her pots and pans than she did of commanding the forever kind of interest, let alone the fidelity, of a womanizing celebrity like Benedict.

"Did you need me for something?" she finally said, and mentally winced when his eyebrows arched suggestively.

"Definitely remind me to discuss those possibilities later," he said and winked. "For right now, though, I thought you'd like to know your mother has arrived."

Pete ignored his lightly flirtatious mood — he was probably that casual with every woman he spoke to — and shot him a surprised look.

"Are you sure? You haven't met her before, have you?"

"Can't say as I've had the pleasure yet."

"Then, how . . . ?"

"Mercedes? Luggage the size of a small Manhattan apartment? It was a lucky guess." Benedict ducked out of the closet door and gestured for Pete to precede him down the hallway. "Shall we? The sooner we wrap up this unsavory business, the better."

Pete sucked in a fortifying breath and dug in her heels. Benedict was now driving down a road she helped to pave, and he deserved to know what they were up against before he faced the family. So she gave him the short version of her run-in with Niles Pollard and the reason he'd sought her out, if that's what he was really doing.

"What did you tell him?" Benedict said.

"Nothing."

"You didn't admit to anything? Not even off-handedly?"

"No, counselor, of course not. I'm not stupid, but . . ."

"But what?"

"While we're on the subject . . . I don't know any other way to say this except straight out — what happened in the boathouse was a mistake, a one-time thing, a moment of necessity."

"Are you referring to the freezer contents or to our kiss?"

"Why, both . . . but especially the kiss."

"I must be getting rusty. I could have sworn you enjoyed yourself. You did, didn't you?"

Suddenly, inexplicably, she felt the room close in and her ears heat up. Now was not the time to be coy. No way she wanted to give the impression she was panting after him as if she were one of the many soon-to-be ex's that he sported about on the pages of the tabloids.

"I did — I mean, that's beside the point."

"And the point being?"

"That I'm grateful for your help, but I'm seeing someone right now."

"Oh. You are?"

"Yes, I am."

"I see. And you don't want him to misconstrue — ?"

"Exactly. You'll be gone in a few days back to Atlanta, while I've still got to live in this town."

"Okay. I'll have a little talk with him."

"You'll do no such thing! I don't need you to rescue me. I can handle my own affairs, thank you."

"Affair? So that's how it is."

Pete wanted to slip through the floor.

"I mean, I think it's best if we leave well enough alone and let the talk die a natural death. Okay?"

"Sure."

She blinked and then blinked again, not expecting him to agree so readily.

"Sure?" she said. "That's it?"

"Yes, okay, sure, I understand," he said, nodding. "Tell you what, so we don't add fuel to the fire, you go on ahead. I'll stay here, count to five, and then walk out. All right?"

He really was being a good sport, Pete guessed, although she was uncertain why that bothered her.

"All right," she said for lack of anything else. "Thanks, I appreciate this."

"No problem." They switched places, and she turned to go down the hall when he said, "Hey, you never answered me."

"Answer what?" she said, turning back to face him.

He had the most seductive smile.

"Do you like to be different?" he said.

Why was he asking her that? Because he was a demented human being.

"Truthfully?" she said.

He chuckled. "Of course."

His hair reflected the yellow light and shimmered like a summer sunset. He was a sexy golden boy with a *GQ* sense of style, and she knew with absolute certainty she could never settle in a million years for being the flavor of the month. She had nothing to lose.

"The truth is," she said, "I come from a long line of eccentrics and oddballs. To be different in my family, I'd have to be a major overachiever." She gave a self-conscious laugh. "And I'm afraid that's more energy than I can muster even on a good day."

Her attention was caught as, quiet as a ghost, Eugenié appeared in the hall and thrust a handful of paper into Pete's hand. She glanced down at a stack of phone messages and floral cards. Her responsibilities were mounting, but returning calls and acknowledging condolence bouquets would have to wait.

"He wants you to take care today," Eugenié added, her bracelets tinkling as she gestured for emphasis.

"His warning comes a few years too late," Pete griped, "wouldn't you say?"

"He wants you to ask and then listen carefully. You do that, missy?"

"Oh, I'll ask all right. I wish he was here right now, I'd ask him an earful."

"Y'hear me, missy? Ask and listen?"

Experience had taught Pete that it did no good to haggle like a camel trader with Eugenié's divinations, so she conceded.

"Yes, yes," she said. "Got the message. I'll listen."

Satisfied, Eugenié barely cut a glance to the broom closet, as if seeing a strange man lurking among her rag mops were a common sight, and padded back toward her kitchen. Pete wondered how much the bones ever really revealed to the housekeeper and how much was owed simply to

Olympic-class eavesdropping.

She pondered the warning, not sure quite how to interpret it, and had almost forgotten Benedict was waiting until he coughed into his hand.

"He?" Benedict said, an edge to his tone.

"My grandfather."

Benedict's eyes widened.

"Lang?" he said.

"The same."

"But I thought he was dead."

Pete scowled, angry anew at the mess he'd left her to clean up.

"He is."

Before Benedict could give voice to the skepticism running rampant across his face and take the conversation where she didn't particularly want to go, his cell phone rang and he reached in his pocket to retrieve it. Pete took advantage of his inattention and tapped the secret panel shut on him. It slipped perfectly back into place, and she stood staring at a solid wall.

She could hear his muffled voice on the other side, and for a second the situation struck her as morbidly funny. Most people had a field mouse or two in their walls. Leave it to a Lang not to be so pedestrian — Pete had a drop-dead gorgeous lawyer in hers.

Just like a turtle that gains ground by sticking out his neck, Pete squared her shoulders and headed at a quick step toward the porte cochere at the side of the house to meet her mother's car.

It was time to get on the right side of this awful business.

The last occasion Pete had seen her mother was when Racine brought around her new husband, Carl.

Some experts claimed that romantic attraction often blinded people to a complete lack of common ground. Not so with Carl. He knew he and Racine were from opposite poles, and he married her anyway.

He had been the Rosetta Stone of patience when she stood on a Beverly Hills hotel balcony in her skivvies, belting out "New York, New York." In turn, she'd fallen in love with him and his raffish, reckless charm on the spot.

They were a perfect pair. Carl wasn't much to look at, but as Racine enjoyed borrowing from Mickey Rooney: "Money makes a man better looking."

So was Pete different, Benedict wanted to know? The man was about to find out.

Poor thing.

Chapter 6

By the time Danny approached the eight-foot-tall double doors that stood open to the porte cochere, the family's private driveway was a flurry of activity.

He halted inside the landing, the summer air caressing him like a lover's kiss, sweet and warm. The high roof extended far out over the adjacent driveway and looked to offer shade and a cool breeze to this part of the house all year round. Six wide, stone steps led down to the gravel drive where two more cars had pulled up while Danny had been inside the house.

"Care to explain what went on back there at the hall closet?" he said, slipping up behind Pete.

She wore a light perfume, floral soft. Scents and flavors were extremely sensual and arousing to Danny. It would be a simple matter to ease her back against him and cage her within his embrace. Simple, but not what she'd care for.

Besides, she was already in a relationship. Danny should have known the odds were against a gorgeous woman like her being unattached. He forced his arms to his sides and slowly committed her scent to memory.

"No," she said, without turning around. "It's complicated."

"I do well with complicated."

"Another time, maybe."

"I'm holding you to that."

He watched Pete step forward and clear the top tread just as a weatherworn geezer helped a full-figured mall princess in a purple cut-to-there dress emerge mouth first from the red Mercedes convertible at the head of the line. She wore a wide-brimmed red straw hat and oversize dark sunglasses and immediately set to holding court with two gardeners in overalls who had been plucked from their work to help with the mountain of luggage that was piling up.

"Your mother?" Danny said.

"Racine in the flesh," Pete said, and Danny heard her take a deep, steadying breath. "She can be a handful at the best of times."

"I take it she doesn't believe in traveling light?"

"For her, that *is* traveling light."

"And who's the older guy?" he said.

"My stepfather, Carl. He's into oil and gas. He comes off as breezy, devil-may-care, but don't let him fool you. Underneath, he's sharp as a tack."

"Sounds as if you like him."

"Yeah, I do. The last one Mother married was a dud, but this one . . . he's been real good for her."

"Where's your dad? Is he coming, too?"
Pete shook her head.

"Ye gods, let's hope not. He died in a skiing accident fifteen years ago."

Danny knew what it felt like to bury a parent. In a wordless gesture of support, he moved up beside Pete and lost himself in the warmth of her gaze when she turned and offered him a heart-stopping smile.

For all her moxie and smarts, Pete carried an air of vulnerability about her that inspired a potent mixture of tenderness and respect in Danny.

Back in the hallway, he'd gotten a sense of her community, the simplicity and elegance of the townspeople, as Pete had shaken hands, kissed, and hugged her way toward this side of the house. Danny had trailed behind her and, by comparison, had met with stiff but polite nods that left him feeling he was under more microscopes than an amoeba.

Despite all he'd told himself, he was enchanted.

The way Pete's eyes devoured him whenever she looked at him. The way her hips moved smooth as ice cream. The way she talked to the dead . . .

Okay, Danny had to admit that talent seemed a little divorced from reality. It wasn't quite as bad as the ethereal housekeeper who channeled Gramps and gave Danny the willies, but it was enough to remind him to keep on his toes.

And speaking of feet, Danny didn't need to ask about the occupants of the black Mercedes sedan. He recognized Jackson Lang — stocky, short dark hair, wire-rimmed glasses, clothes that seemed to strain to confine his energy — and assumed the two guys in cheap gray suits with him were campaign aides of sorts. A person wouldn't know to look at Jackson that he suffered from fallen arches.

It was odd how fate worked. If not for those bum insteps, Danny wouldn't be there. He hoped Jackson had the good sense not to invite his podiatrist fiancée to keep him company.

Behind them, a woman looking to be on the sunny side of forty and a younger man climbed out of a late-model Jaguar. Danny jutted his chin toward the white sports car.

"Who are those two?"

"She's my sister, Phoebe, and he's a jerk."

"The jerk got a name?"

"Stephen McCaffrey."

"McCaffrey?" Danny searched his memory bank of peripheral acquaintances. "As in the McCaffrey Building?"

"And the McCaffrey Library, and the McCaffrey Towers," Pete said, ticking them off as if they were character flaws. "And they also sell all the lighting fixtures in the world."

Danny blew a low whistle. "Nice job if you can get it. What's his problem?"

"His patronizing attitude. So condescending, you wouldn't believe. Sometimes I wonder if it's just me or all women with triple-digit IQs."

To Danny's way of thinking, Phoebe seemed to be holding her own with the guy. She wore a plain silk blouse over flowered capri pants almost as loud as she was. A long-legged, wafer-thin brunette, she was giving lighting boy a list of complaints longer than the Ninety-five Theses Martin Luther nailed to the Wittenberg door.

"They married yet?" Danny said.

"Not likely. He's more of a household

convenience, but the combo plays great in the press: he's a young CEO, she's a Harvard MBA." Pete leaned in close and spoke out of the side of her mouth. "He has the moral backbone of a pretzel, and if his eyes were any closer together he'd wear a monocle."

On a chuckle, Danny said, "Be sure to give her my card when they go for the divorce."

"Gladly."

"Pietra, darlin'!" Racine called and mounted the steps. "There you are, my precious girl. Be a dear and have Eugenié fix me a cocktail. Make it a double. I'd forgotten how dreadfully hot it is here compared to California."

"No way, Mother. Doctor's orders."

"For five years, I've been dry as a camel's ass. Now don't argue with your mama, darlin'."

Then, with international flair, she bussed Pete first on one cheek then the other.

Danny's initial impression was that no one would ever mistake Racine for a mellow matriarchal figure. She looked great from a distance. Up close, she had nothing left to lift. Her cheeks were stretched so tight that one more surgery and her ears would meet.

She pulled off her sunglasses, leaned back, and touched her index finger to the cute little wrinkle between Pete's eyes that Danny had come to adore.

"A spot of Botox will fix that, dear," she said. "Can't let things go. You're not gettin' younger, you know."

Danny could feel Pete shrink beside him. Her mother never noticed.

She was obviously one of those mothers genetically predisposed to wielding makeover advice freely and without guilt. In the next instant, Racine turned her charm on him. He automatically clasped her outstretched hand and returned her collagen-enhanced smile with a practiced one of his own.

"And who is this handsome gentleman?" she said, more excited than Danny expected. "Merely a friend, or perhaps he's a lover?"

"Mother!"

"I'm Jackson's lawyer," Danny corrected. He watched the light in Racine's eyes dim surprisingly quick and didn't know what to make of it. "We were scheduled to meet today but —"

"Of course, you'd be Mr. Benedict then." Her voice fell flat. "I'm sorry we must meet under these dreadful circumstances. It was a shock to us all to lose my former mother-in-law so suddenly. We all loved her dearly. She was such a grand and colorful lady."

"Yes, she certainly was," Danny said, thinking Pete's mom didn't know the half of it. "My condolences on your loss, ma'am."

"Why, thank you. You're very kind. Is your wife with you?"

"I'm not married."

"Oh, my, that is a shame, now isn't it?"

She perked up, stared at him expectantly, and Danny guessed from experience what she was waiting for, so he obliged.

"I can see why your daughters are so beautiful," he added, the fib slipping easily off his tongue. "Y'all look more like sisters."

As he'd expected, Racine sucked up the flattery. She giggled into her hand like a sixteen-year-old attending her first prom.

It was a small white lie.

Over the years, Danny had dealt with a slew of women who kept a plastic surgeon on speed dial. What else was a fun-loving, sun-loving woman to do when she woke up one morning, looked in the mirror, and saw Armageddon?

He'd read an article somewhere that the

reliance on cosmetic surgery usually came out of insecurity or the fear of getting left behind. Frankly, he saw nothing wrong with a woman being fifty or sixty or seventy, except when she tried to look twenty-five.

Carl gained the top step then. He had shock-white hair and a complexion like beef jerky, and it was evident he'd lived a lot of hard years in his face.

"Behave yourself Racine," he said. "Can't you see you're embarrassing the poor girl?" He wrapped a skinny arm around his wife's shoulder and leaned over and gave Pete a peck on the cheek. "Hey, kiddo, long time no see. Too bad about the old gal passin' on. You doing okay with it?"

Pete nodded, and Danny couldn't help but return the lanky fossil's genuinely compassionate smile.

"Hey, yourself, Carl," she said. "Yeah, I'm doing okay. I didn't know you were coming. I thought the Number Six well kept you hopping out there in California."

He grimaced and laid a palm to his stomach paunch.

"Don't get me started. I've got more gas in my gut than there is in that damned well." He extended his hand to Danny in a surprisingly strong grip for such bony fingers. "How do you do, son? I'm Carl Winthrop, and I guess you've figured out this mouthy woman is my wife, Racine."

While they exchanged niceties, Danny noticed Niles Pollard had appeared in the driveway and huddled up with the older of the two guys who accompanied Jackson. The way they both gestured here and there, Danny assumed they were discussing the types of publicity stills Pollard was expected to shoot around the house and in town.

As Pete and her mom and stepfather chattered away, the notion crossed Danny's mind that Pollard might get to wondering why he was standing with the family. Danny inched closer to neutral territory inside the shadowy doorway, just in case Pollard decided to start snapping pictures.

His move didn't do much good, though. The creepy housekeeper materialized at his elbow and garnered his attention by nudging him closer to Pete. With the other hand, the woman balanced a tray with a pitcher of iced tea and several frosty tumblers, so he couldn't very well continue to play Switzerland. He gave ground and could only hope Pollard snapped his best side.

"Do I get anything for drinkin' that concoction?" Racine said, eying the pitcher with distaste.

"For starters, missy, you get past me," Eugenié replied, offering up the tray and not taking no for an answer.

With a grimly pronounced, "Thanks," Racine accepted a glass rimmed with a slice of lemon.

"Dare I hope it's made with real sugar?"

"Hope all you want. But this here is made with substitute."

"Naturally." Racine offered a brittle smile. "Eugenié, you're a treasure, simply a treasure. I don't know how we would get along without you." Then, since misery loves company, she pivoted on the step to face the drive and called, "Refreshments!"

Jackson caught sight of Danny then and bounded up the steps, grabbing his hand and pumping it as if he were a voting constituent.

"Hiyah, Dan. Good to see you. Thanks for comin'. I know this blows your holiday, and I appreciate you makin' the time. Did you get settled in? Where are you stayin'?"

He fired his innocuous questions too fast for an eavesdropping Pollard to glean anything untoward from them and also too fast for Danny to answer individually, so he didn't even try.

"Good to see you again, too," he said. "I'm next door in the cottage."

Jackson seemed taken aback for a moment, then recovered himself.

"Great, that's . . . great. Everythin' okay? Need anythin'? If you need anythin' at all, you just ask —"

"I'm good, really. The cottage is fine, quite comfortable, thanks."

A sheen of moisture covered Jackson's face. The sweat could have sprouted as he emerged from the air-conditioned car into the humidity, but Danny had the sneaking suspicion he'd just upset his client's plans for a randy rendezvous.

Jackson swiped the tea from the waiting tray and downed half a glassful, then angled around and pointed to the two men with him. The older one was now having an animated and stressful conversation on his cell phone, gauging by his jerky hand gestures, while the younger one had his head buried in the car trunk, presumably retrieving the bags.

"Bill Sheldon, my campaign manager, on the phone," Jackson said. "And Tony Gant, recent Columbia grad and a hell of a gofer."

"Speaking of which," Danny said, "we need to sit down later and have a heart-to-

116

heart with — Sheldon, is it? — about his choice of photographers."

"Don't worry about rememberin' their names, you'll meet them later. Y'ready to get to work?"

"Our timing's lousy. You know that?"

Jackson managed to look contrite and raked thick fingers through his hair. He'd put on weight along with self-importance since Danny had seen him last.

"No help for it, though, Dan. I'm workin' a tight schedule between now and November. Grandmother would understand. I want to get the ball rollin' here and see if we can't cut Marjorie loose by election time. I've already interviewed every family law attorney in Tallahassee, so none of them can take her case. Vanessa has her little heart set on a Christmas weddin'. Should be easy, right?"

"Absolutely. Not a problem."

Danny removed his tongue from his cheek and refused to speculate further on the case in front of company, which was fine, because Jackson didn't wait for an answer anyway. He just smiled and greeted his mother, Carl, and his sister before turning back and clapping Danny on the shoulder.

"C'mon in the house," he said. "Let me

press a few palms with the locals and then we'll chow down on some of them good ribs I smell." He leaned in close and confided, "Bad Byron's Butt Rub is the secret, but don't you dare let on to Eugenié that I told you. Sure enough, your taste buds'll be thankin' you. The chipotle powder's what gives it the kick. Say, after we eat, how's about you and me gettin' together 'round mid-afternoon? Sound like a plan?"

"Hold up a minute," Danny said, catching him by the upper arm before he took another step. "I need a private word with you — with all of you. Now."

A nettled, surprised look washed across Jackson's face.

"Now?"

"If not sooner."

Racine heard his remark, lowered her glass, and searched first Danny's face then Pete's.

"Do you know what this is about, dear?"

"Yes, Mother," she said, "I do."

Her face relaxing, Racine said, "Well, there you have it. Whatever the problem is, Mr. Benedict, I have confidence my daughter can handle it. She has my authority to do what she thinks is best. Shall we go in, Carl?"

"Ignoring the problem isn't in your best

interest, Mrs. Winthrop," Danny said.

She stopped in her tracks, clearly unaccustomed to receiving plain speak from employees, and she was getting perturbed.

"Whatever is it, young man? You look as if you robbed a bank. Surely, nothin' is as bad as all that."

"Let the boy talk, hon," Carl said, patting a soothing hand to his wife's shoulder.

"I'm afraid it is bad," Danny said, casting his glance to include them all. "A situation has arisen concerning the late Mrs. Lang that needs your family's immediate attention."

"Be serious." Jackson set his half-empty glass back on the tray, stepped up to the landing, and offered a lazy grin. "The old gal was ninety. What could she have gotten into this time?"

"More than I care to say standing here in the open," Danny said, giving him back a long, hard look.

Jackson lost his smile and speared Pete with a glare.

"She didn't piss away our inheritance, did she?"

"Worse," Pete said.

"Nothin' could be worse. Let's get this settled now. Lead on."

"Not so fast, brother dear," Phoebe said,

coming up behind him and checking her Cartier watch. Her voice was abrasive, her manner brusque. "We've been on the road five hours. If you think I'm sitting down again right now, think again."

With drops of sweat running down his hairline, Jackson swiveled his attention to her as she gained the steps. Danny sensed her type, a deliberate ball-buster, and decided it was wiser not to interfere. Instead, he stood quietly beside Pete and watched the family dynamics unfold.

"Pheebs," Jackson said, "if Grandmother's done somethin' that could impact my reelection campaign —"

"Like I care." She marched up the steps, threw a quick greeting to her mother and sister and Carl, and merely nodded to Danny, acknowledging his existence but obviously wanting to distance herself from any fallout that might be coming Jackson's way. "I intend to freshen up first. Eugenié? My usual room?"

"All ready for you, missy," Eugenié said, scooting out of the way.

"See to our bags," Phoebe said.

Eugenié shook her head and said, "I ain't no porter. Fetch 'em yourself."

"Fine." Phoebe's mouth thinned in irritation a second before she bellowed down to lighting boy who dawdled at the car, "Stephen — the bags, sweetness!"

"Ten minutes," Jackson said.

"In the library," Pete added.

"Fifteen," Phoebe countered, breezing passed him.

"Ten!"

"Bite me."

Once everyone disappeared inside, Danny couldn't believe it when Pete turned to him, flashed a *Mona Lisa* smile, and said, "That went well, don't you think?"

Chapter 7

Grandmother Lang's library was turn of the century: mahogany, crystal, leather-bound books, and hand-tatted doilies; and it still smelled faintly of the imported Dunhill's she used to smoke when she thought nobody would notice. Overhead, an ever-changing play of light and shadow tangoed across the coffered prestplate ceiling as the sun moved in and out of the tree branches outside the French doors.

Near the center of the room sat a scarred cherry wood writing desk that had been used by generations of Langs and their spouses. A high-backed wing chair angled the desk and fronted the black marble fireplace.

On the mantelpiece stood legions of family photos in assorted sizes. Suspended above the mantel, in an ornate frame, Jackson and Phoebe smiled down on the world with the optimism of eternal teenagers, and Pete reigned forever in oil as a gap-toothed first-grader. Her platinum curls would never droop, and her youth would never fade.

And in an open cabinet hung in a lighted recess on the adjacent wall, a soft-tip dartboard sported a full-size picture of Grandmother's late husband.

Pete caught Benedict contemplating the dartboard.

"Oldest woman to make the world's dart championship quarterfinals," she said. The others hadn't wandered in yet, so she indulged herself by coming to stand at Benedict's shoulder.

"Looks like he gave the old girl plenty of incentive."

He studied the board intently, and she studied him. Fit. Elegant. Romantic. Spectacular. She filled her senses with the unique scent of him, musky and sinful and so inviting.

"Dreams die hard," he said.

"Some do," Pete said, nodding, her mind not entirely on her grandparents. "When I close my eyes, I can still see them as they were the last time they were in a room together, but it's difficult to picture the two of them ever being in love."

"At one time, I imagine, they were desperately in love. Otherwise, where did the hate come from?"

"You've very perceptive."

Benedict shook his head. "Not really.

123

I've managed to learn a couple of things in the years since I opened my practice."

"Such as?"

"One is to harbor few illusions about human nature."

"And the other?"

He looked back over his shoulder at her and winked, the sensual sparkle in his gaze sending a warm flush of desire all the way to her red-painted toes.

"Sometimes you lose people you love," he said, "and sometimes they stay with you even when they're gone."

The others started trickling in then, before Pete could further explore Benedict's past.

"Let me handle this," he said, becoming all business.

"Thanks, counselor. I appreciate your concern, but it's my family. The news is better coming from me."

"But your brother is paying *me* the handsome fee. I might as well start earning some of that."

Pete stood her ground, shook her head, and said, "Don't worry. He can afford it."

The job of handling the family belonged to her, not to some outsider. If she'd let Benedict have his way, they'd be featured on the eleven o'clock news as a notorious local family of petty criminals and probably all wind up scrubbing toilets inside some minimum-security prison.

As if sensing her thoughts, Benedict relented and moved farther into the room, leaving Pete to watch old ghosts rise up to haunt her.

Other than the crotch bull's-eye, which was riddled with dart holes, the library was conspicuously devoid of any mementos of her philandering granddaddy.

She missed her grandmother the most in this room.

Pete settled herself against the writing desk, half leaning, half sitting, with her hands resting near her hips. Racine perched in the wing chair to her left.

She had changed into a fashionable cocktail-length black chiffon, Phoebe into comfortable midnight blue tank top and pantsuit, while Carl and Jackson more closely resembled street-corner Bible thumpers in coatless white shirt, tie, and dark lightweight slacks.

Carl lounged in the matching chair opposite his wife. He was present, as he always was, because he was the skycap of Racine's emotional baggage, not because he had a voice in Lang family matters. Their feet rested on a mahogany and brocade gilded turtle, and their expressions mirrored each other, a mixture of curiosity and polite boredom.

Phoebe and Jackson sank into the Italian leather loveseat to Pete's right. Pete didn't know where her sister had left her myopic CEO and didn't care enough to ask, either.

Actually, that wasn't true.

Even feeling indifference suggested a relationship existed between them. She and Phoebe got along well enough but were practically strangers, too far apart in age to share in sisterly secrets and too opposite in personalities to be close.

The oldest of the three kids, Phoebe was born during Racine's writer period, back when the moon was young and she and Christopher Lang ran in the same circles with the likes of Truman Capote and Nelle Harper Lee, who both grew up in nearby Monroeville. Back then, young people nobly sacrificed themselves to artistic poverty and moral superiority while devouring monosyllabic claptrap that passed as expressive poetry.

Once, on a visit to New York, Truman introduced Racine and her then new husband Chris to Jerome David Salinger, in the time before he went into hibernation. Pete often wondered why her mother never spoke about that trip.

Phoebe was smart, well-read, and opinionated. She was also selfish, cocky, and egocentric, a woman determined to have it all and, as far as Pete could tell, very nearly did. She had a good education, a nice figure, substantial settlements from each of her ex-husbands, a son at Choate, and houses on two continents.

If it made Phoebe happy to troll the ranks of the Forbes 100 for big shots, then Pete was content with the status quo.

Benedict had moseyed over to the patio doors and seemed engrossed in something happening in the yard. Pete caught a glimpse of the dogs playing tug-of-war with what she hoped wasn't a slow cat belonging to a neighbor. The mousers Grandmother had allowed on the property knew better than to tempt fate.

Unable to forestall her grim task any longer, Pete took a fortifying breath and looked over the expectant faces congregated in the library.

"This morning I made an awful discovery," she said and then blurted out the no-frills version.

The galvanized silence that followed rang with the echoes of her grandmother's history.

Hoo-boy. Maybe Pete should have eased into the telling.

News of finding Miss Fritz in the boathouse freezer hit the family like a bad odor, and everyone except Benedict gaped at Pete as if she were a three-legged dog with chronic flatulence.

The I-told-you-so expression on Benedict's face said she should have let him do the talking, as he had wanted to do in the first place. Whether he talked or she did, either way, it was too late now to start over.

For what seemed like several long minutes, but were actually only a few seconds, Pete suffered through the stunned silence that followed her account of the floozy in her grandmother's broken freezer.

Then, finally, someone found his voice.

"Y'know why I love it here in the country?" Carl said, smiling benignly at no one in particular. "It's so quiet you can hear the fish fart."

He was such a keen observer of detail.

Unexpected but effective, his remark goaded the rest of the family out of their stupor and set them to bellowing at one another like a herd of sick calves. Yes, it was good to have the family back home again.

"Pipe down!" Pete said, flapping her

arms for quiet. "One at a time, please."

"I don't know whether to laugh or cry," Jackson said, jabbing shaky fingers through his hair.

"What you're doing," Phoebe chimed in, talking over him, "is accusing our grandmother of murder. How insane is that?"

"No, Phoebe, what I'm doing is laying out a family problem and asking for your input on a solution."

"Of course, you are, darlin'," Racine said, quieting her elder daughter with a glower. "And Phoebe understands that. She's just taken by surprise is all, as we all are. You're perfectly right to keep us in the loop."

"Murder," Phoebe grumbled and made a grand show of heavy sighs and crossing legs. "That's the most ridiculous thing I've ever heard of — and don't think you're dragging me into the middle of a noisy, god-awful mess. I'm not going to get mixed up in any scandal that I haven't created."

"Thanks," Pete said with a strained smile. "As always, Phoebe, I appreciate your candor."

"Don't mention it."

Phoebe then folded her arms over her chest, the picture of indignation and justified annoyance.

"I don't believe you're makin' the distinction between correlation and causation," Jackson said. "Just because there might be — and we don't know there is — but might be a relationship between Grandmother and some alleged dead woman, it doesn't mean Grandmother caused the alleged death."

"Alleged dead woman?" Benedict said, speaking up for the first time. He angled around to face the room and ping-ponged his gaze between Pete and her brother. "Are you an old movie buff, as well? Because it sounds as if you two watched the same Mickey Spillane movie."

Pete started to retort *Perry Mason, not Spillane,* then looked at Benedict's tight face and checked herself. Benedict was riled.

She knew he'd had his share of difficult clients, but this time was different. This time the media couldn't be used to gain sympathy for the case. This time, with this family, logical arguments went out the window.

This time Pete had put his ethics to the test.

"For the love of —" Jackson said, flopping back in his seat. "I know these things because I'm a lawyer."

130

"A tax attorney," Benedict pointed out.

Jackson glowered at him.

"I don't think you've found the tone yet that you want to take with me," he said, then added, "I know as much about criminal law as a divorce lawyer does."

Unwilling to sit on the sidelines while the two of them whipped out their measuring sticks, Pete opened her mouth to let her frustration show, but Racine beat her to the punch, putting a much nicer face on it.

"Gentlemen, please!" Racine said, sitting motionlessly, one hand to her chest, her eyes hidden behind thick false lashes. "This is most upsettin'."

There was no need to elaborate. Her silence stretched until they got the point. Then she slowly returned her hand to her lap and turned her attention to Pete.

"What are our options, dear? I'm assumin' we do have more than one course of action."

In nodding to her mother, Pete embraced the familiar mantle of responsibility. Solving problems, taking something torn up and putting it back together again — here was her niche in the family, her raison d'être, her happiness.

"Dan and I have discussed solutions,"

she said, "but we don't agree on any one solution, which is why we're running them by you." She gestured Benedict's way. "You've got the floor, counselor."

"Ladies first," he returned.

She shook her head and stated the obvious. "I have the home field advantage."

"Very well." He stepped up beside her in front of the desk. "My advice is to follow White's Chappaquiddick Theorem."

"Which is?" Jackson said, arching a dark, wooly brow.

Benedict shot him a wry smile.

" 'The sooner and in more detail you announce bad news,' " he quoted, " 'the better.' "

He paused — Pete figured to let that radical idea sink in — then continued, "Simply put, folks, the media loves to seize on this sort of thing. There's no way to win here, so why not make a clean break and concentrate on damage control?

"The story's going to hit the media, it's just a matter of when. Trust me, with the press, it's pay me now or pay me later. So let's save ourselves some headache, not to mention we'd be doing the right thing. Let's call the sheriff, cooperate one hundred percent with the authorities, and issue a public statement through whichever publicity person you choose to use."

He reached into his pants' pocket and pulled out a business card.

"If you need some names suggested —"

"What are y'all tryin' to do to me," Jackson said, sitting forward, forearms braced on his knees, "ruin my campaign?"

Benedict flipped the card onto the coffee table.

"Did we forget to mention that ancient freezer is on its last legs?" he said, hooking a thumb over his shoulder. "Wait much longer to do something, and there won't be a campaign for you to worry about."

"Pietra?" Racine said. "What do you think, dear?"

Stealing a glance at Benedict, Pete wished she could see the situation as black and white as he did. He just didn't understand family . . . especially her family.

"The media circus that would surround this news could be potentially devastating," she said.

"No shit, Sherlock!" Phoebe tossed out.

"And for what?" Pete continued, ignoring her sister's rude outburst. "To what purpose? Whoever the woman is in the boathouse, she's dead, has been for God knows how long, and most likely the people are gone, too, who could shed light on her and the circumstances."

Pete shook her head, her voice going foggy.

"Sometimes," she said gently, "ideals are more important than exposing the guilty. Think what's happened. After seventy years, this town has lost its driving force and its stability. There's not a soul here who doesn't owe some part of his or her life to Grandmother's kindness and generosity. What good is served by defiling her legacy? I think we should let sleeping dogs lie, say nothing, and bury this unpleasant episode quietly."

"You wanted me as your lawyer," Benedict said with a pointed gaze at Jackson, "now listen to me. If you agree to cover this up, go into it with your eyes wide open. Go into it knowing that not only are you committing a crime but probably the biggest PR boner in this state's legislative history."

"Well, I refuse to believe Grandmother murdered anyone," Phoebe said.

"Isn't that for a police investigation to figure out?" Benedict said.

"No, Mr. Benedict," Racine said. "Thank you for your comments, but I must agree with my daughter. What's done is done. It's up to us now to close this unfortunate chapter in our family's history and with as much privacy and dignity as possible."

Pete breathed a sigh of relief and let go of the tension bunched in her shoulders.

"Thank you, Mother."

"You're welcome, dear." Racine gained her feet and clasped her hands in front of her ample chest. "Now that we have that out of the way, we need to get with Eugenié and go over our plans for your Grandmother's barbecue tomorrow."

"You're going ahead with it?"

"Of course. Why ever not? We've celebrated her birthday ever' year with a big barbecue, and I don't see any reason we can't honor her memory in the same way. We'll do the barbecue, then later the parade, and then the fireworks in the evenin' — it'll be a perfectly beautiful Fourth. Just perfect. You'll see."

She stepped close to Pete and squeezed her hand.

"This ugliness with the freezer," Racine said, her voice subdued, "make it go away, darlin'."

Then, without waiting for a reply, Racine extended her hand to Carl and he rose from his chair.

"You're a good kid, Pete," he said, "and

smart. We're countin' on you and Dan there to figure a way to do what's right for everybody."

He blew her an air smooch as he and Racine left to attend the local nabobs collecting like lint in the front room, a role that played to all of Racine's strengths. Pete managed to smile back and nod, wishing she shared Carl's confidence. At about the same time, Phoebe peeled herself off the loveseat and stood.

"We're not even sure there was a murder," she said. "But if there was, I certainly had no knowledge of it and want nothing to do with it."

"The distinction between correlation and causation?" Benedict said, taking in the two of them.

"It's a sound argument," Phoebe said, glancing to her brother for support. "But I was thinking more along the lines of ends and means."

"I agree," Jackson said, rising to stand next to Phoebe. "We have no proof that any of what you're saying is true."

"Tell you what," Benedict said, "how about both of you follow me to the boathouse, and you can decide for yourselves whether we have an *alleged* murder."

"Do we have a choice?"

"Not really. That's why I'm getting paid the big bucks." And before either one could back out, he guided them toward the patio doors. "Let's slip out this way and avoid being seen by the crowd."

Benedict air-conditioned the outdoors while he angled to the side of the doorway and let Phoebe and Jackson precede them onto the rear lawn. Pete held back, knowing what awaited them inside the boathouse and wondering when she'd relinquished control.

"Is this a good idea?" she said to Benedict.

"You have a better suggestion?"

"Well . . . no, but I'm worried about Pollard. We haven't discussed him with Jackson yet."

"That's next on the agenda. Something tells me your brother and sister aren't up to hearing more bad news right now."

"For that matter," she said, dragging her feet, "I'm not all that anxious to see the dead floozy again, either."

She glanced in his face, and the calm strength and encouragement she saw there were enough to help her keep her shredded nerves together and goad her feet forward.

"C'mon," he said, nudging Pete out the door. "We haven't got much time."

"Think she can last in the freezer until

dark? It'll be easier to get rid of her then without being seen."

"If I remember my biology correctly," he said, "freezing damages cell walls, so defrosting tissue becomes mushier faster."

Pete swallowed, hard.

"Oh, lord, you certainly know how to get a girl's attention."

"Exactly. Now, let's get this settled before she gets in worse shape than she already is."

"Promise me something?"

"All depends if I can."

"Afterward, I can find a quiet spot and buddy up with a much deserved bottle."

He chuckled and said, "I may even join you. We'll make that two bottles."

The heat shimmering in his eyes was a delicious temptation. Pete did her best to ignore it.

But her best wasn't good enough.

Despite all she'd told herself, it was there and growing . . . the desire that had been plaguing her since the first moment in the hospital when she'd laid eyes on Dan Benedict.

"Here," she said and dipped into her pocket and handed him the key to the old metal door. "Be my guest. You go in first this time."

Chapter 8

Northwest Florida in July was proof positive that hell existed.

So much hot and sticky air hit them when Danny shoved opened the boathouse door, anyone but a southerner might have thought he'd unlocked Dante's *Inferno*.

As Danny stepped over the concrete threshold first, he had a bad feeling envelop him like a shroud, along with a blanket of perspiration that instantly plastered his knit golf shirt to his back. A flicker of second thoughts went through him, but he reminded himself he owed old Mrs. Lang and, by extension, he owed Pete.

After all, had he taken the old gal's confession seriously that day she'd sat in his office, Pete wouldn't now be acting out a harebrained idea about saving her grandmother's reputation. And he wouldn't be sweating out seeing the disappointment in Pete's eyes when he contacted the local sheriff and revealed Mrs. Lang's awful secret.

Pete. She was definitely a problem, a

threat to Danny's professional equilibrium, an unexpected snag in what was becoming a not-so-routine divorce case.

For the length of half a breath, Danny seriously considered moving to Montana and taking up fly-fishing. Brown trout had no philandering husbands. No beguiling granddaughters. No dead bodies stuffed into old freezers.

At that moment, anywhere held more appeal to Danny than here. He wanted nothing more than to get this chore over and done with before someone got too curious about what they were all doing down at the boathouse.

Their actions, and especially the lack thereof, were going to be hard enough to explain. They could all kiss the sane life good-bye if someone else were to contact the authorities first.

And that was exactly the point Danny hoped to drive home to his bull-headed client.

Jackson and Phoebe followed Danny inside the boathouse single file. Pete followed them. His fishing rod and tackle box that he'd left behind were propped in a corner, but the stringer of bass he'd paid the kid to catch were nowhere to be seen.

"Pete?" Danny said. "You take my fish up to the house?"

She shook her head, glanced around, and said, "They were right here when I left. I guess the cats helped themselves. Sorry."

With no evidence to the contrary, Danny accepted her theory, but the lawyer in him was skeptical. The rest of the interior appeared as cluttered and untouched as when he'd left it earlier in the day, with one exception: a person had to suffer chronic nasal congestion not to notice that the water stain casting from the base of the freezer was matched in velocity by a sour odor that was close kin to moldering peaches.

"The stink!" Phoebe wheezed, pinching her nostrils closed. "That is just nasty. Whoever was in here last needs to start stepping closer to the soap and water."

Jackson mumbled his agreement and added, "Pete, y'all need to clean up and fix up in here before the place falls down around our ears."

"It's on my to-do list," Pete said.

Leave it to a politician to champion easy issues and blatantly ignore the hard ones. What Jackson failed to acknowledge and what Danny worried on was that, taken together, the growing puddle and the smell weren't a good sign of things to come.

"Well?" Phoebe said with an impatient gesture toward the freezer. "If you've got something to show us, then show us."

"Are you always so personable?" Danny said.

"Only when I'm sweating my tookus off, counselor."

Danny took that to mean no.

"Hold onto your stomachs," he said.

But when he reached to open the freezer door, Pete put a detaining hand on his forearm.

"Wait a minute," she said.

He shot her a questioning look, taking in her glistening face and the delicate veins at the base of her hand at the same time. Then she pressed a finger for quiet to those moist and luscious lips he wanted to taste again and cocked her head to the side.

"I think someone's coming . . ."

No sooner were the words out of her adorable mouth than a frantic Albert all but skidded into the boathouse.

"Ix-nay! Ix-nay!" he said, his excited voice sinking to a singsong whisper. "Eporter-ray with amera-cay!"

"Oh, great," Pete muttered. "We can autograph eight-by-ten glossies at our trial."

What happened next was farcical.

Danny figured Albert had gone ahead and opened up the bar at the big house because, if the boozy fumes radiating off him were any indication, he was well lubricated.

"Hey, twinkle toes!" Jackson said, shoving Albert backward. "Go blabber somewhere else. We're busy here."

"Hold up, fellas," Danny said and stepped between them.

In the second the two of them started to square off, Danny resuscitated his long-forgotten pig-Latin enough to decipher the gibberish Albert had first uttered. Then the meanings registered.

He acted too late, though. Pete had already yanked Jackson and Phoebe each by the arm and whirled them toward the offending concrete stain.

They resembled a scene out of *Macbeth* as the three of them huddled around the freezer, Pete launching into an animated monologue on the sins of faulty wiring. *Double, double, broken coils and more trouble . . .*

Danny suspected she rambled, her mind detached from her mouth. With a family as prominent as hers, gabbing on one topic

143

while making mental lists or other was a trick she'd probably learned sitting through many a boring rubber chicken dinner.

As far as Danny could see, there were only two ways to escape the boathouse. One was out through the door, and the other was diving into the empty boat slip.

Neither offered much help. An exodus en masse either way would rouse the suspicions of even the most trusting soul, so Danny didn't bother to suggest they flee.

Instead, he sank back against a warped shelf and wiped the drops of sweat trickling down his neck, ready to bluff his way through. Albert let loose a boozy beer belch and then contrived to keep a straight face.

From experience, Danny knew getting huffy and ordering a reporter to leave was the best way to prick his curiosity and make him stick around. Enticing him to leave of his own accord was a better idea.

Speak of the devil, behind them all, Niles Pollard, clicking camera in hand, erupted in the doorway like a pustule on the butt cheek of Danny's life. Flanking him was the fresh-faced campaign gofer, Tony Gant.

Pollard paused, sniffed a couple of times,

and took in the scene, his glance sweeping over each face.

"Puts me in mind of hamburger I once left thawing too long in the sink," he said, lowering his camera and waving his free hand in front of his nose.

"Sorry to bother you, Congressman," said Gant. He had removed his coat and rolled up his shirtsleeves, and those were his only concessions to the heat. "Sheldon scheduled some volunteers to meet around four o'clock. Is it all right if we get some pictures of the grounds? There's a cottage over there that would make a great backdrop."

Danny expected Jackson to answer, but it was Pete who stiffened her spine.

"I'm the one you need to ask about the house or the grounds," she said.

"Yes, ma'am." Gant shifted his gaze to her. "My apologies, Miss Lang. Is it okay?"

"Tomorrow's better. I'm sure Sheldon will understand. Ask him to reschedule."

Her voice was soft and sensual, and Danny found it both alluring and arousing.

Jackson lost his thousand-mile stare about the time it apparently dawned on him that it was in his best interest to play along with his kid sister. And for the first time since Danny had met Phoebe, she seemed too startled to object to much of anything.

On the outside, Danny pasted on a business-as-usual face. On the inside, he was boiling.

Pollard was Jackson's folly and his responsibility to deal with, not Pete's. Younger than Jackson though she was, he appeared quite content to let her take charge. And gauging by how quickly she'd reacted in her brother's stead, Danny supposed this wasn't the first time Jackson sat back while someone else fixed things for him.

In that respect, Danny had more in common with Pete than either of them had realized.

Their exchange lasted mere moments before Gant skittered off, leaving Pollard lingering in the boathouse, but it was enough time for the seed of an idea to sprout.

Was it Jack Dempsey or Vince Lombardi who coined the sports slogan, "The best defense is a good offense"? Danny couldn't recall. No matter, there was plenty of political truth in the words, and it was a notion worth trying.

"Know anything about electrical wiring?" Danny said to Pollard.

Pete cut a startled gaze to Danny and

then glared as if he'd lost his marbles. Maybe he had.

He'd find out in a minute.

"Y'checked the plug?" Pollard said, sauntering up to the freezer.

"And the breaker box," Danny fibbed.

The reporter grabbed the door handle for balance and squatted on his haunches, giving the stain and the coils the visual once-over. A moment later, he straightened, rubbed his bristly jaw, and shrugged.

"Hell if I know," he said. "Call an electrician. Better yet, chuck the freezer and buy a new one."

And he reached again for the door handle.

Danny slammed his hand against the freezer door, preventing Pollard from opening it and startling him at the same time. Pollard snapped his chin up. His camera banged against his chest with the force as he narrowed his eyes.

"What's in there anyway? What're you hiding?"

Silence.

"A dead body," Danny finally said and decorated his bluff with a long, slow, sublime smile. "Mrs. Lang whacked one of her hubby's bimbos and stuffed the body in there. Next question?"

Danny then proceeded to give Pollard

the most patronizing stare he had, the one designed to make a client's spouse squirm as they sat across the conference table divvying up the Tupperware and the Baccarat crystal.

The first one to talk lost.

If the reporter noticed that Albert and the Lang siblings seemed suddenly stricken with shell shock, he gave no indication. To Danny, their unease was palpable in the stillness.

Seconds passed and his stomach started to cramp. He was sweating like a spit-roasted chicken.

Just when Danny thought Pollard was wise to him, a hiccup sort of giggle exploded from Pete.

It was an excited sound, one Danny chalked up to nerves. She slapped a hand over her mouth, but another extremely rude noise escaped anyway.

"I — I'm so sorry," she managed to utter between gasps of air. "I didn't mean . . . don't take it personally, it's just . . . ye gods."

Pollard's face mottled, and he looked like someone spit in his breakfast.

"Har dee har har," he said, his voice overloud in the small building. "Real cute." Turning to Danny, he pointed his finger and said, "Y'know, there's a reason Shakespeare said kill all the lawyers."

Gotcha.

Relief crept into Danny's shoulders, and he tried to appear amused.

"Where's your sense of humor?" he said. "But seriously, ever been through a hurricane?"

"No."

"Didn't think so. Anyone who has knows you don't open the fridge if the power's out. Ruins the chance to save any of the contents." Danny turned a questioning gaze toward Phoebe and Jackson and added, "Right?"

His emphatic tone prompted them out of their catatonic state to answer with mumbled confirmations and brief nods.

"Yeah . . . okay," Pollard muttered. "Whatever."

He seemed bored enough to leave when Phoebe chose that moment to open her mouth.

"Who is this person?" she said. "And why is he butting into family business?"

Danny fought back the urge to wring her neck. Fortunately for her, Jackson recovered his sense then and said, "Simmer down, sis, Niles works for the campaign."

Pollard nodded.

"The campaign wants publicity shots of the Congressman here to use in the press and in collateral material. Him shaking babies, kissing pets, glad-handing non-incarcerated kin — the whole cheesy home-town show. So do me a favor and smile."

And he raised his camera to his face.

"You're kidding," Phoebe said, pointing toward the door. "It's too hot in here for pictures. Now, out — unless you want to wear that camera as a hat!"

"You heard the lady," Danny said and gave an exaggerated shrug.

"Give us a minute, won't you?" Jackson said, clapping Pollard on the back.

He opened his mouth to retort but didn't have much choice except to move along, because Jackson was gently but firmly showing him the door.

"I'll be along directly," Jackson added. "Better yet, why don't you go ahead on up to the house and get yourself some of Eugenié's iced tea and peach cobbler. You won't be sorry. She makes the best cobbler in three counties . . ."

Once Pollard cleared the doorway grumbling, Danny threw Albert a quiet injunction, "Stand lookout."

Albert hustled to position himself near the door, scanned left and right, and then turned back to give Danny the thumbs-up sign.

"Good grief," Pete said, raking the damp hair off her forehead. "That was close."

"Too close," Danny said. He tilted Pete's chin up with his thumb. "Y'done good. You think quick."

Her eyes sparkled and made his heart dance in his chest.

"Lots of practice," she said.

He had the nagging urge to kiss her hard and deep despite their audience, but he recognized that feeling for the insanity it was.

"Oh, hurry up, will you?" Phoebe said, rudely interrupting his reverie. "I'm melting. Open it before someone else decides to come looking for his sainted congressman."

"Heads up, people," Danny said and yanked open the freezer door.

And then he just stared.

"What in the . . . ?"

"Why, it's empty," Jackson said.

"Slap empty," Phoebe added.

"I can see that," Danny snapped, unable to believe what he saw, or rather, what he didn't see. "I need to sit down."

He upended an old five-gallon paint bucket and plopped his fanny on top of it, resting his forearms on his thighs. They all stared at a big box that was yellowed with age.

Mrs. Lang's dead floozy was gone. Vanished. Kaput. Not even a thread left behind.

"What's happened here?" Danny said, canting his head over his shoulder toward Pete. "I thought you couldn't raise the dead."

"Get real, counselor." Pete adamantly shook her head and held up her hands, palms outward. "When did I have time to do anything with her?"

Not exactly a convincing denial.

"Well, she didn't just get up and walk away."

"Maybe she did," Albert offered. "Maybe Eugenié rolled the bones and put a hex on her, or maybe old man Lang conjured her from the grave . . . or maybe I should go see if I'm needed up at the house?"

"That's your best suggestion yet," Danny said and swiped the sweat off his face.

With no further coaxing needed, Albert slipped out the door.

"There is somethin' seriously wrong with that boy," Jackson said, jabbing a finger in the direction Albert had disappeared. "He's one brick shy of a load." Then he clapped his hands together, flashed a typical campaign frozen smile, and said, "Now, that we've got that settled, how about a bite of dinner?"

"But we don't have anything settled," Pete said. "What are we going to do about the dead woman?"

"What woman?" Phoebe argued. "See for yourself — there's nothing there." She turned to go. "I swear, if you want to cry over past woes and worry about someone who doesn't exist, help yourself. I don't have the time or inclination to indulge your fantasies. C'mon, Jackson. I'm starved."

"Right behind you," Jackson said with a pointed glance at the empty freezer box. "Y'all had me goin' there. For a minute, I actually thought you were serious." He gave a hollow chuckle and then followed his sister out.

Danny stood, slammed the freezer door shut, and shot Pete a fed-up look. The silence was long until she shrugged helplessly, but in her gaze was the shared understanding — *now what?*

"Somebody absconded with Miss Fritz," he said.

"That they did."

"Your brother and sister aren't concerned."

"It's easier for them to dismiss the whole

story if they refuse to believe she even existed."

"We've got to find her and convince them."

"Wait . . . *we?*"

They stepped into the relatively cooler air outside and heard a crowd of voices coming from the screened-in pavilion adjoining the dining room.

"Yes, we," Danny said. "I just crawled out on a very fragile limb to try to prove to your family that they had a big problem."

"And what did it get you besides heartburn? We tried. They wouldn't listen. End of story. You're the rock star of divorce lawyers, and a busy one at that, not a cop or a private investigator. Finding a missing body isn't your job. Don't you have a divorce case to focus on?"

"You're not going to help do the right thing?"

"I would love to," she said, "but my cross requires both hands."

"Have it your way, then. I'll contact the sheriff and let him handle it."

Pete folded her arms at her waist and threw back her shoulders, totally unaware of the sultry effect she had on him.

"There's no body," she said. "No evidence of a crime. Go to the sheriff with what? Tell him what, exactly? Remember, this isn't Atlanta. Not many strangers around here carry tales of murder without getting looked at sideways."

"Three of us saw the body. That should be enough for starters."

Pete shook her head.

"Not without Albert or me to corroborate your story."

Startled, Danny checked up. Her mouth was tight, her stance firm. The woman was obstinate as well as delectable.

"You're serious?"

"Try me."

He admired her devotion to family, but he wouldn't agree with her logic. She was in over her sexy little head, whether she admitted it or not, and he couldn't help the rueful smile that sprang to his lips.

"A few hours together," he said, "and this is our first bump in the road."

"More like a pothole," she said. "No — a sinkhole."

Pete paused at the end of the concrete skirting that surrounded the boathouse, in a patch of shade made by the roof overhang, while Danny pulled the rusted metal door to behind them and perused the doorframe.

"No point in locking it now," she said.

"I was looking to see if the door had been jimmied. Doesn't appear it was. Is there another way in besides this way and from the lake? A secret passage or something?"

"Not that I know of."

He pointed to a set of rickety-looking wooden stairs at the end of the building.

"Where do they go?"

"Up."

After a stunned moment, Danny lifted a brow, grinned, and a chuckle shook his shoulders.

"You bring it on yourself," Pete said, without apology. "Y'know?"

"Yes, I should've been more specific."

"No, counselor, you shouldn't have assumed that stairs lead somewhere."

"Most stairs do. These don't?"

"Nope."

"Of course, they don't. You're right — with your family, I'm wrong to assume anything."

She nodded thoughtfully and took pity on him.

"There used to be a second floor apartment with a widow's walk. I guess about eight, maybe ten years back, a hurricane blew through and — poof! — the whole top was gone with the wind, sheared right off and spread in a bazillion pieces all over the yard. Grandmother refused to replace it, just ordered a roof put on the bottom part here and a gate put at the top of what was left of the stairs. So that's what you see today, stairs that go up —"

Pete stopped and drew in a short breath. Then she and Danny both stared at each other.

"Ye gods," she said. "Are you thinking what I'm thinking?"

"The apartment's the scene of the crime?"

"That's the one."

"Yeah, afraid I am." He shook his head, and they both studied the air the apartment once occupied. "It'd be next to impossible to prove anything happened there now. There's no other way into the boathouse?"

"None."

"Then you know what that means, don't you?"

"Whoever poached Miss Fritz must have had a key?"

"Bingo." He cast Pete a prodding stare. "Moving a dead body equals obstruction of justice, accessory to murder, tampering with evidence . . . We're talking jail time here."

If Danny expected a confession, he was sorely disappointed.

"And there's something else we need to discuss," he said.

She dropped her arms to her sides and stepped closer to him, her hips swaying, her eyes warm and passionate, her skin glistening and inviting, and Danny's thoughts cobbled together. The sight hit him in the heart and excited him in ways he hadn't been excited in years.

He swelled with anticipation.

"Something else?" she said, and he watched her swallow. "What else is there?"

"Publicity," he said. "All of it bad. Can't dance with the devil and then walk away. You know Miss Fritz is real. And like it or not, you know we need to find her before she turns up as the lead story on the eleven o'clock news."

"*We* again?"

"It's your family."

Pete swung her gaze up to the big house, where it appeared dinner was in full swing. Danny was right, but he figured she wasn't in the mood to admit it.

"Sounds like it's time to eat," she said. "People looking this way are going to get curious. We'd better go join them."

"After we eat then? We'll make a few discreet inquiries."

"No blabbing —"

"I said discreet, didn't I?"

She stepped closer and glided her fingertip in an elegant circle through his damp hair and behind his ear. He stared at her and she stared at him. He listened to her slight breathing and inhaled the salty tang of her warm skin, and his breath caught in his throat.

"Pieces of cobweb," she said.

He was a goner.

No man sets out to make a fool of himself over a woman, yet it happens all the same. Danny had tried to define their relationship with parameters, but he could feel his resolve weakening, his good sense succumbing to the gentle pull in Pete's voice and the hot promise in her eyes.

"Dan?" Her voice grew lower, deeper, softer. "Sure we can't drop this whole thing?"

"Afraid not, sweetheart."

Reluctantly, she accepted his stance on the topic of the missing Miss Fritz and moved into the sunlight. As she ambled toward the house, he heaved a heartfelt sigh.

Maybe, if he was lucky, his attraction to Pete wouldn't land him behind bars.

Yeah . . . maybe.

Chapter 9

Pete's inner goddess was clamoring to graze at the buffet table.

No wonder. Given the day Pete was having, she seriously considered dropping her face into the pan of chocolaty Mississippi mud pie and not coming up for air until she hit endorphin overload.

The presence of Vonnie Miller hovering at her elbow, however, suggested she mosey over to the nearest full-length mirror and stand there until she came to her senses. She looked at Vonnie, fence-post thin, looked back at the abundant buffet, and opted to skip dessert. For now. But it was with a certain amount of satisfaction that she perused the rest of the food Eugenié had set up between the dining room and the banquet tables in the pavilion.

The screened-in room and the colonnade connecting it to the main dining room had been Pete's idea. They were added during the renovation to make traffic flows easier at the food stations.

Unfortunately, this was the first occasion

they had to throw open the dining room doors. Still, it did Pete's heart glad to see her grandmother's friends chatting and wandering freely between the outside tables and the house.

No matter the occasion, socializing at the Lang mansion was about projecting image and maintaining it with proper lifestyle. Everyone in the family had a job to do. Racine worked the room. Carl kept glasses filled. Phoebe directed traffic at the door. Jackson guided conversation. And Pete ensured that everything ran smoothly behind the scenes.

Vonnie, wearing his usual stoic expression and dark suit, had arrived while Pete and the family were convened in the library. Now an old woman with a walker and whittled cheekbones claimed his attention, so Pete left them to it and helped herself to a plate and fork.

He hadn't mentioned hearing any rumors about her and a certain appealing lawyer, but Pete figured it was only a matter of time until he caught a whiff of gossip from someone. Rather than worry about it further, it was better if she came clean and told him. But how, exactly, did she broach the subject?

Was there etiquette to cover such things?

Somehow Pete doubted Emily Post con-sidered homicide sparkling dinner table conversation. *Grandmother died and . . . oh, yeah . . . was a murderer. Pass the cornbread, please . . .*

To add to Pete's dilemma, Benedict perched over a full plate in a corner across the crowded room and kept tabs on her, at the same time he engaged in a schmooze-fest with a couple of GED hopefuls and a former state senator just back from a stint at Betty Ford. Pete sensed the full weight of his gaze boring into her.

The attention was flattering yet un-nerving, to say the least.

Racine slipped up beside Pete, speared a green olive from the condiment dish, and said, "It's certainly not Spago."

"No," Pete said and grinned, "it's better. You can't get down-home Southern cooking just anywhere."

Her mother nodded absently, and Pete silently gave her to the count of five to spill what was really on her mind. She didn't make it to three.

"He's an excellent catch." Racine popped the olive into her mouth, nudged closer to Pete, and whispered, "You have my blessing to marry him."

"Who, Mother?"

"Baron von Hardon over there," she said, cutting her mischievous gaze to the corner. "Who do you think? He looks sexy enough to give you an orgasm every night and twice on Sunday. Good-lookin' *and* a lawyer — trust me, there are worse combinations, darlin'. Why, the man is practically undressin' you with his eyes."

"Don't be absurd." To hide her embarrassment, Pete ducked her gaze and latched onto the serving spoon in front of her. "He's simply bored out of his gourd and staring into space."

"Work with me, sweetheart." Racine gestured in the air with her toothpick. "Men need a little encouragement. It wouldn't hurt to offer some eye candy."

"Mother, are you suggesting I go Hollywood and traipse around half-naked at my grandmother's funeral?"

The last thing Pete imagined herself doing was sliding over that slippery fashion slope.

"Nothin' so crude, dear. Heavens, some of the clothes I see out there aren't fashion statements, they're cries for help. I'm merely pointin' out that there are rewards in showin' a little cleavage. And you know I'm right."

"How do you figure that?"

"Because you're doodlin' in the tuna fish."

Sure enough, when the salad bowl in front of Pete came into focus, she had created a pediment by pushing tomato wedges into a triangle and using onion bits as dentil. She released the death grip on the spoon and pasted on a bland face.

"I was simply thinking of changing the roof line on the boathouse," Pete said, drawing an innocent smile from her mother.

"Of course, you were, dear." Something beyond Pete's shoulder caught Racine's gaze then and her eyes turned over bright with politeness. "Why, as I live and breathe. Vonnie Miller!" To Pete, she squeezed out of the side of her mouth, "Think about what I said, darlin'." Then, louder, "You dear boy, where have you been hidin' . . . ?"

As Racine continued her mingling, Pete mulled over her mother's words.

There was more insight in them than Pete cared to admit. Not only had she been trying to fathom why she suddenly wanted Benedict to see her as a sexy, liberated woman, but she'd been trying not to make unkind mental comparisons between him and Vonnie.

Unfortunately, she was failing miserably on both counts.

She lay the blame on raging curiosity and on her own namby-pamby nature.

Vonnie was a considerate and gentle man but not exactly a heartthrob. His looks were average, and his drab way of dressing was a trait that erased him from most women's radar screens. He wasn't well educated, but he could read and write. He never shied away from work, and he was honest.

The unvarnished truth?

There were no flashing lights and fireworks when they were together. It wasn't chemistry that drew Pete and Vonnie to each other's company so much as loneliness.

They both possessed a sad acceptance of the dull life they had chosen.

At one time, she thought common ground was enough for two people to build on, that the sum of a relationship was more important than the parts. That is, until the sight, scent, and taste of Dan Benedict made Pete go weak in the knees.

"Aren't you eating?" she said to Vonnie as Racine moved on to other quarry.

The inquiry was more to divert Pete's uncharitable thinking than any real interest in his delicate appetite.

"I finished a bite or two." He flashed a lopsided grin. "I'm pacing myself. What about you — can't decide?"

The variety of food donations from the community, added to what the house-keeper had cooked, blended Southern with Cajun to create intensely flavored, highly textured fare. Fruit salad, green salad, pasta salad, heaping platters of fried chicken, cold cuts, and sliced country ham were among the usual meats and side dishes covering the main tables.

For the more daring tastes, spicy jambalaya, gumbo, dirty rice, chicken Creole, and boudin balls waited in beaten-copper chafing dishes that decorated the hundred-year-old sideboard. Beyond the sideboard sat a cloth-covered banquet table loaded with glass pitchers of lemonade and pint-size Mason jars of sun tea chilling in a pewter tub of crushed ice.

"Too much stress, I guess," she said, unwilling to share her thoughts with him just yet.

She didn't understand them. How could she expect him to?

Albert passed within hearing, balancing a mug of chicory coffee and a dessert plate overflowing with peach cobbler drizzled with homemade vanilla ice cream.

"Stressed spelled backward is desserts," he said, hoisting his full plate for emphasis. "Coincidence? I think not. Dig in, toots."

And with that diet advice bestowed, he sauntered off toward the less-crowded patio tables out on the verandah.

Pete silently vowed to be good and fixed herself a sampler plate of salads instead. After helping herself to a few home canned baby gherkins and a couple of slices of fried green tomatoes, she grabbed a jar of tea and followed Albert outside, not ready to be left alone with Vonnie.

"Here y'go, Pete." A man with a beer belly and a comb-over helped his plump wife rise from the white porch swing. The creaky chain protested, and Pete made a mental note to squirt some oil on the links. "Y'all can sit here. We gotta head back to work."

She shot a glance toward Albert, hoping for an excuse to decline, but he was chatting it up at a table with some of the members of the Baptist Church choir and didn't notice her SOS. Short of being rude or embarrassing herself, neither of which Pete was inclined to do, there was no way to avoid accepting the offer to use the intimate seat.

"Drop back by for supper, y'hear?" she called as the couple ducked into the house. "We've got plenty to eat."

"Will do," came the reply.

Vonnie shrugged out of his suit coat, tossed it over the back slats, and loosened his tie before settling down beside her on the swing. The underarms of his white shirt were dingy wet with perspiration stains.

At any other time, Pete would've enjoyed the serenity of lounging in the shade of the porch. Behind them, bumblebees darted in and out of clusters of hot pink blooms on the crape myrtle trees. The breeze from the ceiling fans made the heat tolerable, while the whir of the fan blades mixed with the low jumble of voices around them.

"Sweetie," Vonnie said, and Pete mentally winced. "There's really nothin' to stress yourself about. Miz Lang left specific instructions, right up to the last note of music. I'm personally overseein' every aspect of her services, so don't worry your little heart about it none. We'll do right by your grandma, you'll see. I don't aim to let her down, and I ain't partial to lettin' my best girl down, neither."

Best girl? Pete's food stuck in her throat.

"And I appreciate it, Vonnie," she said

between choking down bites. "Grand-mother knew you'd do a good job, and so do I. Really, her funeral is the one thing I'm not worried about."

He offered a sorrowful smile, which Pete knew was genuine and not just because it was an expected part of his office.

"It's your mama and them, ain't it? They're drivin' you crazy again, poor baby."

He stole a gherkin from Pete's plate, bit into it with a crispy crunch, and she didn't have the heart to mention kissing another man and wallowing in the sensual pleasure of his touch, let alone broaching the matter of her grandmother and the dead floozy.

Why did Vonnie have to be such a nice guy?

While he continued to reassure her with compassion and caring and understanding, she was having an aneurysm and waiting for the left hand of God to come down and smite her right there in the middle of the potato salad.

What an ingrate she was. Instead of ap-preciating the fond attentions of a good man, she fantasized over a few moments of mindless hot and heavy with a tasty side dish like Dan Benedict.

So what if he had a gorgeous face and a

beautiful caboose? She refused to dwell on the good glimpse she'd gotten of tight buns packed into an indecently smooth pair of shorts, although it was hard not to notice that the man liked to work out. And so what if he was well spoken, intelligent, and rugged?

None of that mattered, because he'd be gone in a few days and she'd remain there.

And that would be the end of that.

"If I have time," Vonnie said, "mind if I drop in to see you later tonight? I've got something I've been meaning to talk to you about for some time."

"How about now?" Pete said, her curiosity up.

Vonnie shook his head and glanced around as if he were trying to locate a forest fire.

"When we can have some privacy," he said.

The seriousness of his tone made Pete's heart sink with dread. If he uttered a sentence containing the words *ring* or *church,* she was in trouble.

"I know you're grievin'" he added, "so don't be afraid to flat out tell me to go peddle my peanuts elsewhere. I don't wanna be a bother."

He looked so sincere, Pete would sooner

kick a puppy with an army boot. She took a deep breath. Whatever he had to say, she'd meet it head on and deal with it.

What else could she do?

"No — I mean, yes, come eat supper with me if you can. And no, you're never a bother. Really."

"If you're sure now?"

She nodded.

"I'm sure." Then Pete searched for safer ground. "Don't let me forget to contact Jackson's secretary this afternoon and give her the funeral schedule. I should've done it already."

"Becky can see to that," Vonnie said, speaking of the middle-aged mom who did double duty keeping the mortuary's books and answering the phone. "She'd be proud to since your grandma gave her so much help when her husband had that tractor accident. Did I tell you her father-in-law at the *Gazette* called me 'bout runnin' a nice photo tribute?"

"That's so sweet of him. If I don't see him before you do, send him my regards, won't you?"

"Sure thing. Let me go now. I got work to see to."

Then he grabbed his coat and stood. Vonnie represented something fundamentally decent, and he deserved better than for Pete to sit there wishing he were someone else.

"You've done so much," she said. "How can I thank you?"

In reply, he leaned over and gave Pete a quick peck on the cheek.

"No need. Proud to help out. If you think of anythin' else you need 'tween now and tonight, you got my number. Gimme a holler."

Pete smiled her gratitude, watched him leave, then rose from her seat. Deep breaths. And chocolate. Lots of it.

She headed straight for the comfort of the dessert table inside the house. One step over the threshold, she collided with Benedict, who was on his way out.

His stance was demanding, not asking for, her attention.

"What're you doing with that guy?" he said. "Is he the one you were talking about, the one you're seeing?"

"Not that it's any of your business, but yes."

"He doesn't look to be your type."

"Oh, and you do?"

"Me? No, I'm just admiring the view."

"In that case, don't let me keep you."

She had the Mississippi mud pie in her

sights and moved to go around him. Not one to be ignored though, he pivoted on his heel and fell in step with her, holding up his right hand and revealing two paper cups stacked over the neck of an expensive bottle of red wine.

"What do you say? Me, you, and a '96 Syrah?" When Pete stopped to gawk at his nerve and resourcefulness, he smiled and added, "Your grandmother keeps a well-stocked wine cooler."

"Of all the — do you always pilfer booze from clients?"

"Only the ones with good taste. When we're done with this beauty, there's a bottle of '02 we can filch."

Despite herself, Pete cracked a smile. The man was incorrigible and way too appealing.

"C'mon," he said, indolently leaning his shoulder against the wall. "I know a quiet magnolia with lots of shade."

She tried to say no but became distracted. He was endearing with his mouth grinning and his shimmery hair falling over his forehead and his eyes caressing her as if she were the only woman in the room.

Pete had trouble catching her breath. A jolt of desire rushed all the way to her stomach.

"Count to five," he said, "and meet me outside?"

The invitation was tempting. Benedict was tempting. Too much so. Pete cast her glance around to see if anyone were watching, feeling excitement and trepidation and more than a twinge of resignation.

Who was she kidding?

"Why fool ourselves," she said, shaking her head. "It won't work."

Benedict lost the wicked gleam in his eyes and straightened away from the wall. He didn't pretend to misunderstand her.

"How do you know?" He glided the backs of his fingertips down her cheek, and Pete almost sighed out loud. "Why don't we give it a try and see where it takes us?"

She was such a coward.

"I don't think so." She captured his hand to lower it away from her, but he curled his fingers around hers. "Look, I'll be honest." After another quick glance left and right for any eavesdroppers, she lowered her voice so her words carried to Benedict's ears only. "I've been in one relationship since I graduated college. If you've been in more than one, that's one memory more than I care to compete with."

Of course, he had. She knew that much from reading the rag mags.

She watched him open his mouth, but what could he say? She'd left him no wiggle room. Frowning slightly, Benedict eased his hand away and took her dirty plate, stacking it on a pile of others waiting on a side tray to be carried into the kitchen.

"Are you sure?" he said.

She nodded.

"We agreed to leave well enough alone. Now, I believe you have a meeting with Jackson?"

"I've been stood up in favor of a photo shoot with the dancing bears."

"Squares," she said and mustered a chuckle. "Dancing Squares. Don't take it personally. The members of the square dancing group are locals. Their votes count. Yours doesn't. Around here, it always comes down to politics."

"So it is in life," he said. He angled away then turned back and studied her a moment. "Anyone ever tell you that you're the most amazing woman this side of the Mississippi?"

His quiet words made her thoughts go still and clean.

"You should see me on the other side," she said.

And that's when Pete began to fall in love with him.

Before either one of them could say more, Phoebe swept through the dining room doorway like an ill wind and caught Pete by the arm.

"Where have you been? I've been looking all over for you."

"I just finished eating. Aren't you and McCaffrey supposed to be handling meet-and-greet at the front door?"

Phoebe nodded and said, "We were. Now we've got a problem."

"What's up?"

The urgency in her sister's tone conjured all manner of possible trouble for Pete, but only one thought sprang uppermost in her mind.

She gasped and whispered, "The dead floozy showed up somewhere?"

"You wish," Phoebe whispered back. "No, I mean a *real* problem. Did you know Jackson's corn-and-bunion babe is here?"

"I was afraid he'd pull a stunt like that," Benedict cut in.

Pete swiveled her attention between them, but she didn't need to ask which podiatrist Phoebe referred to.

"He invited her here?" she said. "What in the world was he thinking?"

"About getting laid, probably."

Pete frowned at her sister's snorted assessment, even while she silently agreed with her. There was no denying that Jackson possessed more than his share of Granddaddy Lang's randy genes.

Normally, Pete wouldn't interfere between consenting adults. But July 4th was a press junket bonanza. Talk radio. Newspaper. Local television.

The holiday was the primo opportunity for voters to see their candidates give more than lip service to motherhood and apple pie and all the other staple issues guaranteed to strike emotional chords. Now was the time for a politician to appear squeaky-clean.

Parading a fiancée around before he was a divorced man wasn't Jackson's smartest move. As stupid as it was though, on Pete's worry meter, it wasn't on par with colorizing *Casablanca* or with a dead floozy missing from the fish freezer.

Relaxing, she said, "Let's at least hope he and Vanessa exercise some discretion."

"I don't think that's the part of him he was looking to exercise."

"Want me to talk to them?"

"Vanessa's not the problem," Phoebe insisted. "When I couldn't find you, I sent Stephen to round her up and stash her in the library, out of the way for a while until you could figure something out."

"Then, what — ?"

"Hurry up," Phoebe said, dragging her sister along, "before World War Three breaks out at the front door! Large Marge just arrived."

Chapter 10

Marjorie Lang was a silent partner in her husband's successful political career.

She was also his soon-to-be ex-wife. The problem was everyone in the family seemed privy to that impending development except her.

Danny realized the mature and overstated woman was like a mushroom in the dark when he followed Pete and her sister into the visual treat that was the grand foyer to find out what his client had gotten them into.

Large Marge, indeed.

Forget little woman, little feet, little anything. Marge in stiletto heels was at least six-feet tall and a plus-size woman in all the right places. But she wasn't tarty. Wearing a well-cut black suit and a look-at-me hat, she had presence and stature and knew how to use them to make a statement.

No doubt she had selected her outfit knowing it played off the formal black and white checkerboard tile. From head to toe, she looked every inch the socialite wife, the kind who sat this board or that board, who attended glitzy charity functions, and who organized well-attended fund-raising events. She appeared almost regal as she stood surrounded by the foyer's elaborate woodwork, a sweeping circular staircase, and a massive, nine-tiered crystal chandelier suspended from a painted dome three stories up.

So many bereavement baskets and potted plants had arrived that the foyer was a floral tribute spectacular filled with striking, brilliant color. Through the opened mahogany doors, Danny glimpsed large delivery vans bringing more as he approached the front where the air was rich with the pungent perfume of fresh cut flowers.

"Marge!" Pete said, quickly crossing the entry room and extending her hands. "How nice of you to come. What changed your mind?"

"Good manners and breedin'." She clasped Pete's hands in hers and exchanged perfunctory kisses on the cheeks. "Your grandmother was always generous in her kindnesses to me, especially when her grandson wasn't. Besides, this is family values time. No prick making a bid for reelection can afford to be seen marshallin' a

July 4th parade without his wife, now can he?"

Then she took one gander at Danny trailing behind Pete, and he thought he'd stumbled into a Hollywood B movie: *Revenge of the Middle-Aged Woman*. Marge knew exactly who he was before they were even introduced; he could see recognition and suspicion in the narrowing of her flinty eyes.

He figured Pete noted it, too, because she became animated.

"C'mon inside," she said, gesturing with her arm. "Aren't the flowers lovely? I'll bet you're hungry. We've got lots of food."

Marge shook her head.

"I'm not eating any of that Cajun Lucrezia Borgia's food. The woman scares me. No telling what she's sprinkled in it — ground lizard's guts or something."

"Honestly, Eugenié doesn't . . ."

But Marge ignored her sister-in-law's poorly concealed effort to soothe her ruffled feathers and bustle her out of the way.

"I know you," she said, wagging a French-manicured finger in Danny's direction. "I've seen your picture in magazines."

For that matter, Danny was acquainted with high-crass wealthy, too — people practiced in the polite brush-off and for whom writing a check wasn't as much a matter of generosity as it was ostentatious.

Before he could form a reply to Marge, she cast an accusatory glare over her shoulder at her husband, who developed a sudden fascination for the aroma of the white lilies spilling from a tall glass vase on the foyer table.

"Jackson?"

"Yes, dear?"

"Why is a divorce attorney standin' in your grandmother's foyer?"

No one spoke for several seconds and then Jackson reached rock bottom and started to dig.

"Because . . . ?"

"Because," Phoebe said, cutting him off, "being married makes it really hard to date."

Wonderful. No Christmas card for Phoebe this year.

Granted, Jackson could have saved Danny and the rest of them a lot of grief if he'd come clean earlier with his wife about sweating up the sheets with her replacement. But Danny wasn't surprised to find out he hadn't. Truth was usually the first casualty when a spouse decided to stray.

Now what?

Danny's mind sorted through quick-fix

solutions in rapid order.

With a hundred people of varying influence gathered in the house to mourn old Mrs. Lang's death and celebrate her life, now was definitely *not* the time to inform Marge that her flat-footed husband had been rogering the good doctor who was squirreled away in the next room.

Jumping in, Danny cut off Phoebe in a bid to save his client from social and financial suicide.

"She works with glue too much," he confided to Marge. "Say, Jackson, old boy? Fetch your wife's suitcase, why don't you? I'm sure she'd like to freshen up."

Jackson latched onto that suggestion with obvious relief and hit the pavement a second later. If luck were with them, he'd lose his way and not return until they were all collecting Social Security.

But Danny wasn't holding his breath.

When Jackson scurried out the door without refuting Phoebe, Marge changed tack on her sister-in-law and fired her own shot across the bow.

"Don't you have a boyfriend to go burp?" she said.

"You know why I'm single?"

"I can think of several reasons."

"All righty, ladies!" Pete said, staring at

them with varying degrees of impatience and disapproval. "This is not a good time. How about we wait until our grandmother is actually in her grave before we get into a pissing contest, shall we?" And she made a shooing motion toward her sister. "Thank you and bye-bye!"

Phoebe's indecorous expression gave way to a bogus smile, and she dodged out of sight.

Once her sister was gone, Pete turned and muttered in a weary undertone, "Now, where was I? Oh, yes . . . Marge, I'd like you to meet —"

"Pete's houseguest," Jackson said, hardly missing a beat as he rolled a black garment bag and weekend satchel over the threshold.

After Danny picked his jaw up off the floor, he realized his face-saving options were dwindling fast. He could call his client a lying adulterer, but that struck him as self-defeating as well as redundant. Large Marge probably already knew that fact about her husband, anyway.

Not only was Danny not in the mood to referee if his client from hell and his wife decided to go ten rounds in front of God and everyone, but it scored no points for his case to antagonize her right off the bat.

As a matter of routine, Danny preferred to keep things as civil as possible between both parties for as long as possible, and right now, he was willing to do whatever it took to accomplish that, even if it meant enduring the frowns and lecturing of his client's intriguing sister.

To that end, Danny stepped up to Pete when she opened her mouth and draped his free arm around her shoulder, nestling her close to his heart.

"That's right," he said. "Pete and I are . . . friends. How do you do?"

It wasn't exactly a lie. But since he'd put just enough hesitation in his voice to suggest a closer relationship existed between them, it came as no surprise to feel Pete stiffen in his embrace or to see her shoot him a baleful glare.

He heard a few titters coming from somewhere in the rooms behind him, but there was no help for it. Jackson's wife could infer whatever she would.

Pete wasn't about to contradict either one of them. Oh, no, not Pete. He'd figured out that much about her. She was an intensely private individual, but very protective when it came to those she loved, and she would go along with whatever achieved that goal.

Then, simply for panache, Danny ruined her umbrage by kissing her directly on the mouth in front of anyone who cared to watch. Although she accepted his impulsive gesture, he thought she was remarkably constrained compared to their earlier kiss. He waited for her to look up at him and smile, but she didn't lift her head.

Marge considered them a moment, her keen gaze flitting from their faces to the wine bottle and the paper cups in Danny's hand and back again. Then her expression softened and she nodded.

"Good for you, Pete," she said and patted her arm. "It's about time you resigned as general manager of the universe and got yourself a life."

And then she turned her attention to her luggage and her husband. The warmth between the two of them held all the spontaneity of a corporate merger.

For a split second, Danny spied a sad gleam in her unguarded gaze, and in that moment he knew — Marge believed their tall tale because it hurt too much not to. The woman was still in love with her cheating husband.

Danny halted before his thoughts strayed too far afield. His job wasn't to fix what was broken between them. His job was to

186

get his client the spoils of war. Period.

And Large Marge wasn't his client.

Danny needed a drink. Wasting no time on get-acquainted small talk, he hustled Pete out the front doors and didn't stop until they were well past the delivery vans and across the hardpan road.

Once they were lost among the shade of the oak trees beyond earshot of the house, she tugged her hand from his grasp and whirled on him, her cheeks glowing with indignation. Danny leaned his backside against the trunk of an aging tree, yanked a waiter's corkscrew from his pocket, and went to work on the wine bottle.

"Well? What've you got to say for yourself, Mr. Dan *Benedict Arnold?* How could you? You agreed to let the earlier talk die a natural death. Fat chance of that now. Do you know what you've just done?"

He knew, and he wasn't happy with himself for going back on his word to her.

The cork emerged from the bottle on a low, flatulent hiss. Forgoing the paper cups, Danny upended the bottle and took a healthy swig, savoring the smooth, black fruit flavor with meaty element that flowed over his tongue and helped cool his temper.

"Let's see," he said. "If I'm not mistaken, I've just helped you save your lying brother's ass."

"That's not very nice."

"No, but it's honest."

Then, without an apology for breaking their earlier agreement, Danny offered Pete the bottle.

Some truths were inescapable. Sunlight and indecision darted across her flushed face before she released her ire on a pent-up sigh, accepted the wine, and plopped back against the rough tree trunk, shoulder to shoulder with Danny.

This part of the grounds was peaceful and quiet except for the occasional bird warble and the droning buzz of dragonflies and carpenter bees through the yellow flowering weeds. Somewhere in the canopy of leaves over their head two militant squirrels scuttled across tree limbs, complaining to them and each other in shrill *tchrring* sounds. Not a breath of air stirred.

After filling a cup halfway, Pete passed the bottle back, then kicked off her sandals and sank to the carpet grass and clover at the base of the tree. She downed half her drink in the time it took her to lean against the bark and extend her legs out in front of her to cross her ankles.

Danny settled next to her, resting his

forearms on his bent knees. The wine seeped through him like a rolling wave, gently rounding and blurring the rough edges. And since arriving in Langstown, he had so many rough edges to smooth.

To look at Pete, her skin moist and glistening, her hair hanging natural and touchable, her dress good quality but practical, no one would guess she had access to more money than God. Where Racine was the embodiment of a gilded society dame, and Marge reeked of money and influence, and Phoebe fed an addiction to flash and cash, Pete had somehow managed to retain a certain understated detachment from the mainstream that only escalated her attractiveness to Danny.

She had cute toes, too. Shapely legs.

He pictured himself gliding the cloth of her dress slowly up her sweet skin and rubbing and kneading and caressing . . .

Three dogs charged toward them, tongues lolling and tails wagging in greeting. Danny swiveled to scratch one gnarled old mutt behind the ear.

"Friendly critters," he said. "They yours?"

"Grandmother's." Pete gestured to the two Terriers that quickly lost interest in Danny and were nosing a banana spider lurking in the web that hung between two nearby fallen trees. "Meet Patty and LaVerne. The Lab's named Maxene."

As Danny watched, Maxene sniffed in the high grass and briar weeds around a rotting log and lifted a leg, marking territory.

"Shouldn't that be Max?" Danny said.

Pete shrugged.

"He hasn't complained about it."

"How do you know he hasn't?"

"Because LaVerne's the informer of the bunch."

Danny cracked a grin.

"Dead grandfathers *and* dogs talk to you?"

"Can I help it if I'm a good listener?"

"Seriously, what's with that? Is the housekeeper crazy, or do you really believe your grandfather sends you messages?"

Pete played with her cup and eyed Danny thoughtfully, long enough for him to drink in the sight of her fine-boned face haloed by filtered sunlight.

"Don't scoff," she said. "Eugenié's harmless but very serious about the subject. Is she psychic? Intuitive? Perceptive? Maybe, maybe not. Who's to say? But I know she's not crazy."

Pete's mouth beckoned his, soft and kissable. He ached to thread his hands through her hair and feel the silkiness.

"I better get back," she said. "No telling what kind of trouble —"

"They're big kids." Against all good reason, Danny didn't want to let her go, so he stayed her with a firm hand to her shoulder. "They can handle it. Let them."

"And if they don't?"

"*Don't* is my specialty. One way or another, we'll work it out later."

Raking her fingers through her unruly hair, she blew a breath and finally slouched back against the tree again, and Danny felt he'd won a victory of sorts. She worked hard at being the family caretaker. And unless he missed his guess, she was conditioned into thinking her life revolved around other people's important moments.

What Pete Lang needed were a few great moments to call her own, and Danny was just the man to help her out.

On the horizon, blue sky flared above a stand of dark green pines. A gossamer strand of clouds spread over the trees, then gradually faded away into a bright yellow day. Danny sipped from the bottle, enjoying watching the dogs, enjoying Pete's quiet company, and not wanting to intrude on her thoughts.

Inhaling her appealing subtle scent, he floated in a bed of magnolia blossoms. His chest tightened.

"Think Marge was right?" Pete finally said into the easy silence.

"About what . . . you being Miss Fix-It?" Danny cocked his head. "Maybe. It doesn't matter what I think, though. What do you think?"

She let loose a heavy sigh and offered her cup, which he refilled.

"I'm thinking she's right. I'm about as interesting as a dry cracker. I ask you, can I possibly become more boring than I am right now? God forbid." Pete gestured with her cup as she spoke, then took a big swallow. "Gives me a lot to look forward to in my golden years."

"Don't let your sister-in-law get to you," Danny said. "She's an unhappy woman, and she's jealous."

"Jealous? Of what?"

"You."

"Me?" Pete's eyes widened. "No way."

"Of the choices you've made for your life." Danny nodded, leaned over, and splashed more wine into Pete's cup. "You're independent. You live where you want to, work at the job you want to."

"But Marge has choices, doesn't she?"

"Not since she hitched her wagon to your brother. Every day she's stayed with him has been a gamble that he wouldn't replace her for a younger or more beautiful woman. Today, her greatest fear came to pass."

"Which was?"

"Me." Danny took another swig to wash the bitter taste out of his mouth. "She took one look at me and realized she'd let too much time go by. Everything she has now is tied up in being Mrs. Congressman. If he divorces her, she loses him, loses the future she envisioned for herself, her social status, and her only source of income."

"Put that way, I almost feel sorry for her."

"Well, don't. Mark my words, when she finally accepts that it's over, it's going to come down to dollars and cents, and lots of them. I've learned to have a healthy respect for money-grubbing women."

"She's going to watch you and Jackson like a hawk now, you know that, don't you?"

"I'd be surprised if she didn't."

"You came down here to meet in private, didn't you? If you can't, then . . . then will you be heading back to Atlanta first thing in the morning?"

Pete chewed on her lower lip, and Danny decided she'd have to run him off.

"You never know what opportunity will present itself. Let's play it by ear, why don't we? Anyway, I'd like to stay until after your grandmother's funeral. It's the least I can do. Will that be a problem?"

"No. No problem."

"We'll have to continue the houseguest charade."

"Yes, I suppose we will."

"Just to keep things from blowing up until the funeral's over, you understand?"

"Of course, it'll get ugly around here if we don't."

"Exactly. Can you square it with the guy you're seeing?"

"I guess so. I'll speak with him."

When Pete nodded for emphasis, Danny could have sworn she was relieved, or maybe that was what his heart wanted to see.

"Answer me something?" she said. "Why did you agree to represent my brother?"

"Strictly as a favor to your grand-mother." Danny took another swallow of wine. "I usually don't take on politicians as clients."

"Because you think they're too much trouble."

She sounded so positive that he chuckled.

"You don't know anything about me. How do you know what I might think?"

"Oh, I know all about you."

She drank as she talked and glanced at him over the cup rim. He wanted to cover her mouth and taste each crease in her lips.

"I know you were an only child," she said, "born in Georgia. Your father was a symphony musician who passed away of cancer when you were in college. Your mother is a successful designer. And you now spend your time helping women through their divorces, because it makes them happy to feel desirable."

He listened, amused, until she recited the last part, then his eyebrows crashed together.

"Did I say that?"

She nodded.

"I read it in one of the rag mags."

"I know I was quoted as saying that." When she tipped the cup to her mouth again, he watched her eyes shine with a sensuous flame. "Enough about me. What do you think of the wine? Good choice?"

"Not bad for a red," she said and smiled, a warm, friendly, inviting smile. "Next time, steal something in white."

His heart tripped in his chest. Her vital spirit and liveliness drew him in, an image that came across as natural rather than cultivated. He ached to touch her again, to feel her closeness again.

A hint of red wine lingered at the corner of her mouth. Without giving it a second thought, Danny wiped the droplet away with the pad of his thumb and then let his lips follow the path his thumb had forged.

She met his advance, and incredibly soft lips brushed his mouth once, twice. It wasn't enough.

He abandoned the nearly drained wine bottle on the grass next to him and did the same with her empty paper cup. Then he curled his hands around the sides of her warm face, tilting her head, and lost himself in the sheer joy of her touch.

"Remind me," he murmured against her mouth, "I've got ideas about our missing floozy."

"Good," Pete managed to say. "Tell me later."

His heart pounded. Marveling at the taste and texture of her, Danny assaulted her senses. He wanted her. Desired her.

He deepened the kiss, touching his tongue to hers, urging, coaxing her fire.

Her hand crept up his arm and encircled his neck. He groaned his approval.

Not breaking the kiss, Danny lay back in the grass and conducted her with him. She sprawled on top of him, and he had her right where he could free a hand and caress her from her shoulder to her firm bottom.

He traced her contours and urged her closer to his bulging heat. His body clamored for hers.

Too soon to suit him, Pete broke off the kiss. He gazed at the bemused expression on her face while his thumb stroked her lips, moist, slick, and delicious.

At that moment, Patty, Maxene, and LaVerne joined in the romp and launched themselves into the fray. Danny forgot about his uncooperative client, forgot about finding a dead floozy, forgot about everything except the warm sun, the bright day, and the hot woman in his arms.

Pete squealed with delight, and Danny found himself smothered with doggie smiles, covered in doggie drool, and enveloped by the sweetest female laughter he'd ever heard.

No doubt about it, he intended to enjoy being snagged in paradise.

Chapter 11

Supper came and went without Vonnie, but not without incident.

The local pastor stood to say grace, and somewhere between "Dear Lord" and "Amen," Phoebe and the McCaffrey heir got into an argument and he lit out in Phoebe's Jag with Jackson's podiatrist in tow. Vanessa was turning out to be one busy doctor.

Pete never learned the details but overheard snatches of their conversation that led her to believe a convicted airline big shot also figured in the tiff.

Phoebe threatened to call the sheriff and report her car stolen, but Carl persuaded her to simmer down and talked her out of it. He would get the car back.

Last Pete saw, Phoebe was nursing her grudge and a bottle of Crown from deep inside a chaise lounge at poolside.

Twilight closed in around eight o'clock, and by nine it was dark outside. The flow of visitors had trickled to nothing.

Most everyone had gone home, so Racine and Carl had called it a night.

Sheldon had been elated to see Marge and had promptly herded her, Jackson, Gant, and Pollard out to the cars to caravan around the county, with stops at every senior center, nursing home, and convalescent center.

Pete couldn't honestly say she missed them.

Only Eugenié looked as fresh and unruffled as when her day had begun. After helping the housekeeper finish clearing up for the evening, Pete joined Albert and Benedict, who sat at a table on the side patio under the jaundiced glow of fluorescent bug lights.

An assortment of moths and gnats flitted around the light fixtures blissfully unaware that millions of marketing dollars swore the color yellow repelled bugs.

The summer night was a balmy eighty degrees and breezy because of the ceiling fans. Beyond the driveway, moonbeams shone on the grass and fireflies blinked at the edge of the lawn. Every few seconds brought the crackling snap of the mosquito zapper.

Albert dipped into a small cooler behind him and hauled out a longneck.

"Want a beer?"

"No thanks," Pete said. "I'm good."

She sank into the seat cushion and then pulled another chair up to rest her feet in. The metal legs scraped on the brick pavers with a screeching noise.

Turning her attention to Benedict, she lowered her voice and said, "Earlier, you mentioned ideas about our missing floozy. Care to share before Pollard and them get back?"

Both Albert and Benedict leaned forward in their chairs, forearms resting on the glass tabletop. Just as Benedict opened his mouth, Eugenié appeared out of the gloom, carrying a lighted citronella candle.

"Y'all tryin' to wake the dead?" she said.

"I hear that's your job," Benedict returned.

Pete started in her chair. Few people ever spoke that way to the housekeeper; most weren't so brave. They either gave Eugenié a wide berth or tried to stay on her good side.

Eugenié's eyebrows rose, and her teeth flashed white with her grin. She set the candle down in the center of the table. When she spoke, the New Orleans humidity dripped through her mellow, soulful voice.

"The man got him a mouth, ain't he?" she said to Pete.

"He's a lawyer," Pete returned, as if that explained his lapse into lunacy.

To Pete's surprise, instead of backpedaling, Benedict gained his feet and pulled out a chair for the housekeeper.

"Here, take a load off," he said. "Albert, pass this good woman a beer."

Eugenié studied him a moment, and Pete wondered what those shrewd old eyes saw. Was he the one? Or just the one right now?

Would the bones even tell her that much?

Then, with a quick nod and an eerie tinkle of glass bracelets, Eugenié hiked the voluminous folds of her white caftan. Quiet as a nun, she settled in the proffered chair and took a swallow of beer.

"You tryin' to butter me up," she said. "Ain'tcha, boy?"

"As a matter of fact," Benedict said, resuming his seat, "I am. How am I doing? Is it working?"

"Not yet, it ain't." Eugenié took another long, thirst-quenching swallow of beer and then gestured to Albert. "You, boy, pass me 'nother one of those over here."

Albert obliged.

When two chilled longnecks sat in front of her, she said, "Now it's workin'. What's a handsome devil like you want with this old woman?"

"We need your help."

Pete watched Eugenié's sharp gaze circle the table, studying each face. Between reading the bones that morning and being acquainted with Grandmother Lang for thirty years, Eugenié knew what kind of help without any of them having to explain.

"Y'done found her."

It was a statement, not a question.

Pete nodded.

"In the boathouse," she said, "but she's disappeared again."

"Bad juju," Eugenié said, taking another swig. "I ain't got her."

"We didn't think you did," Benedict said, rolling his gaze heavenward. "But maybe you know where she is?"

"And if I do? Whatcha gonna give me t'tell you?"

Benedict frowned.

"What were you in your last life, a camel trader?"

He leaned over and yanked two more beers from the cooler and plopped them down on the table in front of the housekeeper. She waggled her fingers for two more. They appeared in short order.

Satisfied, Eugenié fished in the side folds of her caftan and produced a deck of cards that she tossed on the table in front of Benedict.

"Cut 'em."

"Oh, no, Dan-Dan," said Albert, sitting back. "You've done it now."

Benedict looked at the deck and then looked at Pete with wary eyes. The cards appeared ordinary to her.

"Go ahead, big boy," she said, unable to keep the wry amusement out of her voice. "You started it."

"If you lose," Albert said, "she turns you into a toad. Just thought I'd mention that."

"Thank you for sharing," Benedict said.

"No problem. I'm here to help."

Even after the warning, or maybe because of it, Benedict picked up the proverbial gauntlet and cut as Eugenié had said. Pete marveled to herself that he seemed more curious than intimidated.

"Count twenty-one off the top," Eugenié said to Pete, "and start dealin' three cards face up in three piles."

Pete lowered her bare feet to the patio, sat forward, and dealt as instructed.

"What now?" Benedict said, looking over the cards.

"Pick yourself one," Eugenié said, "but

don't touch it, and don't say what it is. Keep on dealin', missy." And then she completely ignored them and stared out at the yard. "Would you look at all them lightnin' bugs flashin' theirselves a mate? Flashin' and flyin'. Closer and closer, 'til they up and find each other in the dark."

After three sets of three, Pete was told to count ten cards off the top and to put the eleventh card face down on the table.

To Benedict, Eugenié said, "Now tell missy here your card."

Benedict played along without hesitation and said, "Four of clubs."

"It's done then," Eugenié said and gestured to the lone card. "Turn it over."

Pete did. Four of clubs.

She and Albert gaped like dead fish. Only Benedict laughed out loud.

"How did you do that?" he said.

"You and missy there done it, not me." She offered him an enigmatic smile. "Like them lightnin' bugs, life's a wondrous mystery."

Eugenié stood and gathered the remaining five beers in a pouch she fashioned from the skirt of her caftan, cradling the bottles gently in her embrace.

"Wait a minute," Benedict said as she started to walk off. "You didn't say —

where should we look?"

"Try the cemetery."

"The cards told you she was there?"

" 'Course not."

"Then what was all this?"

"That?" Eugenié waved a negligent hand over the table and shot Benedict a look that questioned his intelligence. "That was a card trick that done cost you six beers."

"I think you've just been had, Dan-Dan," Albert said. "Can I get you another cold one?"

"No, thanks," Benedict grumbled.

Pete fingered the cards left on the table, looking to see if they were marked in some way. If they were, she couldn't tell.

After the housekeeper disappeared into the house, Benedict said to Pete, "Have you talked yet with that guy you're seeing?"

"His name is Vonnie Miller, and no. He was coming over tonight, and I was going to talk with him then, but I guess he had work to finish."

"Talk with him about what?" said Albert.

Pete gave her friend the gist of what happened with Marge, deliberately leaving out sucking down half a bottle of wine that almost led to a fling in the grass with Benedict, which was why he kept gazing at her with knowing heat in his gorgeous eyes.

"So what's your idea?" she said to Benedict.

"We already determined whoever took Miss Fritz had a key, so it was someone your grandmother knew."

"That's about everyone in town," Albert said.

"Someone she trusted to keep his or her mouth shut."

"Okay," Pete said, "so that's half of everyone in town."

"It had to be someone who could call on help, because a corpse is — pardon the pun — dead weight and a semi-frozen one isn't easy for one man to handle."

"You think it was a man then?" Pete said.

"Or three or four women," Albert offered.

"Possibly," Benedict said to him, "but it would be hard to miss that crowd. A couple of good-size men could come and go and no one would think twice about seeing them, especially if they were wearing work clothes."

"Muscled guys in work clothes," Albert mused, sipping his beer. "My favorite kind. That narrows the field, but it's still a lot of folks. There are plenty of guys around here who work horses, cattle, lifting heavy farm equipment — that sort of thing."

"So follow the logic back to the freezer," Benedict said. "You were surprised at finding her, right?"

"I would call it shocked white-headed to my ever-loving toes," Pete said. "But that's me. Go on, counselor. I'm with you."

"Given your reaction, I take it she probably hadn't been there since day one?"

Pete shook her head.

"This time last year," she said, "I was using that freezer to store ribs and shrimp for the birthday barbecue, and she wasn't on the shelf. I would have noticed."

"Then ask yourself two questions. Where was she before that? And where did they put her after?"

"Aren't we back where we started?" Albert said, his eyebrows soaring.

Benedict smiled.

"Not quite. The freezer is the key, or more specifically, refrigeration. We find someone with access to cold storage, and we'll find Miss Fritz."

"Not if she's already been buried," Albert pointed out. "No one would ever find her then."

"She hasn't been buried."

"How do you know?"

"A hunch. Why bury her now? Why not years ago? There's a reason. I don't know what it is, but there's a reason she's not buried."

While Albert and Benedict tossed around other variations on that same theme, Pete leaned back in her chair and mulled over the possibilities and the implications. From the old icehouse to the convenience store, half the merchants in town had some sort of cold storage.

Where to start?

How to start?

What was she thinking?

"Do you realize you're suggesting that the town conspired with my grandmother in this murder? Do you know how many people that is? That's too bizarre."

"Not in the murder," Benedict said, tracing an invisible line of dust on the tabletop. "In the cover-up. The old gal had help in keeping this secret for so many years."

Was Pete imagining that Benedict had a hard time making eye contact? Or did he know more than he was telling?

Wait — how could the lawyer know more? He hadn't been in town two days. Pete decided it had been a long day and she was, indeed, imagining things.

"Hold up," Albert said. "Say we do find Miss Fritz. Then what? I mean, what'll we do with her? The only refrigeration big enough we've got is busted. We can't drive around with her strapped to the car like a hood ornament."

"Easy," Benedict said, raising his gaze. "We turn her over to the sheriff."

"Oh, man." Albert shook his head. "Leave it to a lawyer . . . I was afraid you were going to say that."

"We can't," Pete argued. "If your theory proves out, half the town could go up on charges. That's wrong. Just wrong. I refuse to be responsible for opening that Pandora's box."

As Pete gathered more breath for her tirade, voices and car doors slamming brought her up short. Apparently, Jackson and his entourage had returned.

"Sounds like the barbarians are at the gate," Albert said and shoved back his chair. "I hate to eat and run, but tomorrow's going to be busy. Let's figure something then. Right now, I'll say g'night and hit the hay."

"Me, too," Pete said, worn out from trying to find a compromise.

Albert leaned over and gave her a peck on the cheek.

"Sleep tight, toots. Catch you later, Dan-Dan."

Benedict stood when Pete did.

"Guess I'll turn in, too."

When he leaned toward her, she expected another quick peck. Instead, one step and he had her backed against the wide, fluted column.

"Somebody might see us," she said.

"That's the point, isn't it? We've got to keep up the charade, remember?"

She nodded, feeling no pretense at all. Her hands slid up his chest to his shoulders, bringing him closer still until she was flat up against the solid wall of his chest.

Her pulse raced. Adrenaline flowed. A thrust of pure heat ignited a blaze within her.

If they had to play close friends for a while, she thought, might as well shoot for an Oscar performance.

His mouth covered hers and she caved, turning into a creamy, gooey mass of want and need.

The sound of voices growing closer registered in the back of her mind. The rest of her thoughts centered on the sensuous, soft lips nibbling her earlobe.

"Sweet dreams," he whispered, and then he was gone.

The kiss was infuriatingly brief.

Pete slumped against the column for support, still tingling over the memory of his mouth, and watched until he turned the corner of the house out of sight. Their conversation echoed in her head.

The town conspired in a cover-up? What an absurd notion. Not even her grandmother could pull off that one.

Benedict not only had a wonderful imagination, he also had a persuasive way about him. Sleep would be a long time coming tonight.

But if Pete were to dream on a grand scale, that dream would wear the face of Dan Benedict.

Chapter 12

A dancing polar bear knocked on the cottage door.

Danny knew the bear was there because he could see the fuzzy white head and black-nosed muzzle staring back at him when he squinted through the Judas-window. What a mammal living in the circumpolar north might be doing standing on his front porch early on a sweltering July 4th morning was the second question that popped into Danny's mind.

The first question was why the bear was jitterbugging while speed singing the gospel oldie *Let the Sunshine In*?

"Dan? C'mon, up and at 'em! You awake?"

Hearing Pete Lang's voice calling for him answered both questions and sent a funny little jolt of anticipation through him. He'd missed her.

Maybe she'd felt the same?

That was too much to hope for. She enjoyed his kisses, he knew that much. But she'd made it plain nothing else was on the menu.

Dressed only in skimpy blue nylon bike shorts, Danny struggled into a rumpled cut-off football jersey and threw open the door.

"I'm up now," he said, leaning his forearm against the door frame.

Warm air caressed every inch of his body, or was it the heat in her gaze he felt?

The sultry look revved his engine. He watched her brown-eyed regard slide past him and zero in on the unmade bed that sat center stage in the cottage's great room.

Good thing she couldn't read minds. If she knew the slow, steamy delights he'd dreamed of doing with her in that bed . . .

A man couldn't tune out what turned him on. The baseball cap over a ponytail, white pocket T and khaki shorts, and her face natural but for a bit of gloss and mascara suggested Pete was a woman who focused on being comfortable in her body, not on changing it. It was a very appealing package.

He loved her legs.

"What did you do with the money?" he said.

"What money?"

"For singing lessons."

She laughed.

"Is that the best you can do? That is so lame."

"It's early yet." He shrugged, unapologetic. "Wait until I have my third pot of coffee. My repartee shines brilliantly then."

"I bet your nervous system glows, too. That's enough caffeine to launch a rocket."

Then she smiled, and more than his next breath, he wanted to see her in that gauze-draped bed wearing nothing but that seductive smile.

Danny startled himself when he realized just how much he wanted to take her in his arms right there and kiss her senseless, then spend the rest of the day exploring all her sensitive spots and learning all her secrets. She seemed reluctant to venture beyond the porch though, which was wise of her, as randy as he was feeling. He had no desire to glimpse the unrecognizable flaming wreckage that would be his ego if she turned him down, so he wasn't going to push his luck.

Instead, he pointed to the bear she held dear to her chest, wishing he were that bear.

"Would you and your friend like to come in for a cup? I just put on a pot."

"Only if it's not decaf."

"Perish the thought. I'm a man who prefers to live dangerously."

Giving her breathing room, he strolled to the kitchenette and reached into the overhead cabinet for the mugs. She stepped over the threshold but lingered by the opened door.

"Make that three to-go cups," she said. "We're due at the casting tournament by nine."

Halting in mid-reach, Danny angled his head over his shoulder. She was checking her watch.

"Three cups?" he said.

Pete nodded.

"Albert's waiting for us in his truck."

Danny nodded back. At least, that explained why she didn't venture beyond the door.

"Did I forget to mention we're judging all the under-eighteen groups?" she said.

"Yeah, you did."

He resumed rummaging for throwaway cups. Did she actually forget? Or did she not bring it up earlier because she thought he might refuse such a sweaty chore?

Danny couldn't decide.

"Sorry about that," she said. "It was the best I could think of on short notice to keep you out of Marge's line of fire."

"Thanks, but you don't have to look out for me, Pete. I can do that for myself." He watched a sheepish grin appear before she ducked her gaze. "How's Marge doing this morning?"

"On the warpath. She and Jackson had another one of their arguments that carried down to the kitchen."

"Did he win?"

"I scored her an eight point five. Sounded to me like she wiped the floor with him."

"Ouch. Cream and sugar?"

"Yeah, in mine, please. Albert takes his black. He and I figured it'd be better if we all made ourselves scarce today. Give her some time to get it out of her system."

Danny splashed coffee into the last to-go cup.

"How about your sis? Did lighting boy come back with her car, or is he now wanted for grand theft auto?"

"He called her from the airport at oh dark thirty this morning, can you believe? Apparently, he made Vanessa an offer she couldn't refuse, and the rest, as they say, is history."

Danny winced and said, "Tough break."

"So's life."

"Half-and-half okay?"

"Fine. Carl's gone to retrieve her car. Anyway, enough of *As the Stomach Turns*, starring the Lang family. You'll love the casting tourney once you get into it."

"I will? You're sure about that?"

He was teasing her, but the intent sailed over her head and she sobered.

"Giving really is fun," she said. "At least, I think so. I guess it sounds corny, but having purposeful work is happiness for me."

"It's not corny at all," Danny said, flicking the switch to shut off the coffee pot. "I think it's admirable. It fits with the good person you are."

A becoming blush deepened the natural flush in her cheeks as he padded barefoot across the floorboards and handed her the coffee he'd poured for her.

"Thank you," she said.

"You're very welcome. Now, tell me about this tourney."

"It's tradition on my grandmother's birthday. Three tries to cast dead center of a floating inner tube. All the kids receive a little something for participating, but we present trophies to the top three closest to the center."

"Sounds similar to darts. No wonder your grandmother liked it."

"It's kind of hot work, so afterward everyone canoes or floats down the river. That's the best part."

"Everyone?"

"If you want, that is. You don't have to."

"No, I meant everyone as in your brother, the rest of your family, Niles Pollard?"

"No one in my family is into fishing. They host the barbecue."

It figures, Danny thought.

"Politicians come out of the woodwork today," she continued. "Don't be surprised to see wall-to-wall reporters and photographers at the barbecue, too."

"Anyone with cold storage going to be there?"

"Are we still on that?"

"We never left it."

"All right, then. Yes, counselor, many merchants participate in today's activities because they provide the prizes and like the freebie advertising, but I'm telling you, you're barking up the wrong tree."

She raised the bear and jiggled him as if he were dancing on air.

"He's one of the prizes donated for the T-ball set."

"Okay, you talked me into it," Danny said.

"Great!" She lit up, practically glowing, and Danny chuckled at how little things made her happy. "Well, put a move on, counselor! Time's a-wasting."

Flashing her a crooked grin, he grabbed his coffee and headed for the bathroom. "Give me a sec to wash up, and I'll meet you two at the truck."

"Bring a hat and plenty of sunscreen," he heard Pete call. "With your blond hair, you don't want to burn. And wear something you don't mind getting dirty."

Dirt was the least of it.

A storm out in the Gulf brewed up a hint of breeze, but it took more than a hint to make the Florida Panhandle bearable in July. By noon, the temperature at the river topped one hundred and two degrees and was still climbing.

Breathing was an exercise closer to sucking air through a wet wool blanket. The sweltering humidity drew the sweat out of every pore, and it soon built up on skin, ran between eyes and breasts, smudged sunglasses, and pasted hair and clothes to the body. The UV rays were unforgiving.

Mixed with the miserable heat and the salty tang of sweaty bodies was the smell of rich earth, dense woods, and teeming animal life. A picnicker somewhere had a boom box juiced too much, and the sound of swamp funk filtered through the trees.

It was there, near a landing in the sand bottom river, that a happy Pete waited to help Benedict into the truck for the short drive to the local emergency room for a fishing hook extraction.

Wearing flip-flops, she waded up to her knees in the fast-running cold water to catch him up as he floated toward her in an oversize rubber inner tube. He shouted to her with a familiar grin and an enthusiastic wave, and her heart leaped with a joy that touched and colored everything around her.

Sunlight danced on the water's surface. Sugar-white sandy banks punctuated with bald cypress, live oaks, sweetgum trees, and water fern played host to shy wood ducks and graceful egrets. Overhead, the Mississippi kite, a common raptor, scoured the skies and joined flycatchers and other songbirds darting among loblolly pines.

An ensemble of grasshoppers, cicadas, beetles, and dragonflies filled the air with a harmony of wings. Two backpackers cut the trail along the riverbank and trekked farther into the hammocks and slopes of the floodplain woods where white-tailed

deer, bobcats, and turkey roamed unmo-
lested in the summer.

The wildflowers were out, scattered in
the deadfall, yellow milkweed, red pine lily,
and maroons and pale pinks of parrot
lilies. It was too hot in the day for the ot-
ters, beavers, and cottonmouths that called
the river home, but Pete knew they were
there, as were bass and bream and harmless snakes and turtles. Large white sand-
bars contrasted with the water, which
appeared to swirl black around her legs
due to the tannic acid from the leaves.

Jimmy Boswell and a bevy of other kids
of various ages, whose parents either
wouldn't or couldn't chaperone them,
floated alongside Benedict in their own
inner tubes or shared with a buddy. They
were all busy splashing, laughing, and
horse playing as much as kids could in
inner tubes. Benedict was the biggest kid
of all.

Nothing about him resembled the sophisticated and polished attorney Pete had
first met at her grandmother's bedside.

His wet blond hair stood up in sandy
clumps of dishwater brown. Sunglasses
dangled from a leash around his neck and
rested against a fetching neon yellow tank
shirt, airbrushed with an assortment of

fishing flies and the invitation: *Whip Me. Tie Me. Fly Me.*

The sunscreen he'd liberally slathered on wasn't waterproof, so now the tops of his bare wet feet were plastic flamingo pink.

But the injury that added the true insult was the treble hook lodged by one barb in the muscle on the inside of his thigh. Overall, he was the sorriest sight Pete had laid eyes on all day long.

And the most endearing one.

To her surprise, he'd jumped right in and helped set up the target tubes, then scrounged fishing rods for the kids who didn't have one so they wouldn't feel left out. He exhibited the patience of a new saint with the fidgety parents and cranky kids tired out by the heat, and he answered questions as fast as curious five-year-olds could pose them.

When he wasn't wading in the water with the littler tykes and patiently showing them the art of releasing the button on their Zebcos, he was pushing bottled water so no one would get dehydrated and suffer heatstroke. The man could have just opened his wallet and Pete would have been grateful for the donation and managed on her own.

But he'd done far more. Benedict had

fostered an appreciation and concern for the outdoors all the while he taught the kids various casting techniques.

He liked dogs. He liked children. He seemed to like her. A lump formed in Pete's throat, and her eyes puddled up.

This was as close to a Frank Capra movie as she would ever get.

Who could have predicted Benedict's heart and talents would be as diverse as his wardrobe? Certainly not Pete.

Once he made the gin-clear shallows, he beckoned to her with the familiarity of a kissing cousin, which sent the kids into rowdy shrieks and a chorus of helloing. She laughed at the bedraggled sight and then directed traffic with the ease of any beat cop.

"Grab your tubes, everyone," she shouted into the ruckus, "and drag them up here on shore. Be sure they're out of the water before you leave. Find your parents in the parking lot, and don't forget to pick up your certificates from Mr. Albert."

From deep inside his inner tube, Benedict waved and called out, "Thanks, kids. See y'all later at the parade."

And Pete knew he'd meant it.

He'd truly enjoyed the morning despite the sunburn and the casting mishap. She looked down at him and couldn't stop a chuckle from escaping or her heart from expanding.

The two of them made a good team.

"Can't take you anywhere, can I?" said Pete. "You're looking rough, counselor."

"I suffer a war wound," he said with a mock frown, "and you're going to make fun of me?"

"I swear, you bring it on yourself. We should have taken you to the ER as soon as it happened."

"And let those kids miss out on floating down the river? You're a cruel woman, Pete Lang."

"And you're a stubborn man, Dan Benedict. As a reward for your good deed, you've earned yourself a tetanus shot. Does it hurt bad?" she added, trying for contrite but not quite pulling it off.

"Only when I laugh." Benedict dipped his hand in the water and splashed his sweaty face, then grinned and reached for her. "Give me a hand up? My dogs are barking."

She glanced to his bare feet and shook her head.

"Oh, yeah, those puppies are swelling nicely. Soak them in a gallon of white vinegar, and you'll be good to go. Here, put your weight on the other leg and let's do this quickly."

Using Pete for support, he jumped up on his good leg, soaked from the chest down. The movement jiggled the hook, and he growled low in his throat.

Pete sucked in a breath between her teeth, guessing at how much pain he'd just inflicted on himself. She read in his contorted facial expression the overwhelming urge to blast the air with a litany of choice words, but with innocent little ears still in hearing range, he wisely curbed the impulse.

"Remind me to steer clear of the Boswell kid," Benedict said in a forced whisper. "I'd like to make it back home in one piece."

Did he have to bring up leaving?

That Benedict would be gone soon was a reality Pete refused to think about just now. Today was theirs. She'd face unpleasantness later and enjoy his company while she could.

"Jimmy really was sorry," she said. "He didn't see you sitting behind him when he threw that practice cast."

She scooted under Benedict's arm so he could lean his weight on her and not aggravate his hooked thigh. They were a perfect fit. Like conjoined twins, they moved in tandem, ushering each other down the path that snaked through scrub oaks and pine trees and toward the gravel parking lot.

"He was supposed to have a plug on his line, not a lure," Benedict said. "Two inches higher, and I'd be a lot less fun on a date."

"What makes you think you're fun now?"

"Is this a date?"

"Sort of. Kind of. Yeah."

With one finger, he shoved the Costa Del Mar sunglasses down to the end of his sunburned nose and peered at her over the rim. The outrageous wiggle of his eyebrows coupled with the glint in his brown eyes made her crack up.

"In that case, I haven't heard any complaints yet."

"Cut me some slack," Pete said, laughing. "The day is young yet."

Benedict started to chuckle, then pulled up short on the path.

"Damned thing hurts," he said, then shot her a poor-me pout.

"A dog-leg left and we're to the parking lot," she said. "If I know Albert, he's got the AC going full tilt as we speak."

"The least you could do is offer to kiss and make it better."

She took Benedict's face in her hands and kissed him briskly on the lips.

"Better?" she said.

"Not yet."

His eyes filled with breathtaking softness, and the effect created a wild flutter in her stomach. She closed her eyes against the intensity of his gaze.

Gently, he drew her head closer to him, and every nerve sprang to life where he touched. He barely brushed her mouth with his, at first slow rhythms, before deepening the kiss. She took a rich breath of sun-drenched man and basked in the sensuous dance of his lips on hers.

Presently, footsteps sounded on the path, accompanied by a surprised voice.

"What in the h-e-double hockey sticks . . . ?"

Startled, Pete yanked her gaze around.

"Vonnie?" she said, staring eye-to-eye with the last person she expected to see.

"Pete?" he returned.

"What are you doing here?" she said.

Could she dance around an issue any more thoroughly without actually addressing it? Vonnie must have wondered the same thing. He was wearing short sleeves, cutoffs, a layer of zinc oxide on his nose, and a dumbfounded stare.

"I was coming to see if y'all needed any help," he said. "But I reckon you don't."

Beyond him on the path, she could see Albert hurriedly approaching. As soon as he spotted the three of them, he did an immediate about-face without breaking stride and headed back the way he'd come.

Coward. If he was any kind of friend, he'd take her with him.

The atmosphere chilled noticeably. Pete had put off any serious discussion with Vonnie, and now look where it had gotten her.

Untangling herself from Benedict's embrace, Pete said, "Help me get him to the truck, Vonnie?"

"Sure, sweetie," he said. "But once we get that fish hook taken care of, you and me need to sit down and have a chat."

She nodded. Her joy in being with Benedict was tempered with the knowledge that she might have hurt the one person undeserving of such treatment.

It was a notion that shamed her heart.

Chapter 13

One tetanus shot, two stitches, and a cold shower later, Danny donned sandals and clean shorts and returned to the Lang Mansion, where faint white smoke wreathed the house and grounds like heat haze.

He often felt there had long been something mysterious about the South that wasn't found anywhere else in the country. Part of the Southern mystique lay in its dark past; the other part was in the kind of sultry decadence spread before him.

Old Mrs. Lang's annual barbecue feast was in full swing, with food, live music, more food, misting fans, and dozens of smiling politicians gracing deck chairs and picnic tables set up under several large, open-sided tents. He inhaled a deep breath of air, practically arching up on his fried tiptoes to savor every swirling molecule of aroma.

Nothing beat the sear and smell of grilled steaks, ribs, burgers, chicken, hot dogs, and red leg crawdad boil on a sweltering summer day. Someone had worked overtime to spread the word far and wide

— Sheldon and Gant, maybe? — for there was a steady influx of cars and people.

Six men in red, white, and blue aprons kept three industrial cookers and one smoker going full sizzle in a roped-off area that relegated unsupervised kids to chasing each other and playing tag over the manicured lawn. Iced tea and punch were cold and plentiful, it being too hot for beer or spirits, although Danny noticed a few furtive old timers sharing something in a brown bag among themselves as they pitched horseshoes in the shade.

Everyone knew Mrs. Lang had passed, so Danny wasn't sure what to expect and wouldn't have been surprised to see Southern Gothic, but Racine had stuck to her guns and had turned the gathering into a birthday fete.

Patriotic lanterns hanging in the branches added color to the trees and would add light once evening came. Plastic flies and ants were scattered around the tables as confetti and were frozen in the ice cubes. The centerpieces were Mylar helium balloons tied to old-style metal pails filled with small U.S. flags and fancy bottles of barbecue sauce.

He spotted Jackson and Marge working the crowd, shaking hands and passing out campaign buttons with his campaign manager at his elbow grinning like an escaped felon. Pollard and a couple of other younger photographers tripped over each other snapping pictures.

Racine and Carl were both ladling on the charm, chatting it up with a television crew setting up equipment to tape an interview. And at the end of a banquet table, Phoebe nursed a hangover and moped in her cole slaw, putting off do-not-disturb vibes.

As Danny soaked up the familiar sights and sounds and smells, it struck him that here was why the South was all at once charming yet resistant to change.

He made a leisurely sweep around the crowded grounds until he spotted Pete at the edge of the lawn, sitting on a glider beneath the graceful shade of an old weeping willow. His heart leaped in his chest at the sight of her.

He wanted her. All of her.

Just the way she was.

And the realization didn't surprise him in the least.

Looking as hot and sumptuous as when she left him with Albert at the hospital's emergency room, she and that Vonnie guy had their heads together in conference.

Danny couldn't hear what was said, but he could guess they weren't swapping knock-knock jokes.

Both of them wore the sober countenances of people heavy with their own history.

Pete figured she might as well forget historical restoration and start practicing making license plates.

Her hands resting in her lap, she rocked in a slow, steady rhythm on the glider, pondering what she'd just heard. She should have been shocked at what Vonnie had told her, but she wasn't.

Somehow she'd reached down into that trough that God kept in reserve for every Southern woman who ever had to deal with Southern men and rinsed her troubled spirit in the calm waters of resignation and acceptance. The smuggled beer in her hand didn't hurt, either.

Around her, the skies were a cloudless, brilliant blue and the afternoon sun was still shining fiercely. Feathery willow branches swished every so often with what little bit of breeze stirred. Her stomach gurgled in response to the delicious smells drifting from the grills.

Vonnie sat next to her, his feet gently

pushing the seat back and forth. He was idly chewing gum and staring into space, his arms crossed loosely over his chest.

He'd taken her brief explanation of Benedict's presence quite well, even her candid account of the dead floozy, and no wonder.

Pete tilted her head toward him and said, "So the two rednecks from Spiker's Bar took Grandpa's floozy?"

"Yesterday mornin'," Vonnie said, nodding. "Sure did."

"They put her in Otis Murphy's ice-cream truck?"

"Wasn't an easy fit, but they shoehorned her in."

"I guess the floral van wasn't big enough?"

"Not nearly."

"Right."

"Not with all them flower arrangements. I'd a-fetched her in the hearse, but I figured that'd create a stir and you wouldn't want that."

Pete nodded her head in understanding. What else could she do?

She had chafed and fretted about that floozy for nothing. Vonnie had known about her all along, because he was the one her grandmother had truly trusted.

Where better to hide a dead body than in a mortuary?

"When did you bring her over here?" Pete said.

"Night 'fore last. The instructions your grandma left were specific. Y'know, Becky's husband thought that freezer wasn't soundin' right. Them two rednecks he sent over might not have three teeth between 'em, but they know their way around air-conditionin' and refrigeration. They said that fish freezer wasn't worth savin'."

"I know. I'm going to get rid of it."

After a moment of silence, Vonnie turned to Pete, squinting from the bright sunlight, and said, "I reckon we messed up when we took her back, and I'm sorry. The way I see it, your grandma left it to you to decide what to do next."

Which brought Pete back to where she started.

"Why wouldn't she tell me about something as important as this?"

Vonnie shrugged and said, "Some people are so proud, they'd do anythin' rather than admit a mistake. Your grandma was a tough nut to crack."

"But not so tough she wasn't hurt and humiliated a hundred times over during her marriage. I'll do what she wants. I just wish I knew what that was."

"Think on it some," Vonnie said, patting her knee. "I know you'll figure a way out of this."

"You sure?"

"Piece of cake."

She wasn't thrilled to know her grandmother and that other woman were resting under the same roof, but without anywhere better to stash the floozy, Pete kept that complaint behind her teeth. Besides, Albert was right — at this point, her grandmother was past insulting.

But Pete could well imagine her grandmother flipping somersaults in her coffin at the news.

Pete managed to keep a straight face, all the while wishing she shared everyone's confidence in her ability to come up with a reasonable way out of this mess.

From a distance, Danny watched Pete out there with that other guy.

The lack of tears and yelling were an encouraging sign. Were they breaking up? Staying friends? It was hard to tell.

One thing was sure, the guy wasn't pulling out all the stops to hang onto her. He just sat there like a bump on a log, rocking in the glider.

If that were Danny, he'd sweet-talk, wheedle, and cajole before he'd let her go.

He memorized Pete's face, dreamed of her, ached for her, but in the end, he left her alone. There was nothing for him to do but to back off and give her the room she needed.

Joining in the noisy crowd, he grabbed a thick burger and fixings and a glass of tea and hesitated a second before deciding to take a seat across from Phoebe. Danny actually liked her.

There was very little pretense in her. She made her feelings and intentions known straight off.

And right now, she looked like she needed a friend.

"Mind if I join you?" he said. "Or do you still have a head from all the Crown last night?"

"Come to gloat, did you?" she said, looking up.

Danny could see the simmering anger and hurt in her gaze. She was holding it all close to the vest.

"I never take pleasure in someone's misfortune," he said, stacking lettuce pieces and a slice of tomato on the bun, "or in their unhappiness."

"Congratulations. You're the first lawyer I've met who doesn't. Isn't that what y'all are taught — find a weakness and probe it until it's a festering sore?"

"Some do," he said, unwilling to rise to the bait. "I don't . . . not if I can help it, anyway. Care to talk about it?"

"No. If it's all the same to you, I'm taking a hiatus from being an ass."

He packed the bun on, bit into his burger, and almost groaned at the delicious smoky flavor. Heart-healthy eating be damned. Sometimes a man had to live on the edge.

"Fine with me," he said and wiped mustard off his mouth with his napkin and winced at the touch of sunburn. "I heard you got your car back. That was good. In one piece, I presume?"

World-weary eyes expressed a welter of uncertainty and doubt about what Danny was up to. He patiently munched his food, letting her sort it out.

"Men are dogs," she said.

"No argument there." Danny gave her a lopsided grin. "Woof-woof. And have you noticed how often we're struck with delusions of adequacy?"

Phoebe cracked a smile despite herself. She wasn't half bad looking when she came out from under that chip on her shoulder.

"C'mon, McCaffrey wasn't your type," Danny said, "and you know it. Quit wasting time on the schmuck."

"What do you know about it?"

"I know you're miserable. I can see it. You've got a face longer than my bar bill. And I know you're better off with him gone, even if you don't."

She nudged her hair behind her ears, leaned forward, and braced her bare arms on the tabletop.

"Was that pep talk supposed to make me feel better?"

"Give you food for thought, maybe," he said, popping an errant pickle chip into his mouth. "Only you can make yourself feel better — if you want to feel better, that is."

"And tell me, how would you feel, counselor, if the guy you were with dumped you for a younger woman?"

"Is that what's eating you?" Danny returned his burger to his plate and scrubbed greasy hands on his napkin. "Look, so McCaffrey was an immature turd —"

"A filthy rich immature turd," Phoebe pointed out.

"Rich is important?"

"And being great in bed. I do have standards to uphold."

"Naturally. I stand corrected. So answer me this, are you really missing this filthy-rich walking erection? Or are you missing the feelings he evoked? There's a difference, you know.

"It's easy to be in love with the idea of love. It's harder to be in love with the reality of a person. Divorce courts are filled with people every day who discover that little fact."

A flash bulb exploded in Danny's peripheral vision and he turned to see that one of the young photographers had taken their picture.

"Go away, little man!" Phoebe said, ducking her head and waving him off with a jerk of her hand.

Danny jumped up before the guy could move away and was about to tell him to cease and desist when a beet-faced Niles Pollard horned in. His camera bounced against his chest as he got up in the guy's face.

"Hey, hey, you! Stick to the candidates," he said, blocking the guy's view and shoving him off. "The family and their guests are off-limits. Go on. Get out of here and do your job."

The guy had no time to give lip or resistance.

Pollard waited until he stalked off, then turned to Phoebe and apologized, which surprised the stew out of Danny. A fat second later, Pollard forgot her and buddied up to Danny as casually as if they played golf every Sunday.

Now that was more in character.

When Pollard motioned for a private word, Danny's curiosity was certainly piqued. He joined Pollard, and they ambled toward a corner of the tent out of Phoebe's earshot.

"Thanks for that," Danny said, waiting for Pollard to hit him up for something. "I appreciate your consideration for our privacy."

"No problem. But listen, I do you a favor, maybe you do one for me?"

Danny stifled a smile. Nothing in life was free.

"A favor?" he said. "It depends. What do you want?"

"A little insight on her and the McCaffrey kid maybe — they split for good or what?"

"What makes you think that?"

"He ain't around, is he? I got my sources."

"Maybe he went on a beer run."

"To the airport in the middle of the night with a cutie-pie who was not his regular lady? What do you take me for, counselor?"

"That is rhetorical, yes?"

"Go ahead, have fun. I'll find out one way or the other."

Was that a threat? Danny thought he really should butt out. This wasn't his business.

Yet something about Pollard sneaking around raised alarms for Danny. He decided to play the conversation out and see where it took him.

"I believe you would," Danny said.

"So what do you say?" Pollard added. "I scratch your back, you scratch mine?"

"A deal takes consideration. You don't have anything I want."

"Not now, but I might, and when I do, it's yours."

"You want me to accept an IOU?"

Pollard crossed his heart, his expression pawnshop sincere.

"Honest Abe," he said. "Ask and it's yours. So what do you say?"

The idea of Pollard owing Danny was too appealing to pass up, so Danny decided to kill two birds with one stone.

"All right, deal."

"I knew you could be reasonable," Pollard said, clearing his throat and shifting his stance. "Okay, so?"

"She dumped him," Danny said. "Got tired of him. What can I say? His ego couldn't take it, but you didn't hear that from me. Look, I've got to get back before she starts wondering."

"Yeah, sure, no problem. I'll fill in the blanks."

"I trust you will."

Clapping a smiling Pollard on the back, Danny turned to go but couldn't shake off the nagging sense of something fishy. Playing a hunch, he walked only a few steps then stopped, using the crowd as a buffer to visually trail Pollard's auburn head through the people and tables.

The man was on to something.

But what?

Sure to Danny's suspicious feeling, the photographer who'd taken Phoebe's picture intercepted Pollard. They exchanged a few words and Pollard dug in the pocket of his shorts and handed something to the guy.

Danny couldn't see what the object was but, when the guy's face relaxed and he smiled, Danny guessed money had just passed hands.

That wasn't a good sign.

He returned to his seat across from Phoebe, mulling over what he'd witnessed. It cast his recent run-ins with Pollard in a new light.

What if he hadn't fully bought the ruse in the boathouse? If he was paying for photograph setups, it wasn't much of a stretch to think he'd pay for information, especially juicy information.

There was no point in sharing any of this with Phoebe. Danny had nothing concrete to go on, and Phoebe had proven earlier that she wasn't about to believe any dead floozy nonsense without a body to back it up.

So he returned to his burger and, when she stared across the table at him with a jaded eye, he simply shrugged.

"And that confab was . . . ?"

"A PR matter," Danny said. "By the end of the week, I expect the filthy-rich turd to be reading about how you handed him his walking papers. If he rants, let him. The more he whines to the press, the less he'll be believed. You'll come off the class act in the whole thing."

Danny reached for his tea and gestured with the glass in his hand.

"That's my free consult, by the way," he

said, "for what it's worth. Think about it."

She did, long enough to laugh at the irony. After a moment, she said, "Are you a fan of prenups?"

"Yeah, I am." He swallowed the last bite of burger. "Are you thinking of getting married?"

"It won't happen anytime soon, but, yes, I'm thinking about it."

"Do I get a name?"

"When the times comes," Phoebe said with a secret smile.

Definitely not the McCaffrey heir. Maybe that airline CEO Flora had mentioned on the phone? Phoebe wasn't saying so Danny wasn't prying.

"Talk to me before you do," he said. "A good prenup does more than segregate assets. It's up there with preneed arrangements. No one wants to go there because it represents an end, but that's exactly when you want to spell out preferences and expectations — ahead of time, when your thoughts aren't so emotionally clouded. That's what your grandmother did. It saves a lot of headache later."

Speaking of her grandmother, Danny couldn't stop his gaze from straying toward the glider and Pete. Everything about her had his insides in knots. He craved her smiles and her company.

She was the one; that was all there was to it. He'd had the bone-deep feeling since the first minute he'd laid eyes on her.

Once in a man's life he was entitled to fall madly in love. Whatever happened, Danny knew in his heart that Pete was his once in a lifetime.

The problem was what did he do about it?

Phoebe caught him staring and turned her head, following his line of sight.

"You like my baby sister?"

Superlatives failed him.

"She is something else," he said.

"She's a good kid, but out of your league. Why don't you just leave her alone?"

"If she were a kid, I would." Sobering, Danny stared Phoebe straight in the face, his eyes glinting. "But she's not a kid. She's a grown woman, and I can't."

Phoebe pushed back her chair and stood, collected her plate and trash, and then offered Danny the first warm and genuine smile he'd seen her give.

"In that case, please keep this in mind," she said. "Hurt her, and I'll personally rip your balls off."

On that quiet note, she strolled off with

Danny's chuckles following in her wake. He had no doubt in his mind that Phoebe meant exactly what she'd said.

Sitting there for a few minutes more, Danny patted his sweaty face with an extra napkin. His fingertips drummed on the edge of the table in time to the country song blaring above the noisy crowd.

The band was set up on a wooden platform upwind of the grills. Some honky-tonk cowboy was wailing into the microphone about giving his horse a beer, but Danny rarely listened to country and wasn't familiar enough with the song to hum along.

Pete was still in a powwow with that other guy.

What *were* they talking about for so long?

As much as Danny's curiosity was killing him, he decided against disturbing them. They had issues to settle that were best resolved without his interference.

But that didn't stop him from wishing he were a little fly on the bench.

Chapter 14

Since the town's founding, Langstown had held two parades each July, one to celebrate the opening day of rodeo and the other to celebrate the anniversary of our nation's Independence.

This year's annual community July 4th celebration included arts and crafts booths erected under the sprawling live oaks around the city hall park. In the grassy center, Pete had scheduled volunteers to work potato sack races, a balloon toss, backyard baseball, Frisbee, badminton, and other traditional games that culminated in the late-afternoon parade.

The parade always traveled along the park's one-mile circumference, so a few years back Grandmother Lang had moved the start time to later in the day. The change avoided the excessive middle-of-the-day heat, and it gave parade goers a chance to take advantage of the afternoon shade.

Pete had seen no reason to mess with a tried-and-true schedule, especially when the time provided for families to stay after for the fish fry fund-raiser and barn dance before watching the fireworks later in the evening.

Even though it was still hot at the city hall park, it wasn't stifling. It was Pete's favorite time of the day, when the sun lay over the treetops and cast long shadows on the irreplaceable cultural resource that was the fountain in the town square and on perfectly preserved old buildings that resonated with the spirit of people and events past.

She loved this place. It was a two-mule town and ordinary, but she was so very clearly at home here.

Pete ran down a last-minute check of parade participants on her list to be sure they were all accounted for. It was a routine task. This year, as every year, the parade featured a flock of local beauty queens, Scout troops, and homemade floats covered in banners, streamers, and flags that were sponsored by realtors and truck dealers.

The antique car club was out in force with a gleaming Model T, an early Nash, a Rambler, two Woodies, and a pack of muscle cars playing chauffeur to politicians of all stripes. Not to be outdone, the Fez-sporting Shriners zigzagging in their minicars delighted the fans camped out in lawn chairs along the parade route.

Riders and horses from several local stables showed off their finery and would close the parade. That's where Pete had needed Albert and Benedict.

Not riding. Scooping.

The retired rodeo clowns who usually handled the cleanup chore had car trouble returning from Birmingham and had canceled at the last minute. Never one to ask someone to do what she wouldn't do, Pete had enlisted Albert and Benedict to help her push a wheelbarrow and man a shovel.

They agreed to help her out, albeit reluctantly, and she decided it was probably the only time in Benedict's law career when he scooped it rather than dished it. He hadn't questioned her about her earlier conversation with Vonnie, and she was grateful for that.

She didn't want to have to spoil their rapport by lying to him. And she would lie, if push came to shove, without giving it a second thought. That's how committed she was to helping fulfill her grandmother's last wish.

Even if Pete wasn't clear yet what that last wish was.

Until she figured it out, she'd even left

Albert in the dark, so there was no possibility he might accidentally spill the beans to Benedict.

Pete knew where the floozy was. If she shared that tidbit, Benedict would feel obligated to soothe his legal conscience and head straight to the sheriff. Not only would she be handing him the evidence on a silver platter to support his story, but she'd be implicating other people in the cover-up, people who trusted her.

No, that was something she simply couldn't and wouldn't do.

She needed to wait out Benedict, needed to keep her mouth shut and let him go back to Atlanta none the wiser. Once he left, she'd never see him again, and this little episode in her family's history could fade away.

So decided, she returned her attention to her clipboard and tried to concentrate on the parade, but warm and confusing thoughts of Benedict kept intruding.

He really wasn't what she had expected at all . . . and she was going to miss him more than she cared to admit.

None of the schools in the county were big enough to claim a marching band, but there was no lack of noise when the string of brick-red fire department trucks and steel-gray police cruisers led off the parade, hitting their sirens and blasting their air horns.

Once the line was in motion, Pete cut across the park at a run to double-check with the electronics man handling the sound equipment on the amphitheater stage, where the parade would conclude. She watched the line approach from there.

As the parade marshal, Jackson rode in every little boy's dream. He sat next to a dignified Dalmatian atop the old pumper truck's polished roof, all grins and energetic waves. Niles Pollard was right there to capture the moments on film, standing on the running board at the side of the truck and hanging onto the grab bar.

Marge gifted onlookers with a stiff smile and a regal nod from the passenger side of the open cab. Pete doubted anyone paid much attention to her because she was flanked by the more impressive and more interesting tanker truck and aerial ladder truck in which Sheldon and Gant rode.

The parade circled the park and passed in review in front of the wooden bleachers erected between the gazebo and the small amphitheater. Everyone recognized that the torch had passed when Racine and Carl chose to occupy the canopied seats always before reserved for Pete's grand-mother.

The rest of the dignitaries wilting in the packed bleachers were made up of young vets, droopy old soldiers, their wives, church officials, and anyone else too elderly or infirm to walk, ride, or hop on a horse. When the fire trucks slowed and finally halted in front of the amphitheater, two firefighters helped Jackson climb down off the roof, and Pollard snapped pictures the whole time.

Sheldon and Gant hotfooted it to the stage area to coordinate when the speeches started.

Just as Jackson's feet touched ground, someone somewhere discharged a bottle rocket and the air filled with a high-pitched whistle and a pop, pop, bang-bang, pop! that set off a tinny chorus of dogs barking. Whatever Marge said to him was lost as he helped her off the fire truck. He really wasn't reacting to her.

Pete had no time to worry about how they were getting along. Marge was a campaign pro and, no matter how big a hissy fit she might pitch at the house, she wouldn't create a scene in a public place, of that Pete was sure.

Then, too, one of Sheldon's jobs was to

help solidify image and smooth over the rough spots. When it came to rough spots, Marge was his job security.

"Microphone and sound system all workin'," the electronics man said to Pete. Bald and overweight and sweating freely, he frowned and wiped his hands and tattooed arms on a rag. "Mind if I have a word with you?"

His serious tone garnered her full attention. She lowered her clipboard and followed him to the side of the stage, out of the way.

"What's up, Bill?"

"The red-headed guy with the big camera who's doggin' your brother's steps, how well do you know him?"

"Not at all," she said. "His name is Niles Pollard and he works for Jackson. Why?"

"I'd watch him, if I were you. He's been askin' questions around town, pokin' his nose where it don't belong."

"What kind of questions?"

"About Miz Lang and her husband, if he had any girlfriends. That kind of trash."

Pete's stomach dropped to her toes. She had thought they'd rendered Pollard harmless. Obviously, not.

"And what are people telling him?"

"Nothin' yet, but he was hangin' out

over at Spiker's offerin' to pay for stories. 'Fore long, somebody'll take him up on it. I thought you outta know."

Pete's first idea was to have Jackson fire Pollard, but she dismissed that as soon as it popped into her mind. If he was working for the campaign, at least she knew where he was part of the time. She couldn't keep tabs on him if he came and went freely.

At the moment, though, there was nothing Pete could do except be grateful for the warning. She needed time to figure out how to head off Pollard, but time was in short supply.

Patting the man's arm, she said, "Thanks for the heads-up, Bill. I appreciate you telling me."

"Want me to leave the set up and dismantle it after the fireworks?"

"Take it down after the speeches," Pete said, "if you want. The musicians'll be over on the bandstand."

She gestured to the gazebo, but dropped her hand when she heard her name called. Turning around, she saw Phoebe sauntering up the sidewalk, looking fresh from a shower in a yellow silk summer dress and matching platform slide sandals.

"Are we ready for our fine officials to string together tropes, metaphors, and allegories in speeches that will extol our country's freedoms and its successes?"

"Only if they're short speeches," Pete said, wiping her grimy face on the sleeve of her white T-shirt and leaving a dirt ring. "There's enough hot air out here already. You're late."

Phoebe shrugged and said, "I got stuck on the phone. Where do you want me?"

"Not standing next to me. I feel sticky and sweaty and nasty. You in that dress make me look worse than I feel." Pete eyed the keys in her sister's hand. "How about you drive me back around? I need to go help the guys clean up after the horses."

"I've got a better idea." Phoebe sniffed and wrinkled her nose. "How about I drive you back to grandmother's so *you* can get cleaned up and changed in time for a dance or two?"

It was an odd request coming from her sister, but Pete didn't have the time or energy to ponder her motives.

"Can't, Pheebs. I've got too much —"

"Sure you can. Learn to delegate, kiddo. You don't have to do it all yourself. There are at least two dozen volunteers here, any one of whom can fill in for a bit. For that matter, mother's good at givin' orders."

Phoebe was not taking no for an answer.

Clamping onto Pete's hand, she called to the electronics guy and turned on the come-hither smile and the charm.

"Excuse me, sir?"

"But I told the guys I would —" Pete cut in.

"Apologize later for crappin' out on them," Phoebe said, breaking out in chuckles at her unintended joke. "Sir?"

Pete rolled her gaze heavenward. The parade would be over by the time Phoebe let go. Might as well give in, Pete thought, and then find Albert and Benedict later and apologize.

"Bill," she said. "His name is Bill."

"Excuse me, Bill?" Phoebe called, and this time he jerked his head up and flushed when he realized she was speaking to him. "Will you do me a huge favor? Would you tell Pete's mother to cover for her until she gets back? I'm goin' to borrow her for just a moment. Thank you so much, darlin'. You're a peach."

Then, with a radiant smile that gave him no chance to even consider declining the chore she'd thrust upon him, Phoebe turned on her heel.

"Men are so easy," she grumped and yanked Pete's arm until she had no choice but to follow.

Once the sun set, hundreds of tiny lights outlined the grand Victorian gazebo against the muggy twilight sky.

Danny watched an eight-member band in short sleeves and jeans mount the band-stand and then liven the air with the sound of zydeco. They played tunes with ele-ments of Caribbean music and the blues, sometimes a soulful sound, the same rhythm that cotton-field workers once used to chop cotton in the Mississippi Delta.

In no time, what looked to Danny to be half the adults in town were on the dance floor doing two-steps and waltzes. The other half were busy laughing, talking, and chowing down on fried fish and fixings.

Rug rats darted in and out of the tables, playing tag and squealing at the top of their little lungs. Future delinquents bran-dished sparklers as if they were light sabers and harassed insects, plant life, and each other.

It had been a busy and exhausting day, but Danny wouldn't have missed it for the world. No wonder so many stressed-out city dwellers headed south.

The town's friendly style and slower pace appealed to Danny. He'd lived too many years in the hectic exurbs, and he was tired, burned out, ready to slow down and make a few lifestyle changes.

Apparently, it worked for these people. Why not for him?

He'd noticed they shared a close sense of community along with a stronger sense of personal identity. They knew they were a part of something that lay beyond their front door. No one had to remind them. They weren't simple, and they weren't parking themselves in front of the television in an effort to stay away from each other.

Danny would have to give the matter serious thought, but the idea of cutting back and putting down roots held a great deal of appeal.

Beer in hand, he and Albert were outside the realm of the gazebo's light, leaning against a table and enjoying the music. They had struck up an easy friendship, and Danny could see why Albert and Pete were so close.

"Say, Dan-Dan, you followed up on your cold storage theory?"

"Not yet. Pete wore me out today. If I didn't know better, I'd think she did it on purpose. You?"

"Count me out. If I wanted to dig up ancient history, I'd be an anthropologist."

"Archaeologist."

"Whatever. You know what I mean." Then Albert nudged Danny to get his attention. "Will you look at that?"

He turned and spotted Pete and her sister strolling up the sidewalk.

Pete was a sweet and sultry vision in a hot pink halter dress. Whisper-light material kissed her gorgeous legs with every step she took, and the shape-hugging top revealed her figure to perfection.

Intelligent, funny, big heart, down to earth, beautiful — what more could a man want? That she was independently wealthy didn't hurt, either.

"My, oh my," Danny said, his heartbeat accelerating.

"For fifty dollars," Albert said, "I'll run interference with Phoebe."

"Fifteen," Danny countered.

"Twenty-five."

"Done."

Albert slugged back the last drop of his beer, dumped his truck keys in Danny's lap, and said, "You can settle up with me later," then headed toward the sisters. He practically tackled Phoebe when he swept her off her feet and started dancing on the sidewalk.

Without taking his gaze off Pete, Danny set his beer down and pushed away from the table. He stuffed the keys in his shorts pocket.

"I wondered when the most beautiful woman in town would arrive," he said, extending his hand to Pete. "Would you care to dance?"

She looked surprised and smelled like heaven.

"Why, thank you."

Smiling, she nodded and followed him onto the dance floor, where she stepped into his embrace as if she belonged there. He curled one arm around her, and that's when he discovered her dress had an open back.

His fingers caressed warm, satiny skin. She relaxed and he pressed her close to him, feeling every subtle curve of her body. The touch awakened his physical sensations, and the warmth and sensuality gave him something to fantasize about.

"Guess I don't have to ask where you got off to," he said, guiding her around the crowded floor and wishing they were alone.

"I'm sorry." She leaned her head back to look at him. "I didn't mean to leave you two in the lurch —"

"No problem. You didn't. I'd much rather see you like this."

"In a dress?"

"In my arms."

When she blushed and idly caressed his neck with the back of her hand, he chuckled and whirled her around the floor.

"Did you know that gentle touches are the most effective form of flirtation to me?" he whispered in her ear.

"No, I didn't realize."

"Of course not," he said, watching her eyes turn smoky. "You're leery of getting involved with a man who seems unresolved about the past."

"Are you making fun of me?"

"Not a bit. I'm wishing we were in my living room, just the two of us, sharing a candlelit meal and some makeout music. I'd show you a man resolved about his future."

She furtively glanced to the ears close around them.

"Can we change the subject?" she said.

He tried not to breathe too deeply of her seductive scent, but it didn't work. His body responded to her without any help from him.

"Change to what?"

"Did I mention I helped restore this gazebo?"

"Why no. But I assume you'll tell me what restoration is."

"It's recapturing the finishes, detailing,

form, and features."

"I adore your features, every cute little one of them, and I'd love to capture your form. If I weren't so tired, I'd hie you to my tent like Valentino and make mad and passionate love to you all night."

"Oh, please, I saw that movie. Rudy spent the entire film wide-eyed, flared nostrils, and smarmy grin. I have no idea what women saw in him."

"Well, he couldn't have been all teeth and eyeballs. He was the heartthrob of his day. What do you say? Let's go get wild."

"I thought you were tired."

"I'm getting my second wind. Isn't that why you wore this sumptuous dress, to tempt me?"

She offered him a wicked grin.

"How am I doing?"

"Quite well," he said. "And I'm flattered, by the way, that you went to so much trouble."

"Okay, down boy. There are children present."

One twirl later and they were dancing next to Jackson and Marge.

"Time to switch," Marge said, brightly, too brightly, and before Danny could object, she'd edged Pete out of the way to grab his hand and step up to dance.

Pete shrugged and took a turn around the floor with her brother, while Danny scowled at her sister-in-law.

"I wanted a word with you," Marge said.

"I gathered that. What can I do for you, Mrs. Lang?"

"You can handle my divorce."

Danny missed a step and apologized for almost tripping them. He couldn't tell her the truth, and he wracked his brain for a good lie.

"Money's not an issue," Marge continued, apparently misinterpreting his hesitation. "I know you don't come cheap, and I'm willing to pay handsomely as long as you agree to stick it to him. I want to make it as long, drawn out, and miserable for him as possible. Can you do that?"

"That's a very tempting offer," Danny said, grinning. "You have no idea how tempting, but, no, I'm afraid I have to decline."

"Why ever for?"

He stared her straight in the face and lied.

"Pete," he said.

"What about her?"

"Jackson's her brother . . ." Danny sobered. "It's just not kosher. I'm sure you understand. Tell you what I can do — I can recommend a colleague."

"No, I don't understand, but call me with his name when you get back to Atlanta. Wish I were there now."

"Don't you like it here? I'm enjoying my stay."

"The cows have more to say than I want to hear."

He watched Marge chew her lipstick, then he said, "Was there something else?"

"Watch out for the photographer," she said. "The one working for my husband. Something's not right there. He's a little too nosy."

"He's a tabloid photographer," Danny said, and Marge nodded.

"That explains it."

"I meant to talk to Sheldon about him. Has he caused problems?"

"Not that I know of. Doesn't mean he won't. I caught him questioning people about you and Pete. She's a good kid, stays out of the limelight, and doesn't deserve to be tabloid fodder. You might want to look out for her."

"If she'll let me," Danny said. "I will."

"Good luck. She learned the stubborn streak at the knee of the master. Her grandmother was the same way."

When the music ended, Marge excused

herself and headed toward the refreshment table. Danny stepped to the sidelines and glanced around for Pete, just in time to see Jackson winding his way toward him with Pete in tow.

"What do you think you're doing here?" Jackson said.

The worried expression on his face amused Danny. Let him sweat. It would do his character a world of good.

"Your sister asked me to come," Danny said, taking Pete's hand. "Don't worry, I'm billing you for it."

Jackson opened his mouth and then closed it again when he saw Marge make a swift about-face and head back to them. The band started in on the next song, so Danny wasted no time in whirling Pete onto the dance floor again, leaving her brother to deal with his suspicious wife.

Danny cleared his throat and pasted on a bland face, ignoring the moistness of Pete's lips and the way her mouth beckoned his attention.

"You were saying before we were rudely interrupted?"

"Where was I? — oh yes, restoration is a four-step process of historical research, documentation, inventory, and stabilization. Are you listening?"

"No, I want to kiss you. Let's go some-where —"

"My job's not done for the evening yet. I'm committee chair and have responsibilities to see to."

She was teasing him without mercy, and he loved it. Two could play that game.

"Fine," he said. "I'll kiss you right here in the middle of all these people."

"Don't you dare. Pollard's right over there. He's been snapping pictures all afternoon like he's being paid by the print."

"Let me worry about him."

Three steps and a couple of turns and Danny had them sandwiched between Racine and Carl to their right, Jackson and Marge to their left, and Pollard with a Nikon shoved up his nose right in front of them. Danny gave them all big smiles.

"A kiss here or somewhere else, Pete," he whispered. "You decide. But you'd better hurry up."

Chapter 15

The promise in Benedict's voice thrilled Pete to her toes.

He probably thought she'd give in and agree to slip away rather than cause a stir. And at one time, she would have opted to stay in her comfort zone, to go the safe route.

But not tonight.

Tonight, Pete wanted to live. She wanted some fun, some memories. She wanted . . . Dan Benedict.

Was he in for a surprise.

Maybe it was the expensive dress or the frilly undies she wore beneath it or the sultry way he looked at her that gave her the confidence to act. She wasn't sure.

All she knew was that she felt as beautiful and sexy as any woman ever could, and there was immense power in that feeling.

She rose to his challenge eagerly. Right there in the middle of the gazebo's crowded dance floor, Pete Lang, the low-key town sweetheart, gave them all something to talk about when she latched onto the placket of celebrity attorney Dan Benedict's shirt and yanked his blond head down for a kiss.

Then she barely brushed her lips on his, teasing, taunting, tantalizing him beyond measure. He was having none of it.

While the music swelled to a finish and the band wrapped up, he wound his arm tighter around her middle and yanked her close, then dipped her backward, holding her steady within the wall of his embrace and supported by the strength of his arm. He took advantage of her captive pose in the next instant and covered her mouth in a kiss filled to overflowing with raw sensuality.

Her heart raced and her blood roared in her ears. This was the stuff of fantasies, what Pete imagined scores of ordinary women must have felt when they sat in movie theaters and watched the silent screen star Agnes Ayres in the passionate embrace of Rudolf Valentino.

Flashbulbs went off behind Pete's eyelids at the same time she heard the crowd erupt with catcalls and hoots overlaid with shooting rockets and the first musical strains of "Ode to Joy." She was still clinging to Benedict's neck when he swooped her upright in a billow of pink chiffon.

Fading footsteps and voices registered in the back of her mind. Way in the back. She opened dreamy eyes in wonderment and met the smug smile on his face.

They were alone in the center of the lighted gazebo, pressed together from breastbone to pelvis.

"Well?" he said. "Will you give me a chance?"

Flashing lights, fireworks, and Beethoven. What more could a girl ask for?

"I've always played it safe," she said and sighed, feeling his erection growing against her thigh. "I've never gotten wild in my life."

"Maybe it's about time you did?"

"Yeah, I think maybe it is."

"Pete!" called a volunteer waving a cell phone from over the side rail. "They started the fireworks early. S'okay?"

In a laughing, noisy rush, the last of the dancers were scrambling down the stairs to watch the sparkling bouquet of fireworks displayed against a clear night sky.

"Sure," she called back, her gaze glued to Benedict's beautiful face. "Tell 'em thanks and I'll see 'em tomorrow."

"Albert lent me his keys," Benedict said.

Pete smiled at his suggestive tone and rubbed the strawberry lip gloss off his mouth with her thumb.

"In that case . . . your place or mine?"

With thought so close to becoming reality, she debated the wisdom in her move while they walked the short distance to Albert's pickup. By the time they pulled up at the cottage where Benedict was staying, she knew she had only one choice.

In a couple of days, he'd head home to Atlanta. He'd be gone, and she'd go back to the way her life was before he showed up.

And she'd live each day hoping to see his picture in the magazines.

That prospect held no appeal. She had no desire to go into old age with nothing but a litany of regrets.

When he killed the engine, she said, "May I have the keys, please?"

"Cold feet?"

"Not hardly." She waggled her fingers. "C'mon, give 'em over."

He did, and she unlocked the console between the bucket seats, looking for the fresh stash of condoms she knew Albert always kept in his truck. For all his grousing about a lousy social life, he was a big believer in being prepared.

She rummaged through loose change and junk and came up with a small white plastic bag imprinted with a drug store's logo.

"It occurred to me," she said, "that we might need these."

They held hands as comfortably and tenderly as high school kids as they walked up onto the porch, and Benedict halted before unlocking the cottage door. Under the glow of the yellow porch light, he leaned over and kissed her, and she inhaled the aromas of barbecue smoke and sunscreen and tasted hungry promises.

"Are you sure?" he said.

That he'd still offer her a chance to back out was gallant and endearing and totally unnecessary. She'd renovated the cottage with a lover in mind.

Only fate knew why she had never used the cottage until now.

Pete wondered if Benedict's heart beat as fast as hers did at that moment . . . not from nerves but from giddy anticipation.

There would be no backing out.

She saw the fatigue in his eyes and traced the shadow of beard around his delicious mouth with her fingertips. And Pete knew exactly what she intended to do.

"Yes." She nodded. "I'm sure."

In the epitome of luxury and self-indulgent pleasure, Danny leaned his head back on the towel lying against the tub rim.

His big toe played in the running water, a wide liquid sheet reflecting the white ceramic. He was fast discovering the fun it was to revel in a sensuous candlelight soak that someone else had prepared for him.

Thousands of tiny bubbles floated on the water's surface and surrounded him, lifting the heady fragrance of cinnamon and sweet orange and filling the bathroom with the power of stimulating aromatherapy. The soft, romantic sounds of violin and cello strings drifted in from the great room.

Rather than turn on the overhead fixture, Pete had lighted votive candles and set them on the sink, the window sill, and all the flat surfaces so the stark white tub and walls were awash in a subdued amber radiance. Just when he thought the bubble bath couldn't get any better, Pete padded in and handed him a snifter, two fingers deep and neat.

"Southern Comfort," she said, kneeling on the plush beige rug beside the tub. "Sip, don't gulp."

Her hair spilled over her shoulders in a brown curtain when she shut off the water, her bedroom eyes darkening to a sexy, smoky hue. He cradled the glass in his soapy palm and inhaled the pungent vapors.

No woman had ever pampered him before — it was usually the other way around — and he could get used to this kind of attention real easy.

"How about a shave?" she said. "I promise not to cut you."

Danny rubbed the whisker stubble on his jaw, now softened by the bubbles and the steam.

"Don't bother. It can wait 'til morning."

Her eyes searched his, then she nodded and said in a breathy murmur, "Lean up."

Gently, she sloughed his wet neck and back with the loofah sponge. He arched his spine, giving her greater access, and couldn't stop the groan of pleasure from escaping.

"You have a gift for the personal touch," he said, canting his head to the side.

The shy grin she offered was both innocent and sexually exciting. She was a woman of many surprises, and Danny wanted to learn them all.

"It's so much more fulfilling to give."

Shaking his head, he leaned back in the water and reclined against the tub and said, "You make it more special to receive."

He sipped his drink, feeling the liquid's warmth slide down as easy as silk, and shot another quick look at Pete. She wanted to take it slow, build the excitement, and he wanted nothing more than to please her in return, even if he keeled over from the pleasure.

"Pete, I don't want to push. How about we have no expectations for tonight except to relax and be together? Anything else that happens can be spontaneous and optional."

"Cold feet?" she said, and he had to smile.

"At this moment, nothing about me is cold."

"Good."

She combed her fingers through his wet hair and returned his smile, with enough tenderness in her gaze to make his teeth ache. This was turning out to be the best day of his life. If Danny died in the next minute, he'd die a happy man.

Then Pete stood, and he panicked.

"Don't go," he said, sitting up and grasping her by the wrist, "please?"

He'd never said that to a woman before, never had reason to, because he hadn't known a woman he ever wanted to hold fast to him.

"Can't get rid of me that easy," she said, slipping her hand free and easing him backward with a little push to his shoulders. "I want you to sit there, relax, and watch."

Watch what? he almost asked.

In the next instant, he found out.

She unhooked the V-straps of her dress from around her neck. Then she crossed one arm over her chest to hold up the flimsy material while she reached around back with the other hand and unzipped her dress.

Danny was speechless.

When she moved her arm, the dress slithered to the floor in a frothy puddle of pink, leaving Pete in nothing but a sheer hook-and-eye front strapless corset and thong panty. Danny had a hard time catching a breath.

"You like?" she said, using her toe to scoot the dress out from under foot. "The lady at Victoria's Secret recommended it."

"I like very much," he managed to choke out.

He made a mental note to write a fan letter to the lingerie behemoth. The corset silhouetted Pete's curves perfectly and fired his imagination.

But Danny didn't have to wait long to

see what else Pete had planned.

Starting at the top of the corset, she flicked the hooks free of their eye. One by one. Slow. Sure. Steady.

He watched her nimble fingers, watched their unhurried progression down the corset, unable to look away. His mouth went dry.

Her breasts were revealed bit by bit, her skin so translucent he could trace the delicate blue veins beneath. He swallowed, waiting for her to peel the corset flaps completely away from her body and display all of her to his hungry view.

"Ready?" she said and slowly licked her lips.

It took him a second to gather enough moisture around his tongue to respond.

"You're killing me," he said, his gaze tracing every crease of her luscious mouth. "But you know that, don't you? Go ahead . . . keep on. Payback is coming."

A becoming pink flush spread across her chest and up her neck to her face. Rather than revealing, she turned her back to him instead, threw the corset sides wide open, and dangled the frilly top out to her side by one hand before flinging it to the floor to join the discarded dress.

Danny stared at Pete's naked back and two well-rounded cheeks that topped impossibly long legs. He'd dreamed of those cheeks, of kissing his way down her spine, of wrapping those legs around his hips, of cupping her bottom while he explored all her sensitive spots.

He tossed back the rest of his drink in one gulp and almost scorched his liver. Or was that steam coming from his smoldering libido?

"Please," he said. "Are you going to put me out of my misery?"

Angling her head over one bare shoulder, Pete flashed him a wicked grin.

"Not yet, big boy."

She grabbed the monogrammed white bath sheet off the wall rack next to her shoulder and whipped around, draping it in front of her like a matador's cape. Danny groaned. All he could see was from her neck up and her knees down.

The best parts were hidden by fluffy towel. She was killing him.

"Time to get out," she said.

He surged up out of the tub before the echo of her voice faded. Bubbles slid down his arms and legs and dripped off his fingertips.

While she wrapped the towel around him, he wrapped his arms around her and crushed her mouth under his.

Chapter 16

Pete sprawled naked atop cool beige satin sheets in the center of the king-size bed.

On the ceiling beam above her, a paddle fan rotated in lazy circles, stirring the filmy gauze netting that surrounded the bed frame. She was marooned on an island, buoyed by the music, listening to the inner world of tones, motifs, and sequences that danced with elements of joy and triumph and passion, especially intensity of passion.

It was too late for coyness. Too late for modesty. Too late for timidity.

She kicked the fluffy duvet aside. Nothing felt more right than being with Dan Benedict at that moment.

Without asking, he knew she wanted to take it slow, to stretch out the anticipation and savor every unhurried nuance of their time together. But he didn't know she needed to take it slow because this was probably the only night they would ever have, the only memory of him she would ever store to bask in later.

The viewing tomorrow, the funeral the next day — both would demand her energy and attention, and he'd leave soon after to return to Atlanta.

Knowing Jackson, he'd finagle a way to meet with Benedict at his office. There would be no reason for him to see Langstown again.

After availing himself of one of the condoms, he laid the plastic bag on the café table within easy reach, and padded toward her. Two candles remaining as centerpieces silhouetted him in dim light.

The warmth and desire in his gaze filled her with anticipation. His equally naked body stood at attention.

A rugged beauty lay in the hills and valleys, from well-shaped calves, up solid thighs to the taut roundness of bare hips. He had a swimmer's body — broad shoulders, tapered waist, and corded muscles.

Her gaze traced the golden brown curly hair that sprinkled his chest and tapered into a darker thin line below the flat plane of his abdomen. The path ended in a thicker patch of wiry curls.

"You're beautiful," she said, pushing up on her elbows. "You know that?"

"I was going to say the same thing about you."

"But you've seen hundreds of beautiful women."

"No. I've seen hundreds of women, but none of them were anything like you. Not even close."

With one knee on the bed, he drove his fingers into her hair and anchored her head. She felt his hand tremble and, when he kissed her, she tasted his hunger, his mouth gently punishing her lips.

She clasped her arms around his shoulders and drew him down on the bed with her, wallowing in his strength and determination. Her greedy hands explored the differences between them, tracing the tantalizing expanse of warm skin and firm muscle that coiled beneath her fingers.

"Pete?"

"Yes?"

"Do you know how good you feel to me?" He kissed her eyes, her nose, her cheeks. "How much I've thought about doing this?"

"Dan?"

"Yes?"

"You talk too much," she said, threading her fingers through his hair and bringing his mouth back to hers.

When his insistent tongue demanded access, she parted her lips. A throaty moan escaped her. Delirious sensations assaulted her from every angle, gathering force and leaving her powerless to capture a thought.

His questing hands explored her body slowly, deliberately, and knew just where to touch to ignite her hidden fires. She learned how sensitive her ears were when he circled the whorls with the wet tip of his tongue and sent tremors of excitement down her spine.

"You like that?" he said.

"It's nice."

"Only nice?"

"Maybe a little better than nice."

When he trailed fiery kisses down her throat, his lips teased the erratic pulse at the hollow, his breath hot and ragged against her skin. He fondled and cupped her breast, and she gasped from the delicious contact on the sensitive nub.

She buried her face in his shoulder and breathed in the light scent of orange bubble bath clinging to his skin. Her eyes fluttered closed while she wallowed in the sensual delight of his fingers rubbing small circles around her erect nipple.

He slid his hand lower, past her ribs to her abdomen, and then his knowing fingers grazed inside her thigh and upward to explore the apex of her sex. She arched her back and sucked in a ragged breath.

As he expertly rubbed spots sensitized to

his touch, she squirmed beneath him. Her breath came in pants, matching the slow rhythm of his hand.

A low whimper escaped her lips as the sweet pressure built. Desire pounded. She eagerly reached for more, wanting, arching, kneading his neck, his shoulders. Before she could catch her breath, he settled himself between her thighs.

Now, Danny thought, kissing her lips at the same time he entered her, pressing his hips in a slow, teasing glide. Planting his hands on either side of her head, he raised up and balanced his weight on his palms, watching her in her passion.

She was beautiful, and she was his. He could see them together, their future filled with more lusty nights like this, and the image made him smile.

Advancing and retreating with short, teasing strokes, he inhaled the floral essence of her perfume and the heady scent of their loving. The amber glow of the candles bathed Pete's delicate profile in flame and shadow that invited Danny to explore more of her joys.

His gaze focused on her luscious breasts, and his mind centered on one thought, pleasing her as she had pleased him.

He saw her lips part seductively, her

breath coming in short gasps, and the sultry picture she embodied weakened his control.

"You feel too good, Pete . . ."

"Don't stop, Dan. Don't stop!"

His pulse pounded a deafening beat in his temple. Her arms encircled his back, slick with perspiration.

Sliding his hands under her cheeks, he lifted her bottom and thrust deep into her, feeling her inner muscles clinch around him in pulsing waves. As her climax rose, he caught her cry of release with his mouth.

He kissed her, savored the taste of her on his tongue, flooded his senses with her scent, and let go. The starry light streaked within him, and his own climax chased hers into the night.

In the predawn hours, Pete lollygagged on the rumpled bed in the shelter of Dan's arms, her back resting against his warm chest.

He was propped up on pillows against the headboard, one leg bent, his fingers idly dragging back and forth from her hand to her elbow. She had the duvet pulled up to keep their damp bodies cozy in the air-conditioning.

Should she feel embarrassed about spending the night making love with him? Awkward? Uneasy? She didn't. She was happy, sated, and putting off returning to her grandmother's house and her responsibilities.

Imagine, she'd left before the fireworks were over and the grounds cleaned up. A week ago, Pete wouldn't have dreamed of abandoning her obligations like that to someone else.

But that Pete was gone now.

It felt wonderful to be irresponsible and wild, if even for a short time. And she was going to enjoy every fantastic second of it.

The candles on the table had long since gutted, their light replaced by the moonbeams shining through the window transoms.

"Comfy?" Dan said close to her ear.

"Very. A shiatsu would go good right now." She pointed her toes and stretched, smiling at the newfound soreness in her thighs. "I don't want to ever get up."

"Who says you have to?"

Pete giggled and turned her cheek into his fuzzy chest, hearing his heart beat strong and steady.

"Well, at some point, we'll have to eat."

"We'll order room service."

"This isn't a hotel."

"Minor detail."

"How about when you have to go back to work?"

"I've got a cell phone and an assistant at the other end of the line. I can do business from the bed."

"Wish I could. I'll have to go back to work, starting with burying my grandmother."

He had no snappy comeback for that one.

"Pete, is it too much to ask for your family to help carry the load?" he said.

"You don't understand. It's not their job."

Before the lighthearted feeling disintegrated and before Dan could bring up the dead floozy, Pete changed the subject.

"Did you know my real name is Pietra?"

If Dan wondered about the swift change, he kept his own counsel.

"I heard your mother call you that," he said absently. "Italian?"

Pete nodded and said, "It means 'rock.' It's from mother's Italian period, when she adored all things Italian, the designers, the architecture, the skiers."

"She's a character, your mom. In fact, your whole family —"

"It'll be dawn soon," Pete cut in.

This time she watched his eyebrows shoot up.

"Sweetheart," he said, "the problem of Miss Fritz won't go away just because we don't talk about her. You've done a good job of tap dancing around it."

"Maybe I'd better be going," she said.

The spell was broken. Her grandmother and the dead floozy were there just out of range. Pete didn't want to talk about them, didn't want to think about them, but she couldn't help it. She was foolish to imagine there was a way to keep the world from intruding.

"I don't want you to go yet," he said, nuzzling her hair and nestling her closer to him. "Stay with me. I'll treat you to breakfast."

"That's tempting, but no," she said on a resigned sigh. "I can't. It's going to be a busy day, Dan."

She leaned up to go, and he pulled her back down next to him.

"The biggest problem you have to solve right now," he said, "is deciding which one of us will buy Albert a new box of condoms."

"Having delusions of grandeur, are we?" she said and chuckled. "I don't recall we used *that* many."

"Want to use one more?"

"You're not serious?"

He heaved a heavy sigh and said, "No, I'm not. I'm too tired to draw it back. I just wanted to see your reaction."

"Poor baby, I've worn you out, haven't I?"

"You're a slave driver."

She turned in his arms, her gaze brightening.

"I have an idea — want to go watch the sun rise? We've got time."

As soon as the words were out of her mouth, she felt a pang of guilt for keeping him up most of the night. She was just so reluctant for their time to end.

"Or, if you're tired," she added, half-heartedly, "I'll slip out and leave you to sleep."

"Don't you dare go," he said, kissing her on the tip of the nose. He cupped her face and then nudged her hair behind her ear. "If you want to watch the sun rise, sweetheart, that's what we'll do. Wait right here."

He rolled out of bed, heedless of his nudity, and sauntered to the bathroom. She did as he'd asked and waited to see what he was up to.

The next thing Pete heard was the

shower running. She smiled. Then Dan strolled back to the bed and swept her up in his arms before she could put up much of a protest.

"What are you doing?"

"It's payback time," he said, turning toward the bathroom. "We'll shower first, then dress."

"*We?*" Pete said. "As in together? The shower's awfully small, isn't it?"

"We," he repeated and gave a naughty grin. "Trust me, you're going to love it."

The horizon over the cow pasture burned as hardy as any sinner in hell.

With a beignet covered in powdered sugar in one hand and a foam cup of latté in the other, Danny and Pete cuddled next to each other on a stadium blanket spread across the tailgate of Albert's truck and watched the red-hot rays of the sun creep over the treetops.

She was wearing the hot pink number from last night that had Danny replaying her arousing strip tease in his mind. He'd never again see that color without calling Pete to mind and remembering the feelings she ignited.

"I like a guy who goes all out when he promises a girl breakfast," Pete said, munching into her beignet.

"My pleasure," Danny returned. "Nothing's too good for you."

Pete smelled good and felt better. He'd felt her warmth and tenderness in every word and touch.

She had a musical laugh that Danny would never tire of hearing. But what Danny liked most was how she shared herself with him. Her emotions were so honest.

That was a precious gift, her honesty. She softened his edges and quieted his restless spirit.

Bellowing cows, cawing crows, one lone whistling quail, and a million tiny wings beating to their own rhythms serenaded them. Dragonflies strafed mosquitoes and each other across the pasture.

"It doesn't get any better than this," Pete said, taking in a deep breath of air rich with earthy smells. "I wonder what the poor people are doing today."

Danny didn't have to wonder.

"They're sitting in the middle of a stinky pasture," he said, "watching ugly cows give them the evil eye."

"Worried they'll attack?" Pete said, giggling. "Don't be. Cows are vegetarians."

"That's a rumor they want you to believe," Danny said, studying big hooves and bony rumps.

"A pickup to them means treats, and they're waiting for us to toss them some food."

"Do they like beignets?"

She rolled her gaze heavenward and nudged him with her shoulder.

"Dan, they're cows, not dogs."

"What do I know?" he said and waved his empty hands for the cows to see. "Sorry ladies. The cupboard is bare."

His ringing cell phone interrupted them. He pulled it out from the pocket of his shorts and recognized the caller.

"Excuse me," he said to Pete. "I need to take this."

She closed her eyes, turned her face to the warmth of the sun, and said, "Go ahead. I'm fine."

Danny scooted off the tailgate and tiptoed around cow patties to sit in the cab of the truck to answer his phone.

"It's like a minefield out here," he griped.

Angling himself on the leather bucket seat, the door left open, he was careful to prop his sandaled feet on the running board rather than mess up the carpeted floor mats.

"Mary Ruth," he said into the phone.

"Hey, Danny-boy," answered his chief investigator. "Sorry to call so early, but you did say get back to you pronto."

"Don't worry about it, I was up."

"Geeze, it sounds like your social life has taken a nose dive. Where are you staying, at a petting zoo?"

"I'm a regular Marlon Perkins. Now tell me something good. What have you found out?"

"Not a damned thing. Sorry."

"That's not what I wanted to hear."

"Tell me about it," she said. "If anyone's looked for your Jane Doe, I haven't turned up any evidence of it."

"Nothing in missing persons?"

"That's not how it works, Dan."

"I don't follow."

"Let me make it easy for you. When you decide to get gone, three things have to happen. First, someone has to file a missing person report. Second, it's the reporting agency's responsibility to enter the info into NCIC."

"So what's the problem?"

"We live in a litigious society, that's the problem. When it comes to adults, authorities aren't tripping over themselves to bother people who might have left home on their own. And people leave for all kinds of reasons. Bottom line, police don't routinely look for them. They dump the info into the database and forget it until there's some kind of run-in with the law or a body turns up."

"I don't have the body yet but —"

"Not so fast. That's where the third thing comes into play."

"And that is?"

"Expiration dates."

"You mean like milk? Bodies have expiration dates?"

"Some days I feel like mine does, but I was actually talking about the missing adult entries in NCIC. They have automatic expiration dates, usually about three years out. The kicker is, it's the reporting agency's responsibility to renew the entry."

Danny cupped his palm over his face and dragged his fingers down from forehead to throat.

"Oh, brother, so if they don't . . ."

"You're getting the picture," Mary Ruth said. "Gotta love bureaucracy. If a report wasn't made, I'm wasting my time and your money. If it was made, somebody dropped the ball — it wasn't renewed, and too many years have gone by."

The possibilities were numerous. But

Danny couldn't let it go until Mary Ruth had exhausted every reasonable avenue.

"Do me a favor? Keep digging, will you?"

"The chances are slim to nil I'll find anything to go on," she said, her tone offering even less hope than her grim words.

"You know the saying, in for a penny . . ."

"Only it's a nickel now. Inflation."

"But it's my nickel."

"You got that right, Danny-boy. I hold a special fondness for clients who continue to pay their bills."

"Keep me posted?"

"Sure thing."

He flipped the phone lid closed and shaded his eyes against the glare of the sun. Pete was standing at the end of the truck, stadium blanket gathered in her arms, leaning against the bumper and staring in his direction with a million questions in her beautiful gaze.

Now that the sun was out, the temperature was climbing. Danny had sweat beading on his face, even as a chill went across his heart.

"My investigator," he said and sagged against the seat back.

Although Danny hadn't exactly lied to

Pete, he hadn't been entirely truthful either. He couldn't be and still keep her grandmother's confidence.

Pete wasn't stupid. She'd overheard enough to know Danny was talking about Miss Fritz and to realize he'd gone behind her back to try to force the issue of reporting a crime.

He owed her at least the gist of Mary Ruth's findings.

When he finished, Pete nodded, her expression moving from thoughtful to resigned. She glanced at her watch.

"Thanks for breakfast," she said. "I've got to go."

On the short drive back, Danny searched for something to say to her, but he was helpless to come up with anything. He parked in front of the Lang mansion, and Pete was out of the truck before Danny could get his door opened and come around to her side.

Rolling down the window, he called, "Tell Albert I'll give him his keys when I see him."

Halfway up the walkway, Pete stopped and marched back to the truck. Danny had come around to the side by then.

"Explain something to me?" she said.

"If I can."

"Why do you want to look for someone no one wants to find?"

Danny felt like a heel.

"Because it's something I have to do, legally and morally."

"You would do better to serve your client and not your cause."

"I don't mean to hurt you or cause you more grief. Please believe me."

She searched his face.

"I believe what you've said . . . as far as it goes. But I also believe you know more about Miss Fritz than you're telling me."

Chapter 17

Carl was dressed in a white terry bathrobe and having coffee and scrambled eggs at the glass-top wicker table in the breakfast room when Pete walked into the adjacent kitchen looking for Eugenié.

After all, when one had a problem with the dead, one needed to go straight to the horse's mouth. Pete's late grandparents started this mess, and hearing that Benedict had hired an investigator renewed Pete's determination that her grandparents were going to finish it.

Why couldn't the man mind his own business?

Yes, she was angry, and with a right to the feeling. Just when she thought things might have a chance to work out, he had to go and spoil it by reminding her he was a meddling lawyer.

She kicked off her sandals and shoved them into a corner, padding across the cool hardwood floor in her bare feet. Meeting Carl was a surprise.

Since the full day yesterday, Pete hadn't expected the family to be awake at daybreak. She'd hoped to skip the whole morning-after questions that were inevitable coming on the heels of such a public display as she and Benedict had engaged in at the dance.

The naked glass on the tabletop was Pete's second surprise. Fingerprints drove Eugenié nuts, so a Wedgwood damask table linen usually covered the glass.

"Ketchup get away from you?" Pete said.

"How did you know?" Carl said, offering a startled smile.

"Lucky guess."

"Around here, it's hard to tell," he said, canting his head toward the laundry room and dropping his voice a notch. "She's in there doing her mumbo-jumbo."

"It helps her remove the stains," Pete returned just as low.

Carl considered that a moment, seemed to think it plausible, then nodded and said, "You're up early."

If he noticed Pete was still wearing the pink dress from the night before, he didn't give a hint.

"So are you," she said. "Can't sleep?"

"I'm on West Coast time. Haven't been to bed yet. After your mother turned in, I caught up on some frac paperwork and neutron density reports on the lower

McClure shale that I had my office fax over."

To look at Carl, white-haired and shriveled, Pete could almost forget how sharp he was until he rattled off about his gas wells with such ease.

"And Mother slept through all that?" Pete shook her head and leaned over the pass-through counter. "The excitement we miss. So does all that mean everything is okay, or do we need to pawn the family silver to pay the light bill?"

Carl's face wrinkled more than usual when he laughed and said, "Everything's just peachy."

"Hey, peachy I understand."

An awkward hush followed as Carl continued to eat his breakfast and Pete stood there feeling embarrassed but not sure why.

Prodded by the silence, she said, "Dan Benedict and I were watching the sun come up . . . in case you wondered, that is."

"I watched it over the pond. Glorious wasn't it? It's going to be another hot one today."

He grinned, and Pete relaxed and grinned back. Then she walked over and kissed Carl on his papery cheek.

"What was that for?" he said.

"For not asking."

He blushed and dug into the last of his eggs with flourish.

"You're a grown woman, Pete. How you choose to spend your time ain't nobody's business but yours. You remember that."

Turning to the refrigerator with a lighter heart, Pete helped herself to a glass of orange juice and then bumped the fridge closed with her hip. She carried the glass and the carton with her as she joined her stepfather at the table.

"Yesterday was a good day," he said, reaching out to pat her hand.

"Did you have fun?"

"You betcha. Your mom and me both. The parade was a hoot, and the dance and fireworks were first-rate. You've got a real knack for planning and organizing."

"Thanks, Carl. I guess we've all got our talents."

"You and that young lawyer make a good-looking couple, too."

Pete downed her juice and then said, "Don't get used to it. I'm not."

"You two have a fight?"

"No, not directly."

"Then why do you talk like that?"

Pete's hand fluttered in the air as she

sought to put her thoughts and emotions into words. She had gone to college; she was educated. So why was the ambition a lot tougher to realize than she expected?

"We're way too different," she finally said, her hand dropping out of the air and landing on the table like her scattered feelings. Splat.

Carl arched a skeptical brow.

"And that's a problem?" he said.

A practical credo from Grandmother Lang reverberated in Pete's head: *If your budget allows for a two-hundred-dollar dress, don't fall in love with a two-thousand-dollar gown. It will only break your heart.*

"Dan Benedict is my two-thousand-dollar gown," Pete mumbled.

"I don't think the boy cares what you wear," Carl offered.

Pete didn't bother to correct his assumption.

"Don't you see?" she said. "We had a nice night, and that's all it was. He belongs in the city. I belong here. End of story. Don't make more out of it than there is."

But Carl wouldn't let it go.

"So commute. It's not that long a distance from here to there."

It was if she was in prison as an accomplice after the fact.

With that little nugget in mind, Pete said, "He doesn't understand family, especially our complicated family. His picture's always in the rag mags with big-chested women hanging on him like buzzards to roadkill, and I'm not like that. I'm a homebody. It just wouldn't work out."

Not to mention Pete refused to set herself up for heartbreak.

Benedict said all the right words, but face facts, the man had lots of practice. With all the worldly, sexy, and glamorous women he had to choose from, it was naïve to think she could compete on that level.

Carl finished the last bite of his eggs, let his fork clatter to the empty vintage plate, and then pushed the plate to the side.

"I see," he said. "Is he married?"

"No. It's nothing like that."

Pete yanked open the orange juice carton out of sheer exasperation with herself and splashed juice on her hand and the table. Carl passed her his napkin to sop up the spill.

"Then it appears to me that you don't have much to lose by being blunt with him about your feelings."

She blotted the mess and then rested her chin in the palm of her hand.

"And what feelings are those?"

"You tell me."

She couldn't, because she wasn't clear on that herself. She loved talking with Benedict, working on projects with him, and laughing with him; and making love with him was certainly right up there on her list of favorite things to do. But was she anything more than a lusty holiday diversion? Could she be more?

Pete was too afraid of the answer to find out.

Fast on the heels of that thought, a voice popped into her head.

Ask and listen carefully.

Suddenly, Pete sat up straight in her chair. Is that what her grandfather's warning had meant?

Eugenié glided in from the laundry room about then, sporting a basket of towels, and saved Pete from having to ponder the revelation. She watched the housekeeper's eyebrows raise as her charcoal gaze dropped to Pete's feet and trailed back up again.

"It was a long night," Pete said.

" 'Pears to me it wasn't long enough." Eugenié plopped the clothes basket on the countertop. "Want breakfast, missy? It's gonna be a busy day for you, need to start it out right."

"Had a bite already. Thanks." Pete put a hand to her mouth to cover a yawn. "Give me a couple of hours of shut-eye, and I'll be good to go."

"I second that," Carl said, rising from his chair. "If you ladies will excuse me, I think I'll go check my eyelids for cracks."

"First viewing starts at eleven," Pete called to his retreating back. "Want me to wake you?"

"Don't bother." He waved a dismissing hand over his shoulder. "Racine'll get me up when it's time."

As he disappeared up the stairs, Pete started folding towels while Eugenié cleared the table and loaded the dishes into the dishwasher. Once she was done wiping down the table and grumbling, she turned to Pete.

"So what's troublin' your mind, missy, that has you comin' to me so early?"

"I need advice."

Eugenié nodded and sat on a bar stool to fold the rest of the towels.

"Want to know 'bout your young man?"

"He's not my young man, and no, he's not what I want to ask about . . . at least, not right now." Pete slid onto the next bar stool and grabbed another towel. "Grandmother has left me a chore to take care of,

303

only she didn't leave word how I'm supposed to handle it."

Pete piled her folded towel on top of the others and turned worried eyes to the housekeeper.

"I want to do what's right," she said, "for everybody. But I'm torn, because I'm not sure what the right thing is."

"Missy, y'can't always fight other people's battles."

"I have to try." Pete rose from the stool. "It's my job."

She collected her shoes from the corner and then stopped to give Eugenié a peck on the cheek.

"I'm hitting the hay," Pete said. "Let me know what Grandmother says."

Once, not too long ago, bodies were laid out at home, and somber family and friends gathered in the parlor to commiserate and share recollections of the dearly departed's life.

Pete was glad that custom was history, because she preferred to sidestep death's ickier exigencies. Observing all the rituals took more organizing than she cared to tackle.

Her part was limited to simply locating and boxing certain cataloged items and transporting them to the funeral home.

Setup was Vonnie's responsibility.

Thankfully, in her preplanning, Grandmother Lang followed one philosophy: as long as death was fatal, it might as well be interesting.

She chose to celebrate life by sharing her memories through music and pictures. It was a moment of honest expression of feelings.

When preparations were done, the chapel doors at the Langstown Mortuary were thrown open and all were welcomed. Jackson and Marge were stationed at each end of the threshold, handling meet-and-greet, seemingly together while managing to remain apart.

Gant hovered at Jackson's elbow, ready to fetch and carry, while Sheldon spent his time in an out-of-the-way corner attached to his cell phone. Wearing a pair of Dockers, a navy blazer, and his Nikon, Pollard exhibited the good sense to move discreetly through the pews and aisles to snap pictures of visiting dignitaries.

Since any good Southern hostess feeds her guests whether they wanted to eat or not, refreshments were offered in the lobby: coffee, iced tea, finger sandwiches, and fresh fruit. Replenishing the stash was Eugenié's job.

Overhead the sound system played a CD with dedicated songs, mostly country favorites of her grandmother's with a little Satchmo jazz thrown in and all lively. Albert manned the CD changer, and his enthusiasm became evident when "Ahab the Arab" started playing.

Racine and Carl parked themselves down front of the cushioned pews, quietly asserting their claim as heirs apparent to the family's position in the community. As a couple accustomed to power, wealth, and fame, they had a natural interest in keeping their social and material advantages within the bloodline.

Behind them, Grandmother Lang reposed in a thirty-two-ounce gauge solid bronze casket with red velvet lining and pillow. The material color was a trifle loud for the occasion, but Grandmother hardly minded and certainly no one else was in a position to dispute the fashion faux pas.

Flanking her were lei-strewn tables filled with mementos — dart throwing trophies, favorite fishing rods, vacation pictures, and scores of photographs detailing more than seventy years of the history of the town and its citizens. Framed newspaper clippings recounted the political history of the area. Here, Pete was to play tour guide through the memorabilia, a task that was close to her heart.

Near the front of the tables rested a silk bird of paradise arrangement. *Bring a living plant instead of dying flowers,* Grandmother Lang had often said. Pete had compromised with the colorful silk.

Leatherette-finished memorial registers, with artwork inside from none other than Kinkade himself, were on lecterns scattered along the sides of the tables. Phoebe stood ready with tissues and extra designer writing pens.

For Pete, the viewing was celebrating the gathering of many friends to recognize one. It was a time when the community, family, and friends pulled together to express sympathy and support.

And it was the biggest conspiracy of silence since the Watergate break-in.

"Nice turnout," Vonnie said in Pete's ear. "The six-to-nine viewin' should be just as packed."

She looked out over the crowded chapel and nodded to familiar faces as well as to people for whom contact was too seldom to qualify as sporadic. One thought was uppermost in her mind.

"Do they all know?" she said out of the side of her mouth.

"Not all of 'em." Vonnie rocked back on his heels, looking shy, earnest, and boyishly slight, with an endearingly lopsided grin. "But enough do. Your grandma might've been a humdinger, but she was *our* humdinger. She was well loved, Pete, and people here sorta felt protective of her."

As Vonnie talked, Pete brushed a stray lock of hair behind her ear. That's when she noticed Pollard staring in their direction.

His protracted gaze made her decidedly uncomfortable and reinforced the fact that Pete had yet to find a solution for Miss Fritz.

"Walk with me," Pete said to Vonnie and slipped her arm through his.

They headed down the carpeted hallway, past cozy seating areas that resembled someone's living room. Once in the quiet of Vonnie's office, Pete shut the door behind her and leaned against it, crossing her arms over her chest.

"Is the floozy still tucked away here?"

"Sure is."

Vonnie propped his hip against the edge of a ruthlessly organized cherry wood desk. Not a speck of dust marred the gleaming surface, and not a paperclip was out of place.

"Take care, then," Pete said and inclined her head toward the chapel. "The guy out there taking pictures for Jackson? He's a reporter. He's been nosing around town, trying to uncover any dirt he can."

"He ain't gonna learn nothin' from me."

"Just keep an eye open for trouble." Out of curiosity, she had to know. "How is it you agreed to help my grandmother in the first place? What could she have possibly said to persuade you?"

"She asked me," Vonnie said simply.

Pete waited for the rest of it and then realized from his silence there wasn't any more coming.

"That's it?" She dropped her arms to her sides and stepped forward. "Grandmother asked, and you said sure?"

"Pretty much," Vonnie said, running his fingers over the shiny crease in his slacks.

Wasn't blood supposed to be thicker than water?

Pete being Pete, it frosted her cupcake to know her grandmother felt more comfortable taking a stranger into her confidence. Okay, so Vonnie wasn't exactly a stranger, but he wasn't an attentive and loving granddaughter, either.

"You didn't have to think about it?" Pete said. "You didn't question her?"

"Weren't no reason to."

"No?"

"Your grandma gave me my start-up money interest free and told me not to worry 'bout it. She had faith I'd pay her back as I could. That's a mighty strong incentive, faith is.

"She gave me a livin', gave me her trust, and she never asked for nothin' in return. How was I to refuse her the one time she begged a favor of me? I couldn't."

"No, put that way," Pete said, "I suppose not."

"Y' figure out what your grandma wanted you to do yet?"

He glanced at his watch, stood, and stepped toward the door.

"I'm working on it," she said, reaching for the doorknob. "Something will come to me."

A few moments later, they were back at the photo tables and Pete was hoping a solution would come to her, for heading her way was the Deep Throat wanna-be in her conspiracy.

"Morning, Pete," Benedict said, giving her a killer smile and looking scrumptious in a double-breasted gray suit and tie. "Sleep well?"

His hair was attractively bedhead tousled, and he was clean-shaven and rested. No man should be allowed to look so yummy after only a couple of hours sleep.

Her heart tripped in her chest. He smelled of sandalwood, leather, sweet sin, and impossible dreams.

"I slept like a log," she said.

What a lie. She had tossed and turned, reliving her time in Benedict's arms and in his bed. Pete tried not to blush, but she felt her neck warming up.

"And you?" she added.

"No problems to speak of."

They were careful of each other, probably overly careful of each other's feelings — which was silly, wasn't it? — given that half of her world saw them checking tonsils on the dance floor. He and Vonnie shook hands and made small talk before Vonnie excused himself and moved on to chat with other people.

Benedict tipped his head in Vonnie's direction and said, "Did you two square things away okay?"

"We have a solid friendship." Pete nodded. "He has a big heart, treats people with respect."

Unnerved by Benedict's steady regard, she let her gaze wander over his shoulder. She caught sight of the sheriff and two of his deputies at the door to the chapel, shaking hands with Jackson.

Seeing them wasn't unusual. Of course they would come. Grandmother Lang was a big supporter of their department, but Pete didn't need Benedict getting any ideas about chewing the fat with them.

"So there were no problems this morning," she repeated for lack of anything more clever.

"Only one," he said and offered a cordial smile to several ladies with Slurpee-blue hair who stepped up to Pete's table to chat among themselves over the pictures.

"And what was that?"

"I was alone in the bed."

"Ye gods —"

Pete clamped her lips shut before she said something embarrassing. Was the man insane?

She glanced quickly to the older women. Had they overheard him?

Apparently, yes.

They abruptly quit talking to each other and stared at her with curiously narrowed eyes and stiff backs.

Whispering through a forced smile, Pete edged Benedict away from the table and said, "Would you like a microphone so you can tell the whole town what we spent the night doing?"

He stepped closer, invading her personal space, while she stood her ground.

"I need to talk to you," he said.

"Can we do this later?"

"It's important."

"About what?"

"Us."

His timing sure needed to be finessed.

"I may not be the most sophisticated woman," Pete said, "but I can think of a more appropriate setting for this conversation than in a mortuary, and one more private to boot."

"Look, I —"

"No, you look, counselor. When you and I talk about something serious — if we ever talk again, and I'm not guaranteeing we will — I want something like I've seen in magazines. I want moonlight and champagne, not stale coffee and the lingering odor of formaldehyde — wait! What am I saying?"

Disgusted by her runaway mouth, she grabbed his arm and urged him toward the seclusion of a side door. Just in front of it, she let go and drew in a deep breath.

"There is no *us*," she said in a fierce whisper.

"What was that last night?"

She didn't intend to perform a post-mortem on what was a wonderful memory that she wanted to keep untouched.

"This is not the place —"

"Maybe you're right." He finger-combed the hair that fell over his forehead. "At least let me apologize for not telling you earlier that my investigator was running down missing persons."

"Dan —"

He held up his hands in surrender.

"I should have said something. You had a right to know. I realize that now."

"The guilt of what you did or didn't do has no place at this funeral. Now, may we please talk about all this later?"

"Fine. When?"

"I don't know —"

"Give me a time." She opened her mouth and he repeated, "What time?"

"Tonight," she snapped. "Visitation's over at nine. I should be back at the house by nine-thirty."

"I'll wait for you at the cottage."

"Don't. If I get held up —"

"I said I'll wait."

Without sticking around for a reply, Benedict pushed the metal bar on the side door and disappeared outside. Pete inhaled a calming breath.

One problem at a time, she told herself as the door swung closed.

Right now, she had no choice but to paste on a serene face, give her full attention to the people attending her grandmother's viewing, and wait for the day to drag by.

What did Pete mean, *there was no* us?

Of course, there was an *us* — Danny had known it from the first moment he'd clapped eyes on her. He'd just gone about telling her the wrong way.

Pete wasn't your run-of-the-mill debutante mining for diamonds. A night built around red-carpet premiers and celebrity parties wouldn't impress her. And unless she had been prom queen, she had never been the belle of the ball.

That was about to change.

If a man wanted to bring out a woman's inner Marilyn Monroe, he needed the personal touches — music, flowers, hors d'oeuvres, drinks *de la nuit* — the more individual, the more memorable.

Back at the cottage, Danny wasted no time in calling in favors to plan a perfectly urbane evening. It was less than an hour flight from Atlanta to Langstown, plenty of time for him to choreograph a beautiful seduction, one executed with elegance and taste.

He had the location. And he knew just the person who would jump at the chance to help him pull the design together.

When the voice on the other end of his cell phone answered, Danny smiled and said, "Hello, Mother. I know you've waited a hundred years for this call, so I'm about to make your day. Can you drop whatever you're doing this afternoon? I have a rush project for you."

Chapter 18

The hour neared ten o'clock by the time Pete had finished boxing up her grandmother's mementos and had pulled up to the front of Danny Benedict's cottage.

Pete was tired, yes, but that's not the full reason why she was dragging her feet. She was embarrassed about jumping the gun earlier and opening her impulsive mouth.

They'd known each other how long?

Not long enough.

She hadn't expected anything when she met him, but a tiny part of her sure had dared to wish.

What she felt about him was deepening into a yearning for something long-lasting. Yet it was too soon to nibble anywhere near the exclusivity topic, especially with a man who wasn't known for being an exclusive type of guy.

Ask and listen carefully, her grandfather had warned.

Now that the opportunity was upon her, Pete wasn't sure she had the courage to ask.

She had considered postponing her talk

with Danny, but it was beyond rude not to call and let him know not to expect her, particularly when he said he'd be sitting there and waiting. Because she had forgotten to ask for his cell phone number, calling was out of the question.

Pete started to climb out of her car and stopped. For the past two hours, her panty hose had been creeping down her ankles like ivy on a trellis. So a couple of quick moves later and she breathed a relieved sigh to be rid of them.

After she balled them up, she tossed them into the center console, hoping she'd remember to take them out later, and got out of the car. That was when she noticed the music.

Into the quiet night floated the melancholy notes of a lone guitar playing "As Time Goes By," something unusual in itself, considering the nearest neighbor was at least a half a mile away.

Partway up the brick path, Pete stopped again and listened, amazed that the sound carried so well on the night air. She could imagine coming upon Bergman and Bogart somewhere in front of her, dancing under the old magnolia tree.

Actually, that's where the music seemed to be coming from — the back of the cottage, where the private porch was, rather than from inside. Was Danny entertaining?

What if he was? She had no claim on him.

Even so, Pete's heart sank a little.

Maybe it wasn't a good idea to interrupt. Maybe she should quietly turn around and leave him to whatever he was doing and whomever he was doing it with. Maybe she should have her head examined for even thinking she might have a glimmer of hope.

Hold up a minute. Why would he be entertaining when he said he'd wait no matter what time she arrived? That didn't make sense.

Nothing she was doing made sense anymore, not from the moment Danny had walked into her life. If Pete weren't careful, she'd drive herself bonkers before she could get her grandmother decently buried.

She reached for her mirror and lipstick to make herself more presentable and realized she'd left her shoulder purse on the front passenger seat. Pivoting on her heel, she headed back to her car. She was grabbing for the door handle when she heard Danny call her name.

Was he watching for her? Or had he

heard her car tires on the gravel?

With a fortifying breath, she turned around and sensed something had changed. She couldn't put her finger on what, though.

Danny was still the most handsome guy she'd seen on or off the magazine pages, and tonight he looked every bit the lady-killer in soft white linen slacks and a matching V-neck big shirt that emphasized his blond hair and rugged tan. How he missed being saddled with a wife, ten kids, and a minivan to go with them was the mystery of the ages.

For a few seconds, the expression on his face reflected panic, so Pete chose to err on the side of caution.

"I'm sorry," she said. "I didn't realize you had company. We can talk tomorrow." She jabbed a finger toward her car and lowered her voice. "I'll just be going now."

Was that cologne or aftershave he was wearing? He smelled so provocative.

His gaze relaxed into a smile, and he shook his head.

"Stay, please. I don't have company. Why do you think I would?"

"The music?" Pete said, pointing behind them.

"Speaking of which . . ." He extended

his hand to her and angled back the way he'd come. "C'mon. Let me show you something."

Pete hesitated a moment, knowing this foray could wind up in his bed, which would not be a good idea for her heart if she was going to have to cheerfully wave good-bye to him after the funeral tomorrow. Too curious for good sense, though, she put her fingers in his steady hand and followed the brick pavers around back . . .

And stepped right into Casablanca.

"What do you think?" he said.

Pete was startled and dumbfounded. Before her astonished gaze sat a Moroccan salon on the patio terrace, mingling against a backdrop of twinkling lights and tinkling ice cubes.

"Oh, my gosh, this is fabulous," she said, groping for words. "I'm speechless."

And she was. All she could do was gawk.

Nubby-textured Dupioni silk panels in blue draped from the ceiling of an open-air tent. The same panels in rich plum were gathered to each of the four corners and tethered with a gold-fringed sash. On the tent floor, Oriental rugs layered over terra cotta tiles.

Elegant teak and iron outdoor furniture

was outfitted with pillows and a throw on the table in a mix of vibrant red, gold, and yellow. Large woven baskets were artfully scattered at the edges of the tiles and held flower arrangements in the same brilliant desert sky colors.

Ornately carved wooden accents graced small beaten-brass side tables. A collection of highly fragrant candles dominated the center of the table and livened the warm air with the smell of market spices.

Off to one side of the tent, beyond the rim of the string lights, sat a heavyset man in an immaculate white dinner jacket and black tie playing the guitar that was serenading Pete. He was dressed identical to the middle-aged headwaiter? butler? — Pete couldn't decide which — who stood adjacent to him with a cocktail shaker in his hand.

She couldn't have been more astounded by the elaborate scene if Bogie himself moonwalked out of Rick's Café Americain and into her living room, yet her practical side refused to remain quiet.

"Never sit in a tuxedo," Pete mumbled to herself, "you'll break the crease."

"Ever tasted an appletini?" Danny asked.

Pete forgot about her fatigue as she swung her gaze back to the tent.

"I don't believe so," she said.

He ducked his head to clear a silk panel and sauntered toward her. In each hand, he carried a chilled cocktail glass filled with a cherry skinny-dipping in a light amber liquid.

"I figured you could use one of these about now," he said, offering her a glass.

Her stomach did a funny little jump. This wasn't moonlight and champagne — it was better.

Don't read more into the evening than there is, she warned herself.

But it was too late.

The man was going to break her heart when he left. Pete knew that and accepted it as well as she knew that Danny was a great kisser.

Thanking him, she accepted the drink, clinked her glass to his in a silent toast to illusive dreams, and took a big sip.

"Apple juice with a zing," she said, surprised.

He sported an irrepressible smile.

"An appletini."

She gestured with her glass to encompass the tent, the guitar player, the staid butler hovering at the edges, and said, "Who else are you expecting?"

Pete wanted to hear it from his lips to be

sure. She wasn't going to embarrass herself by assuming anything.

"The only person I want to see has just arrived."

Her stomach came alive with butterflies, and she was helpless to stop a sappy grin from appearing on her face.

When Danny led her into the silk tent, the butler executed an abbreviated bow and greeted her in dulcet tones. Feeling very regal, she acknowledged his greeting with a nod and let him seat her.

Danny pulled one of the small brass tables over and plopped a pillow on top of it. Using the table as an ottoman, he knelt and gently lifted her achy feet, slipped off her sling-back sandals, and placed her bare heels on the pillow.

"Better?" he said.

"Oh, my, yes." She sighed. "It's wonderful. I can't remember when I've been so pampered."

"You deserve it."

The music had changed. Pete recognized "Dream a Little Dream of Me" playing now.

"How did you know?" she said.

"Know what?"

"That *Casablanca* is one of my favorite movies?"

Danny seated himself in the chair next to her and gave a negligent shrug.

"Wild guess."

An inelegant snort sprang to her lips and she said, "Do you always go to so much trouble on a mere guess? What kind of lawyer are you?"

"You've caught me," he said on a chuckle. "I confess I called Albert and grilled him over hot coals until he spilled his guts and told me what I wanted to know. Other than that, it was a good guess."

"Now that sounds more like it," Pete said and laughed. "Nosy to a fault."

"In my own defense, I figured anyone who likes old movies has to be a romantic." He sipped his drink. "And what's more romantic than two lovers in an exotic place, standing on a fog-shrouded runway?"

Pete sobered, the reality in his statement crashing her back to earth.

"Too bad they don't end up together," she said. "He goes his way; she goes hers."

"The movie couldn't have ended any other way," Benedict said.

And neither can we.

Pete almost voiced her thought aloud, but what was the point? Saying it didn't change a thing.

The butler presented a green glass tray from which he lifted a gold napkin and revealed hors d'oeuvres hidden underneath. On the tray was a small glass jar of caviar in a bowl of crushed ice surrounded by toast points spread with what looked to be cream cheese or crème fraîche.

Pete thought the butler's next move would be to offer her the tray, but he served Danny instead. Danny seemed right at home when he used the mother-of-pearl spoon to top the toast with a dollop of caviar and then garnish with capers from a smaller tray of condiments the butler held.

Once Danny was satisfied with his combination, he turned to her.

"Open up," he said and brought the hors d'oeuvre to her mouth.

She did. The delicate texture and salty taste of the chilled caviar danced on her tongue, and the feel of his fingers on her lips conjured erotic images of satin sheets and steamy bodies.

"Beluga?" she managed to say.

"No, Osetra."

Then he raised his finger and thumb to his mouth and slowly slid them one at a time between his lips and sucked the cream off. She watched his move, her gaze caught by his half-lidded, sensuous eyes, desire rolling like a heat wave throughout her every pore.

"Osetra is smaller than the Beluga," he added, "but a fine quality."

Who cared? At this point, he could recite the phone book and she'd melt.

Pete oozed further into the furniture, all of her heated to flaming, right down to her tender toes. She swallowed more of her drink and watched while Danny fixed himself some of the Osetra.

The sultry night, the caviar, the soft light, the market scents, the ambient music . . . experienced together, they were an aphrodisiac.

And were further testimony to the very real differences between Pete and Danny Benedict.

This was his world, not hers. Hers was sunrises in a cow pasture.

Take mental pictures, she told herself. There weren't too many eligible men in Langstown and none with Danny's physical stature, charisma, and flair for the seductive.

According to the old saw, she couldn't miss what she'd never had. But now that she'd experienced an elegant, self-possessed man who was so very attentive to her and who knew all about fly rods, she was going to miss him like crazy.

In the next moment, she polished off her drink, handed up the empty glass to the efficient butler, and said, "Danny? What are you doing?"

Before answering, he nodded to the butler, who correctly interpreted that as the signal to back away. He moved to a discreet distance, giving them a semblance of privacy.

"I thought it was obvious," Danny said, taking her hand and lifting it to his mouth. "I'm wooing you."

"Wooing?"

"Wooing. You know, seeking the affections of a woman . . . making amorous advances toward a woman. How do you feel about it?"

"I know what the word means," she said, hoping to sidestep the question, except he then turned into a lawyer on her.

"That's nonresponsive."

"Okay, I don't know how I feel. Confused, I guess, and that's the problem."

Pete swung her feet off the pillow and stood, searching the corners to see where he'd stashed her shoes. Danny gained his feet, too.

"What problem?" he said.

Swiping her sandals off the rug, Pete

turned to the butler. Did one express gratitude to a butler? She didn't know. She'd never seen a butler before, let alone had occasion to speak to one.

Falling back on her upbringing, Pete decided a display of manners was never gauche.

"Thank you," she said to the man. "It was all quite lovely. Good night." As he smiled and bowed in acknowledgment, she then waved to the guitar player and called, "Your playing was beautiful. Thank you."

"Wait a minute," Danny said. "What problem?"

She cleared the tent and he followed.

"No one's ever gone to such lengths for me." She flung her arms wide. "This is so fabulous, and I'm more appreciative than you'll ever know."

His expression grew serious.

"Do I hear a 'but' in there?" he said.

They were standing on the brick pavers under the canopy of the giant magnolia. The guitar player had shifted to a throbbing song where time moved slowly and echoed the steamy rhythms of the night.

"But," she said, hugging her shoes to her chest, "this is you. This isn't me. Dan, maybe it's better if we don't start something we can't finish."

"Too late, sweetheart. We've already started. You should have thought of that before you kissed me in the boathouse."

"You kissed me," she said, dropping her gaze to her bare toes. "I simply kissed you back. That was my mistake."

He cupped her face in his hands and lifted her chin up so she could look him in the eye. The music drifted around them, each soft note fading into the other and romancing the sultry darkness beyond the tent.

"No, sweetheart," he said, his voice tender and enticing. "Your mistake came way before that."

"It did?"

"At the hospital, when we first met."

"What did I do?"

"You smiled at me."

And then he covered her mouth with his.

Chapter 19

I can resist everything except temptation, Oscar Wilde had once quipped.

Wilde had never met Pete Lang.

She was Danny's temptation. Any other woman would be making an invitation list and picking out a china pattern by now. Not Pete.

Not his Pete.

His? He wasn't sure when he started thinking of her that way — maybe from the first — but she was, and would always be, his someone special as surely as he needed air to breathe.

With her, he'd broken all his personal work rules, but he felt a deep, heart connection that made all the rest of the problems they might face less important. What he was taking was a big step.

Toward what, he didn't know.

But there was magic in her heart that gave him the courage to face the journey. Being with Pete was an adventure in pure joy.

There was a forever promise in her smile, her touch, the way she looked at him with those bedroom eyes as if he'd walked out of her dreams. That was heady stuff, that look of hers.

Even the problem of her grandmother's dead floozy faded beneath the brilliance of Pete's honest warmth and tenderness. Danny and Pete worked well together, and together, if she'd let him, they would find a way to face the problem head-on.

Danny recalled that Wilde had also said *the only way to get rid of temptation is to yield to it.* What a smart guy he was.

It was good advice then, and better advice right now.

Still kissing Pete breathless, Danny slid his hands down her luscious curves until he cupped her bottom and lifted her off her feet. She needed no convincing.

"I want you, Dan," she said.

"God, I hope so. Hold on, sweetheart."

She clutched her arms around his neck, her shoes falling to the ground, forgotten. He carried her through the privacy of the French doors without breaking stride.

Once inside the dim interior, he banged the door closed with his foot, knowing he'd never make it across the room to the bed — he wanted her right here, and he wanted her right now.

The kitchenette was closer.

He didn't bother turning on lights. There was no need. Enough light from the patio filtered through the transoms to blanket them in intimate shadows.

Her legs cradling his hips, he propped her on top of the counter, his arm snaking out and sending paper napkins and cups and plastic plates scattering to the four corners.

"You okay?" he said.

He kissed her neck, her nose, her eyes, her cheeks.

"Fine," she said, grasping his face and dragging his lips back to hers. "I love your mouth, Dan. You have a great mouth."

She moaned his name again and tore at his shirt. He had no time. They could worry with removing clothes later.

Shoving her dress up, he was elated to discover she wore no panties. He was even more electrified to feel her sultry heat against his hand.

She let loose a throaty sound, as ready for him as he was for her. In one smooth motion, he freed himself from his slacks and entered her, her skin pressed against his, their bodies moving together in an age-old rhythm.

When he lifted her hips in his palms and slightly spread her tush, it gave him the deepest, most intense sensation. Between her gasps of delight and the inner shudders he could feel, he knew she liked it, too.

"Wrap your legs around me," he said, "and cross your ankles."

She did. Throwing her hands up by her head, she groped against the cabinet until she latched onto the bottom valance for leverage and support. Then she performed the most incredible feat.

As Danny moved inside her, Pete rubbed against him and squeezed her thigh muscles together. That decision certainly earned his lifetime vote of approval. The friction of the snug fit magnified every sensation.

Their coming together was rough and fun, passionate and hot, slippery and sensual.

And quick.

When the firestorm was over, Pete collapsed into him, all loose-limbed and lushly sweet, while he bowed his forehead on her shoulder and held her so tight she was lucky to draw a breath. He was reluctant to leave her, feeling he'd never get enough of her beautiful softness.

Still inside her, he wiggled his hips and nibbled his way up the side of her neck to her ear lobe. She started giggling.

"Oh, my," she said, her hand flying to cover her mouth.

"What?"

"Listen."

He did and heard the throbbing strains of the guitar coming from outside.

"We're within moaning distance of those poor guys," Pete said, swiping hair off her damp face. "You don't think they heard us, do you?"

If they didn't, they probably had a good idea of what was going on, but Danny kept that to himself. There was no need to embarrass Pete anymore than she might already be.

"Don't worry about them. They're being well paid for their discretion."

Danny kissed her, buried his nose in her neck again, and skimmed his lips and teeth over the pulse racing under her delicate skin. He could envision a thousand such nights spent in her arms, and the idea pleased him immensely.

"I love the way you smell," he said.

In the next instant, he felt a gentle tap on his shoulder.

"Excuse me, Dan?"

"Yes?" he said, his voice muffled in her hair.

"We have a problem."

He raised his head, offered a sheepish smile, and said, "I wondered when you'd notice."

This was the most irresponsible move he'd ever made in his entire adult life. He was a grown man, not a kid. An attorney. He knew better.

The condoms he'd bought earlier were still on the table. Unopened.

"I know I'm clean," she said with a surprising calm. "And I assume you —"

"As a whistle," he hastened to add. "I'm sorry, I wasn't thinking. You just felt too good. You're on the pill?"

"How did you know?"

"The calmness. I don't think you would be calm otherwise."

"You got that right." She cupped his cheeks and kissed him, hard. "Now, let me down from here, lover, so I can visit the facilities. I think I have a plastic spoon permanently embedded on my spine."

Danny tried to act and feel contrite but failed miserably. Instead, he laughed and helped her scoot off the countertop.

When her bare feet touched the floor, he smoothed her dress down for her.

"By the way," he said, as she padded to the bathroom, "you are so hot without the undies."

She winked and flashed him a foxy smile over her shoulder.

Once in the bathroom, Pete closed the door behind her and flipped on the light over the medicine cabinet. She stood for several seconds and just stared transfixed at the woman in the mirror.

Pete barely recognized the wild hair, the chafe marks on her neck caused by Dan's beard, and the lips dark and slightly swollen from too much kissing. This woman with the dreamy, adore-me eyes and flawlessly glowing skin was a stranger, but she was someone Pete wanted more than anything to get used to seeing.

Who was it said the pure and simple truth was rarely pure and never simple?

How right he was.

The truth was, Pete no longer cared if Dan Benedict had known one or a hundred women before her, as long as she was a part of his life from now on. She loved him, every bit of him. In that respect, she finally understood what motivated her grandmother to stay with her grandfather for so many years.

After a quick wash and finger-combing her hair into some semblance of normalcy, Pete emerged from the bathroom to find the cottage empty. A brief glance around and she found Benedict outside on the terrace.

The night air was quiet except for the bugs.

"The guys leave already?" she said, finding her shoes and putting them on.

"It's late," he said. "I figured they could use the time off; besides, I wanted to spend time alone with you. Hey, where do you think you're going?"

He snared her within his embrace and caressed her chin with his forefinger.

"You're right," she said, dangling her shoes to her side and circling his shoulder with her other arm. Her fingers idly played with the silky strands of hair at the back of his neck. "It's late. Thank you for a memorable evening. I can't believe you went to so much trouble, but I'm glad you did. Now, I need to go to bed."

Kissing her on the tip of her nose, he said, "Want me to turn the covers back?"

"Let me rephrase that . . . I need to go to sleep."

"I promise not to snore. C'mon. Stay with me."

"Oh, no, you don't. Carl's an early riser, and I'm not up to greeting him tomorrow wearing the same dress I wore today. This morning's encounter of the strange kind will do me for a while."

Benedict swept her hair back behind her ears, and it seemed all the light was reflected in his beautiful eyes.

"I want you, Pete."

"You already had me."

"It wasn't enough, wench."

"You romantic dog, you."

"I want you," he repeated. "All night. Do I have to steal you away to my tent again?"

She chuckled and playfully pushed against his shoulder.

"Dan, you are incorrigible."

"No." He wiggled his eyebrows. "I'm a lawyer."

Pete sobered.

"That reminds me," she said and then filled him in on what she'd learned about Pollard's recent nosiness.

"I heard the same thing from Marge, except he was asking about you and me, about our relationship."

"And that doesn't bother you?"

"It does, but it's a lot less sensitive subject than if he were to stumble on information about Miss Fritz."

"Oh, well, there's no worry there. He'll never find her."

When Benedict pulled back and studied her, his eyes flat, Pete could have kicked herself for letting that slip out.

"You sound pretty sure," he said. "Do you know where she is?"

"Well . . . I mean . . . that is . . ."

Dropping his arms away, he stepped back and waited.

"Yes, you do know. I can read it in your face." Pivoting on his heel, he faced the cottage and then whirled back to her again. "Dammit, Pete, were you even going to tell me?"

"Truthfully?"

"Of course."

"No, I wasn't. And don't be putting on the ugly with me. You're the guy who said he wasn't interested in truth."

Pete sensed she was trying his patience when he pressed his palms together in front of him and inhaled a deep breath.

"Let me explain something, sweetheart. Bald monks in bad togas spend their lives freezing their butts off on cold mountain peaks, searching for a greater truth than a factual truth. For the rest of us, we're stuck with what can be proven, not on what might actually be true. Now, where is she?"

"Shhhh. Not so loud."

Sealing his lips with her fingers, Pete glanced around, searching for any possible eavesdroppers. She didn't think anyone lurked about, but there could be a herd of elephants nearby and she wouldn't know it.

Not much could be distinguished in the trees that lay beyond the tent lights. A night that had been a haven in a harsh world such a short time ago now seemed less than inviting.

Benedict's warm breath seeped through her fingers as he mumbled and conjured sweet images for Pete. She dropped her hand.

"Are you going to tell me?" he repeated.

"Why? So you can march straight to the sheriff?"

So much for her grandfather's *ask and listen*. Rather than waiting to hear an answer she already knew, Pete crossed the brick pavers to her car and tossed her shoes inside. Benedict followed her.

"It's better if your family faces the music before things get much more out of hand," he said. "If you don't want me going to the sheriff, then you do it."

Pete stared at him as if he'd grown another nose.

"Easy for you to say. You're asking me to risk everything that's important to me. That is so unfair. Now, excuse me. I've got a funeral tomorrow morning, and I need some sleep."

She climbed in the car and turned the engine over, then rolled down the driver's side window at Benedict's insistent signal.

"I'm only trying to help," he said, leaning in the window.

"And I appreciate it. I really do. But sometimes, Dan, the best way to help is to leave things alone."

"Sorry, sweetheart, I can't," he said. "Nothing would please me better than for all of us to sit around the campfire singing 'Kumbaya,' but I don't see it happening this time."

His expression looked as dubious about Miss Fritz as Pete felt. What she needed, she decided, was an echo from the grave.

Chapter 20

Langstown boasted twenty churches for the town of five thousand people. Depending on your outlook, the number was either overkill or hedging your bet.

Pete woke early the morning of her grandmother's funeral service, showered, and dressed in a simple black sheath. She headed downstairs before any of the rest of the family, because she had slept badly, as much as to fend off getting the third degree about her evening visits with Benedict.

Why couldn't he understand what he was asking of her? Too many lives would be ruined, and for what? For a fleeting sense of justice?

Who was the justice for, when everyone directly involved with the murder was already dead? Even Benedict's investigator had failed to uncover anyone who cared.

The questions swirled in her head as she walked into the sun-bright breakfast room. Unfortunately, there were no ready answers.

As usual, Eugenié was the first one up

and busy in the kitchen. The homey smells of brewed coffee and frying bacon permeated the air, interrupted by the acrid stink of burned toast and the piercing screech of the smoke alarm going off.

Patty, Maxene, and LaVerne were in the adjacent mudroom and set to jumping on the gate that separated them from the rest of the house and to howling like demented banshees. If anyone had been sleeping, they weren't anymore. Pete scrambled to let the dogs outside while Eugenié rescued the toast and started fanning a dishrag in front of the brayingly obnoxious smoke alarm.

Once Pete opened some of the windows to let out the smoke, the alarm shut up on its own, never guessing how close it had come to an early demise. She grabbed up another dishrag and the two of them did the NASCAR checkered flag guy proud as they waved in the fresh air.

"Coffee's ready, missy," Eugenié said, tossing her dishrag to the counter. "You close them windows, and I'll pour you some."

"Thanks," Pete said, rummaging in the cabinet for a cup.

"Your young man doin' okay this mornin'?"

Halting in mid-reach, Pete winced, but what had she expected? She seldom, if ever, had a love life to speak of, so was it any wonder it was open season when she finally did get one?

Then again, that ice in the desert lasted longer than her love life was not even worth bringing up.

"He does fine," Pete said, which was an understatement given his performance last night, but one she figured was generic enough to appease without getting into embarrassing specifics. "Any vibes yet from Grandmother?"

"Not a thin'," Eugenié said, cracking eggs into the skillet of bacon grease, "and I don't like it."

"Bad juju?"

"Somethin' gonna happen today, missy. I feel it."

Oh, no.

Pete really didn't like the sound of that.

As she was finishing her first cup of coffee, Racine and Carl came down dressed in their bathrobes, holding hands like newlyweds, and joined her at the breakfast table. The coy looks and grins the lovebirds kept passing between them left no doubt of the joy they found in each other.

They sparked a tinge of envy in Pete. Why couldn't that be her and Danny one day?

Before she finished the second cup, Phoebe, Jackson, and Marge had trudged down, wearing faces like three rooms of gloom, and joined them. If no one knew they were going to a funeral before, they did now.

Jackson and Phoebe had both thrown on comfy T-shirts and shorts, and Marge had tossed on a knee-length, yellow terry bathing suit cover-up. Pete was the only one dressed in black and ready to go.

While Jackson and Marge helped themselves to a plate of bacon and eggs, Pete cornered her sister by the coffee pot.

"What's with you?" she said. "I've seen wilted houseplants sporting happier faces."

Phoebe wobbled a bit on her feet, squinted, and said, "Do me a favor? Not so loud, okay. I'm a little ginger this morning."

"Ginger? You look like a reject from a twelve-step program. My God, those are some boozy eyeballs, girl."

"So I'll wear sunglasses. Get me some ice, will you? This coffee is too hot."

Pete fetched a cube from the nearby

icemaker and said, "Where did you go, bar-hopping?"

"Albert and I went to play Texas hold 'em in the back room at the VFW club."

Now that was a group of old farts well known in the county for sharing a boisterous esprit de corps.

"Oh, lord . . . did you two embarrass the family?"

" 'Fraid so. We lost our shirts, but those boys sure know how to have a good time."

Albert was ensconced in the garage apartment, his usual haunt when he was in town. Pete hadn't thought anything about his nonappearance as long as Jackson was around.

"Should I take some breakfast over to Albert?" Pete said.

Phoebe shook her head.

"Coffee, maybe, and lots of water, but I wouldn't offer him greasy food unless I wanted to die ugly."

Wonderful.

The day was getting longer by the minute.

"Pietra, darlin'," Racine said, returning her cup to its saucer. "You haven't said, how is Mr. Benedict?"

This soft grilling is what Pete had wanted to avoid, but it didn't look like they were going to let her slip by. The phone rang, and Carl rose from the table to answer it because he was closest.

"I haven't said," Pete pointed out, "because there is nothing to say. Lettuce has a longer shelf life than me and a guy."

But her mother had waited too long for Pete to find someone with a healthy six-figure income, and she wasn't about to be deterred when it appeared her goal was in sight.

"Oh, come now, darlin', you can tell us. We're family. Are there any plans for an announcement?"

"Them two?" Jackson jerked his chin up and stared at Pete with the expression of a man who suddenly found himself in a perfectly strange place with grave responsibilities he knew nothing about. "When pigs fly. The old boy'll be heading out soon, and you won't see him for dust."

That was exactly what Pete knew, but hearing it tossed out, a raw wound on her heart, open for the picking . . .

"How do you know?" Marge said, quietly. "After all, he came all the way down here to be with her, didn't he? That says somethin' about him and his feelin's."

Jackson had no ready comeback for her veiled barb — how could he? — so he settled for shoveling in more eggs and mumbling something unintelligible.

"Thank you, brother dear," Pete said, propping her hip against the rim of the counter. "You've always got a way with words. But while we're speaking of heading out . . . The mayor is hosting a reception in the high school gym after the service today. Do y'all want to put in an appearance, or what's your schedule?"

"I think a quick hello is in order," Racine said. "Otherwise, Jackson and Marjorie can represent the family. Don't you agree, dear?"

"Suits me," Pete said and glanced to her brother for his opinion.

"Yeah, fine," he said, using his toast to sop up the last of his grits. "There's no such thin' as shakin' too many hands."

If Racine noticed that Marge sat and drank her hot tea in silence, she made no mention of it.

"Good," Racine said and patted her husband's hand as he regained his seat at the table. "Then it's settled. Carl really must get back to his wells, so we thought we'd fly out this afternoon."

"Oh, that was Vonnie Miller on the phone," Carl said to Pete. "He asked if you'd come early so he could go over things with you."

Pete nodded and said, "Phoebe? You staying or heading back?"

"Heading back. I've got a five-hour drive by myself, and I'd like to get in before dark. You know how I hate driving after dark."

Pete pushed away from the counter and said, "Get cleaned up and dressed, and I'll go check out what Vonnie's done for us. See y'all later at the chapel."

Today, Florida's A-list would be in attendance. The political, intellectual, and financial elite would arrive early and pack the chapel Pete's grandmother had endowed.

Pete parked in the empty lot around back of the church and was greeting Vonnie a few minutes later. He led her into a small curtained antechamber where an inexpensive-looking wooden casket rested between two floor candelabra.

"You got here quicker than I thought," he said.

"I was ready when you called," she said. "It's no problem. What have you got for me?"

She followed Vonnie up the short carpeted aisle to the closed casket. The coffin looked even cheaper up close. He then spread open what appeared to be a hand-stitched ivory sheet adorned with a single cross appliqué in the upper third portion. A flick of the wrist and the cloth draped nicely and covered the entire casket.

"This is simply exquisite," Pete said, fingering the hem of the cloth.

Vonnie beamed and said, "Irish linen. Your grandma had good taste."

"Very nice," she agreed. "Can I see it on grandmother's casket?"

Frowning, Vonnie shifted his feet and blinked rapidly.

"Pete, this is your grandma. Right here."

"This?" She tossed back the corner of the cloth and revealed a casket that she now noticed wasn't even real wood. "No, really, no kidding. I mean her real casket. The beautiful bronze —"

When Vonnie caught on to Pete's confusion, he relaxed and smiled.

"That was her viewing casket . . . y'know, just for the viewing."

"This one is for the burial?"

"Burial? No, sweetie." He chuckled and then proceeded to give her his best sales pitch. "This is our top of the line, environmentally friendly woodlike casket, made of recycled corrugated paper, with no metal or noncombustible components."

"Recycled? Back up a minute. Are you telling me my grandmother is in a cardboard box?"

Pete couldn't believe her hearing.

"Yes, ma'am, it burns one hundred percent without producing pollutants."

"And what am I supposed to do now, Vonnie, plant her in the backyard like a dead goldfish? Fertilize the azaleas with her? Wait . . . *burn?* I've got to sit down."

Stepping over to the first pew, Pete slumped onto the cushion. Silence filled the antechamber for several moments before Vonnie's quiet voice broke into Pete's rambling thoughts.

"I thought you knew she decided on cremation."

"No." Pete pinched the bridge of her nose. "She forgot to clue me in on that one."

"Oh." Vonnie lowered himself onto the cushion beside her and let his clasped hands dangle between his knees. "Well, ain't she just full of surprises?"

"Oh, yeah, she's come up with a couple of doozies here lately."

"Well, y'reckon we go ahead here or what?"

The thought of cremation gave Pete the willies, but now that she'd had a moment to get used to the idea . . .

"If that's what Grandmother wanted, let's go with it. It's too late to change it now."

Pete rose and started back up the aisle, Vonnie falling in step with her.

"I can't believe my grandmother would rent a pretty coffin for the viewing, rather than —"

Vonnie shook his head.

"Can't rent a casket," he said. "The day she come in, she asked all kinds of questions and then bought the bronze one cash money. I tried to talk her out of it, but she wouldn't listen. When your grandma got a bee in her bonnet —"

Pete clamped a hand to Vonnie's arm, her grandfather's warning suddenly gelling in her mind.

Ask and listen.

"Say that again," she said.

"When your grandma got a bee in her bonnet?"

Vigorously shaking her head, Pete said, "The other thing. The bronze casket. She bought the bronze casket?"

"Sure did."

Ask and listen.

"Where is it?" A hysterical giggle exploded from Pete. "What did she do with it?"

"I still got it —"

Pete slapped a hand over her mouth, but another rude noise escaped anyway.

"That's the answer," she managed to utter between gasps of excitement. "Ye gods, that's it."

Chapter 21

As Grandmother Lang's service drew to a close, lively strains from the gospel classic, "I'll Fly Away" filled the chantry and floated out on the muggy air through the opened stained-glass windows and filled the surrounding garden.

Pete sat on an ornamental concrete gossip bench under a sprawling live oak and listened.

In her head, she heard her grandmother singing along in a twanging voice to the Ferlin Husky record. *Like a bird from prison bars has flown, I'll fly away . . .*

Besides being appropriate, the words and music were simple and direct, reflective of the depression era that spawned them and that helped shape her grandmother. With the call-and-response dynamic that was built into the verses, the people present in the chapel seemed to dive right into the song.

Pete thought the old gal would have delighted in the sight of all the chauffeured Town Cars that had snaked northward along the cobblestones on Main Street.

Her memories wandered until she heard her name called softly and she looked up to see Marge, impeccably dressed in a black A-line suit, coming toward her.

"I don't want to intrude on your grief," she said.

"You're not intruding." Pete scooted over to make room on the hard bench, and Marge sat beside her. "I've said good-bye in so many ways already, this time was for everyone else."

They listened quietly to the last of the songs wind down. Over their heads, squirrels played in the tree and a light breeze rustled the leaves.

"I'm leaving him," Marge said with equal parts conviction and anguish. She turned to look squarely at Pete. "I stayed too long as it is. I wanted you to know."

"I'm sorry," Pete said.

"Don't be. I'm sitting on a stockpile of Treasury bonds Jackson knows nothing about." With that confession out in the open, she rose. "I won't be going back to your grandmother's house. I just wanted you to know."

Pete reached for her sister-in-law's beautifully manicured hand and squeezed it.

"Thanks for coming, Marge. It was so

very kind of you," she said and meant it. "Take care."

Albert came looking for Pete just as Marge disappeared around the front of the church. He nodded to her as he passed, but they didn't speak. The singing had stopped and Pete could see people now pouring out of the church.

"I wondered where you'd got off to, toots," he said. "You okay?"

"I'm fine. How about you? You're the one looking a little puny."

"Jeeze, don't ask." He plopped onto the bench, pale and sweating freely under his suit. "I almost killed myself trying to keep up with your sister. I need a nap, big time."

Pete patted his knee and said, "Go on, go back and catch some z's. They're all leaving this afternoon, so it'll be just you and me tonight. We'll rent a movie. How's popcorn sound?"

"Hey, you're talking to a man who considers popcorn a hot meal. A movie it is." He kissed her on the cheek and rose from the bench. "It was a nice service, toots. Real nice. Your grandmother would have been proud." He blew her an air smooch, said, "See you later," and was off.

Pete abandoned her intimate corner of the garden to mosey over to the front door of the church and help her family bid good-bye to the assorted mourners. Niles Pollard was there snapping pictures as politicians and other notables grabbed a chance to smoke and mingle before joining the mayor to share in a sense of fellowship and community at his reception.

Few state politicians, Jackson included, would miss the opportunity for tributes to be made on her grandmother's life. Sheldon and Gant would be in their element. It was good public relations.

When Pete finally caught sight of Benedict, he was talking with the sheriff. Her heart trembled.

She couldn't stop him from reporting what he knew, and she didn't try. His ethics were part of why she loved him, loved him like crazy, and she wouldn't change him for anything.

But she refused to mourn lost opportunities — he had to accept her as she was as well.

He saw her watching him and strolled over to speak with her.

"Pete," he said, reaching for her hand.

"Counselor," she returned.

"I had to do it, Pete," he said, rubbing her fingers, lightly, sensually, "before it blew up in our faces. Please understand."

"Strangely enough," she said, "I do."

"And? What do we do now?"

Pete knew the promise of intimacy was a powerful incentive for bringing someone back. So she lifted his hand up to her lips, kissed his palm, let her gaze linger a moment longer on his, and offered him a tender smile.

"I don't know about you, counselor, but I intend to be humble and accept that I've done what I can."

Later that afternoon, Pete woke from a nap and came downstairs to the library to answer the sheriff's questions.

When she walked in, she spotted Racine and Carl on the loveseat, lingering until their flight. Both her brother and sister had already departed. Albert was still ruined from his night on the town with Phoebe and was sacked out over the garage.

Pete had been expecting the sheriff, just not so soon. And she definitely wasn't expecting to see Niles Pollard pacing outside on the patio or Dan Benedict leaning nonchalantly against the fireplace mantel.

Sheriff Tate stood in the center of the room. He was past middle age, with deep-pitted weathered cheeks, a forehead full of crevices, and the square-set shoulders of a man used to being obeyed. Contrary to his looks, his voice was low key and soothing, probably an asset in his line of work.

Once the polite niceties were observed, Pete leaned a hip on the arm of the loveseat next to her mother. Tate got right down to business.

"Miss Lang, are you aware of the information that Mr. Benedict here has brought to my attention regarding your late grandparents?"

Pete felt her mother's hand resting on her back in silent support. She cut her gaze to Benedict's impassive face, and he met her scrutiny without flinching. It was all she could do not to smile.

"Yes, sheriff," she said. "I am. Dan Benedict is a student of truth. He told me he was going to talk to you before he did it."

"And? Do you have anything to add that might clear up this matter?"

"I know rumors," Pete said, which was true. "My grandparents lived long and colorful lives and met many people along the way. There are so many interesting stories told by so many people it's difficult to separate fact from fiction."

The library doors opened then and Eugenié ushered in Vonnie Miller, who carried a bronze urn in his hand.

"Pardon me for interrupting," he said. "I can wait outside until you're finished."

"Nonsense," Racine said, and rose to greet him. "Look, Pietra, isn't your grandmother's urn simply beautiful?"

"Yes, it's a very lovely urn."

Pete smiled at Vonnie and he nodded back, and then she returned her attention to the sheriff.

"Now, I will gladly open the house and grounds to you, Sheriff Tate," she said, "whenever you feel an investigation is warranted. Is there anything else I can do for you?"

With no body, no weapon, and no witness, Pete figured there wasn't much the sheriff could do. Time was on her side.

They waited patiently while Tate shifted his stance and looked down at a notepad in his hand, his jaw working as he studied the paper. When he glanced back up, he cut his gaze to each of them in turn, ending with Pete.

"No, Miss Lang, nothing right now. I may check back with you later. Thank you for your time. Please, don't bother. I can see myself out."

As the sheriff departed, Danny sidled up next to Pete. She turned her face to his, so close they breathed the same air.

"You know," he said, putting his lips intimately close to her ear, "you did in ten seconds what your grandmother couldn't do in ten years."

"What was that?"

"Bury her guilt . . . permanently."

"Are you saying Miss Fritz is in that urn?"

"Isn't she?"

Pete grinned, "Do you really want to know, counselor?"

"No," he said, his gaze softening. "I don't think I do."

What a dear man. He accepted without verification or proof that Pete had finagled something. Maybe one day, if he ever asked, she'd tell him who was in the urn and who was in a beautiful bronze casket. Until that day arrived though, Pete would keep her own secret.

"What do we do about Pollard?" she said. "I thought he left with Jackson, but I see he hasn't. How do we nip his social vigilantism in the bud?"

"Leave Pollard to me." Danny offered a reassuring smile and a conspiratorial wink. "He owes me a favor."

Chapter 22

Danny's care and concern for Pete went beyond lust.

He'd spent until the early hours of the morning thinking about what mattered in his life. In that, Flora, his confidential assistant, had known him better than he knew himself — he was getting older and wanted stability, a family, someone to talk to when he come home at night.

But he wanted more than that, too. He wanted a helpmate and a lover.

He wanted Pete Lang.

They complemented each other. Where Danny could help Pete be more involved in living and see the depth of ideas rather than only the surface, she could help bring fun and excitement into his life.

It was a perfect match . . . that is, if she'd listen long enough for him to explain it to her.

He and Carl were in the library killing time while they waited for Racine to finish packing and come down. Carl had something on his mind, but Danny soon figured out the old guy would get around to it in his own sweet time.

"Drink?" Carl said, hovering near the bar.

"No thanks."

"Suit yourself. Mind if I . . . ?"

"Not at all. Go ahead."

Danny waited while Carl splashed two fingers of scotch in a rocks glass and topped it with a whisper of water.

"My stepdaughter Pete," Carl said, turning around with the drink in his hand, "is a good kid. Smart. Like when she talked to that sheriff about you being a student of truth."

"No argument there, sir," Danny said. "Pete is a special lady."

Carl gestured Danny to the leather sofa, then settled in the wing-backed chair opposite.

"You're a lawyer," he said.

"Yes, I am."

"Have you ever considered that there's no such thing as truth?"

"How do you mean?"

"Simply that. Have you ever considered that truth might be nothing more than impressions and memories we interpret according to our own experience?"

"Sure, every story has two sides. Truth sometimes depends on which side you're on."

Carl took a swallow of his drink.

"My old man," he said, "was a hard-nosed son-of-a-bitch."

"Are you a chip off the old block?"

"Not quite. He spent his life blowing money on fast women and slow horses, and the best thing he ever did was to sit me down one day and gave me his truth. And now, son, I'd like to pass it on to you."

He downed the rest of his drink in one gulp and then scooted to the edge of his seat, which enticed Danny to lean forward with interest.

"If you never remember nothing else in life, Dan, remember these truths: never pass up a bathroom . . . never trust a fart . . . and never waste a hard-on, even if you're by yourself."

Carl rose from his seat and punctuated the air with the empty rocks glass in his hand.

"When you get to be my age," he added, "you'll appreciate that those three things are all the truth you'll ever need. The rest of it . . . it's just details."

He jerked his chin toward the verandah where Danny saw Pete gliding back and forth in the swing, glistening hot and smoochy.

"You two look good together," Carl said.

"Maybe you should have some babies. She's not getting any younger, y'know."

"Think she'll have me?"

Racine swept into the library then, all big red hat, sunglasses, and purple print dress of her, ready to head to the airport.

"If you're lucky," Carl said, grinning at his wife. "When you meet someone special, son, chase after her."

A few minutes later, Danny stood with Pete on the top step of the porte cochere to see her mother and Carl off. The sky was clouding over, and the air was muggy, heavy with the smell of rain, cut grass, and change.

He wrapped his arm around Pete's shoulder and nestled her close to his side as she waved good-bye. They stood there as long as they could hear the tires crunching on gravel and watched Racine's little red Mercedes fade into the horizon.

"Pete?"

"Yes, Dan?"

"I guess you're going to ramble around this big house all by yourself now?"

"I guess so."

"Want some company?"

"For how long?"

"Forty, fifty years or so."

She nodded and said, "I think we can

find room. Are you offering?"

"I promised myself that when I found the right place and the right time and the right person, I would ask her to marry me."

Pete finally turned her face to him, and the love he saw glittering in her bedroom eyes wrapped around his heart and wouldn't let go.

"And do you feel you've found all those?" she said, her eyes puddling up, her mouth trembling.

"Yes, I do."

"Are you sure?"

A tear escaped down her cheek, and he wiped it away with the pad of his thumb.

"I've never been more sure of anything in my life. This is the right place, Pete, and the right time and you are the only woman for me. I'll shout it to the world if you want me to. I'm in love with you, Pete Lang, and I want to spend the rest of our lives proving that to you."

On a soft cry that was half laugh, half sob, she wrapped her arms around his neck and gathered him to her heart.

"I love you, too, Dan Benedict. You're infuriating and incorrigible, and I love you like crazy."

Then she cupped his face in her hands

and brought her mouth to his in a kiss overflowing with passion and promises. Only the ringing cell phone in his front pants pocket disturbed them.

"Get that, will you?" he said, circling Pete in his arms. "I've got my hands full right now."

She dipped in his pocket and pulled out his phone.

"Hello? . . . no . . . yes, it is . . . that would be great . . . fine, see you then."

Then she closed the lid and slipped the phone back in his pocket.

"Who was that?" Danny said.

"Your mother." Pete's eyes were misting up again, and the sun shone when she smiled. "She invited us to dinner this Friday night."

"And what did you say?"

"I said yes."